SWEET
SORROW

Titles in this series
(listed in order)

Sweet Poison
Bones of the Buried
Hollow Crown
Dangerous Sea
The More Deceived
A Grave Man
The Quality of Mercy
Something Wicked
No More Dying
Sweet Sorrow ✓

SWEET
SORROW

A murder mystery featuring
Lord Edward Corinth and Verity Browne

DAVID ROBERTS

Constable • London

Constable & Robinson Ltd
3 The Lanchesters
162 Fulham Palace Road
London W6 9ER
www.constablerobinson.com

First published by Constable,
an imprint of Constable & Robinson Ltd 2009

First US edition published by SohoConstable,
an imprint of Soho Press, 2009

Soho Press, Inc.
853 Broadway
New York, NY 10003
www.sohopress.com

A copy of the British Library Cataloguing in
Publication Data is available from the British Library

UK ISBN: 978-1-84529-691-9

US ISBN: 978-1-56947-615-4
US Library of Congress number: 2008028595

Printed and bound in the EU

Mixed Sources
Product group from well-managed
forests and other controlled sources
www.fsc.org Cert no. SA-COC-1565
© 1996 Forest Stewardship Council
FSC

For Jane, first and last

How dost thou, Benedick, the married man?

Shakespeare, *Much Ado About Nothing*

_____

Parting is such sweet sorrow . . .

Shakespeare, *Romeo and Juliet*

August 1939

Prologue

Byron Gates was a poet. As he used to say, with that characteristic chuckle women seemed to find so attractive, what else could he be with a name like that? Ever since he had first read – though not understood – *Childe Harold's Pilgrimage* at the age of eleven, he had determined to be a poet and to honour his namesake. As an undergraduate at Oxford, he adopted a poetic personality which he spent what remained of his life refining and perfecting. He began to dress like a poet, modelling his costume on Oscar Wilde and Dante Gabriel Rossetti, developing a taste for silk shirts and bow-ties. He wore a black or purple cape when he ventured out, the colour depending on his mood. He smoked Gitanes through an ivory cigarette holder and, when he could afford it, he sported a buttonhole – for preference a white carnation. He wore his hair just an inch or two longer than was thought decent and he had a way of combing it with his fingers when he was in the throes of creation which, he had read, was a mannerism of Tennyson's.

His mild eccentricity was indulged by his college, Christ Church, and he was only o. ucked in Mercury, the college fountain – a passage of arms he wore thereafter like a medal. He was suspected of being a 'pansy' but this was far from the truth.

Although he was a pastoral poet, writing lyrically of the mountains and lakes of his native Cumberland, he was essentially a city man and was never so happy as when he was sipping at his pint in some smoky, stale-aired public house in Fitzrovia. On leaving the university, with a disappointing third, he attempted journalism but the life of a cub reporter did not suit him and, reluctantly, to pay the bills, he took a post in a preparatory school near Marlborough. As his literary reputation grew, he became increasingly impatient at having to teach small boys Latin and English; necessarily ignorant or at least unheeding of the favour he was doing them, they sensed his dislike of them and ragged him unmercifully. It was a minor compensation that the under-matron was pretty and receptive to his overtures.

By the time he was thirty he had published three slim volumes of verse, the first of which had been described as 'promising', the second as 'daring' and the third as 'significant', though *what* it signified the reviewer – a drinking companion of his – would have been hard put to say. Brief poems extolling natural beauty and platonic love appeared in small magazines with even smaller circulations on a regular basis. He reviewed poetry for the *Telegraph* and *The Listener*, for which he also occasionally set the crossword, writing sharp-edged criticism of his elders, praising his friends, particularly his Oxford contemporaries. *The Listener* brought him into contact with BBC programme makers and he was commissioned to give a series of lectures on how to read poetry, which proved surprisingly popular.

With the approach of war, he wrote a sequence of sonnets expressing his disapproval of violence in any shape or form, bravely declaring to a largely indifferent world that he was a pacifist, like his mentor W.H. Auden. Indeed, he would have gone to America with Auden and his friend Christopher Isherwood to sit out the coming conflict in safety had he been able to wangle an invitation from a respectable American university. As it was, he

4

had reluctantly shut up his house in Flask Walk and left Hampstead for Sussex. Virginia Woolf, the celebrated novelist and an old friend of his, had found him a small cottage close to where she lived in the village of Rodmell just outside Lewes, and to this he decamped with his wife and their two daughters.

Whether it was his name or his fame, if he could be said to be famous, or his pallid good looks and small-boy appeal, he had always enjoyed – even at the university – considerable success with women. His first wife, to whom he had been unfaithful from the day of their marriage – with her sister, as it happened – had died five years earlier of cancer, though some unfriendly folk spoke of a 'broken heart'. With Marion dead, he had remarried almost immediately a moderately well-known actress called Mary Brand.

He discovered that the act of marriage was death to romance and immediately began an affair with Frieda Burrowes, an aspiring actress young enough to be his daughter. They had met when she had interviewed him for the BBC and she had signalled her devotion by attending several of his 'readings', staying on after the – usually small – audience had dispersed to tell him how profound he was and how affecting his verse. No one ever said that his poetry was memorable – it wasn't – and he winced when his women chose to quote from poems by his more famous namesake, instead of a line or two from, say, his moving elegy for his dead wife.

Ada, his daughter by his first wife, now aged twelve, was a shy introverted girl, 'not particularly pretty', as her father used to say to her face, who was left very much on her own. Her stepmother was by no means an uncaring woman but she had her career, mostly on the London stage but occasionally in Hollywood. She, too, had a daughter, Jean, from an earlier marriage, now aged fifteen. Jean was everything Ada was not – outgoing, noisy and showing every sign that she would be a beauty. Ada worshipped her stepsister and Jean repaid her devotion with casual friendliness. She had a soft heart and the ugly duckling was so obviously in need of mothering that she did what she could to provide it.

Ivy Cottage to which the Gates family moved was not large and, to Jean's chagrin, she was forced to share a room with Ada. The girls did not quarrel but it was an uncomfortable arrangement.

Byron's young admirer, Frieda, remained in London. Fortunately, he had to go up to town quite frequently. With war almost a certainty, the government, rather late in the day, decided to do what it could to foster patriotism and, as part of that effort, Byron was invited to give a series of talks for the Home Service on what it meant to be British. These proved to be even more popular than his talks on how to read poetry.

However, the BBC only paid a pittance and, since he never earned more than fifty pounds a year from his poetry, Byron had been forced to find an alternative source of income. He had tidied up his lectures on poetry and Victor Gollancz had published them as a book which had made him a hundred pounds. Then, in 1937, his publisher, who had a thriving list of crime fiction in its famous yellow livery, suggested he might try his hand at a detective story.

To his own and his publisher's amazement, *Just Like a Coffin* had sold very well. Setting crosswords had prepared him for constructing the puzzle at the heart of most detective stories of the period. He hardly bothered to invent a detective, merely providing the reader with an idealized portrait of himself. Nicholas Shelley, the name he sportively gave his detective, was wise, good-looking and 'philosophical' – by which his creator meant that he was given to spouting platitudinous opinions on life, death, patriotism and other great topics – but he did solve crimes. Bulldog Drummond might be the man you needed beside you in a rough house, but Nicholas Shelley had brain and a way with the ladies which made many a middle-aged female's heart flutter on the way out of Boots lending library.

There was a certain irony, upon which Byron himself had remarked, that as an avowed pacifist he should prove so good at describing murder – bloodless though it usually was. A much greater irony, particularly in view of the trouble he had taken to remove himself from London and the danger of being bombed – an irony which, unfortunately, he was unable to appreciate – was that, even before the war he so much dreaded had broken out, he met a violent death where he least expected it, in the peaceful Sussex village in which he had made his home. It was just such a murder as Nicholas Shelley might have been called upon to investigate but, with the fictional detective's creator dead, the onerous duty fell to the newly married Lord Edward Corinth.

1

'But it's perfectly all right as it is, Mrs Brendel,' Verity said firmly. 'I much prefer the walls white and I know my husband has an aversion to flock except in relation to sheep.'

Verity enjoyed referring to 'my husband'. She had determined that as she had, against all her principles, got married, and to Lord Edward Corinth rather than to plain Mr Snooks, she might as well revel in her sin. She would not try to pretend that marriage was merely a slight error of judgement for which she could hardly be blamed. And here she was employing staff for the first time in her life. Edward had insisted on appointing a cook/housekeeper on the grounds that, as he put it, Verity was quite without any domestic skills – hurtful but undeniably true – and because she would be away for long stretches of time by nature of her work – she was a foreign correspondent for the *New Gazette*. Edward had accepted an ill-defined but interesting-sounding job at the Foreign Office, so he was likely to be at home more often than she and would need someone to run the house for him.

'Do you mind that I can't darn your socks, Edward?' she had asked him, rather abashed.

'Nor boil an egg or make a bed . . .' He saw her face fall and stopped teasing. 'Of course not! You know very well that such a woman would bore me rigid. That is why we will employ Mrs Brendel. And we have the added

8

pleasure of knowing that we are helping someone less fortunate than ourselves. Oh dear, does that sound impossibly smug? But you know what I mean.'

Mrs Brendel was a Jewish refugee from Nazi Germany – a friend of their near neighbours, Virginia and Leonard Woolf. Leonard – a Jew himself – had been active in helping refugees find work and somewhere to live.

'You can decorate the house how you like, V. The only thing I insist upon,' Edward had continued, 'is that you keep it clean and simple – no wallpaper. Wallpaper reminds me of dull London drawing-rooms and is totally inappropriate to a country vicarage.'

Verity, feeling almost dizzy with virtue – was she not behaving like the wives she had read about who treated their husband's slightest whim as an order? – opened her mouth to ask Mrs Brendel what she was planning to give them for supper. She was arrested by a cry of 'Cooee!' from the French windows.

'Verity, I hope you don't mind me coming at you through the garden but I could hear you talking . . .'

She had very few female friends – she found most women irritating. They tended to disapprove of her wandering the world as a journalist, unmarried and unchaperoned. Now that she *was* married they would disapprove of her all the more. A wife's place was in the home looking after the children and preparing supper for the man of the house when he returned from the City. She had no children, had no intention of having children and, under pressure, confessed to not liking children. As for waiting at home for Edward to return from town – she had never waited for anything, least of all Edward. At dinner parties, she objected to being sent out of the room with the women to discuss children and 'the servant problem' while the men sat over their port and cigars discussing money and politics. However, she had one woman friend to whom she was devoted – Charlotte, a novelist married to one of her oldest friends, the painter, Adrian Hassel. They lived in a cottage just across the field and it was they who had found Edward and Verity their house.

'Of course not! Come in. It's so hot that Mrs Brendel and I decided to open every window and air the house while we can. It's wonderful to have escaped London. I really thought I should die, it was so oppressive.'

'And how do you like it here?'

'I adore it! I can't tell you how grateful we are to you. I don't think we would ever have found anywhere to live without your help. You know, I feel like a child playing with a doll's house. I just can't believe it's all real.'

'Well, I'm pleased, though somehow I can't ever imagine you playing with dolls,' Charlotte replied. 'Is there anything I can do to help you settle in?'

'No, thank you, Mrs Brendel is so efficient. The furniture we brought from Mersham arrived yesterday. It's all a bit of a muddle now but I'm sure by the end of the week we'll feel we have lived here for years.'

'And last night . . .? You could have come and stayed with us.'

'I know we could. You have been so kind but we decided we had to "take possession" so to speak. Now, are you coming to dinner tonight? I was just about to discuss what we might eat with Mrs Brendel.' Verity looked doubtful for a moment. 'We have got some food, I suppose, Mrs Brendel?'

Charlotte had to laugh at the hopeless way she looked about her as though expecting a leg of lamb, perfectly roasted, suddenly to appear in front of her.

'Never mind that,' Charlotte said. 'You are invited to dinner tonight with the Woolves. They so much want to meet you. Do say you'll come.'

'Gosh, yes!' Verity's faced cleared and she smiled with relief. 'We'd love that. Edward and I are already struggling to find things to talk about when we are by ourselves,' she joked. 'The Woolves . . .? You mean . . .?'

'Leonard and Virginia – round here, they are always called the Woolves. It's affectionate, you understand.'

Verity turned to the housekeeper who was standing patiently waiting for instructions. 'It seems we'll not be dining at home, Mrs Brendel. I hope you haven't bought anything that won't keep?'

'No, mam. There's a shoulder of mutton but it will keep in the larder until tomorrow, even in this heat.'

'Oh, you've been into Lewes . . .?' Verity sounded surprised.

'No, mam. The butcher calls every Tuesday and Friday, the fish on Wednesday and the baker's boy calls daily except Sundays.'

'Goodness! Well then, there's nothing for me to worry about, is there?'

When Mrs Brendel had departed, Charlotte giggled. 'I'll have some difficulty thinking of you as "mam", Verity.'

'She wanted to call me "my lady",' Verity responded defensively. 'I told her I couldn't live up to that so we compromised on mam or madam. Do you think it too absurd?'

'No! We'll soon get used to the new Verity – with a big house and servants and a title . . .'

'Now you're teasing me again. Why does everyone think it so funny? I can't get Edward to take me seriously and now you. You've got to give me support or else I'll run away.'

'Nonsense!' Charlotte said firmly. 'Don't be such a ninny. Where is Edward, anyway?'

'He's walking Basil.' Basil was Verity's curly-coated retriever. 'They've gone up on the downs. Stay and have some tea. I expect they'll be back in a few minutes.'

'Haven't got time. I have a book to finish. My publisher says that, if the war comes, no one will want to buy books – at least not ones like mine.'

'About family squabbles . . .? Oh, I don't agree. I think people will always want to read novels about normal life

11

to remind them what they are fighting for and as an escape from the horrible present.'

Charlotte looked rather hurt. 'I don't think it's fair to say my books are about family squabbles. I try to write about more important things.'

Verity did not hear her friend's protest and continued her lecture. 'During the last war, soldiers read in the trenches. In Spain, books and cigarettes were used as currency. Don't forget that even in the most beastly wars, most of the time people sit around waiting for things to happen. War is a combination of boredom, fear and exhaustion.'

'What about courage?' Charlotte asked, still rather put out. 'People are brave in war, aren't they?'

'Some people are brave but most just endure,' Verity replied soberly.

'Well, I've still got to finish the damn thing – the book, I mean. I'll see you at Monk's House around eight. Don't dress up – it'll just be us and maybe Byron Gates, the poet. Do you know him?'

'I think I met him once, very briefly.'

'Well, anyway, Adrian will probably insist on wearing his smoking jacket with paint on it and Leonard wears a moth-eaten corduroy thing.' She looked at a pile of black cloth on the floor. 'What's that?'

'It's for the blackout. Colonel Heron dropped in and reminded us that, when war is declared, we'll have to keep any lights from showing. He took one look at our curtains and said they were much too thin. Next week he's expecting to receive a new batch of gas masks to distribute. It's so awful. One can't think of war when it's like this – the sun shining and the birds twittering and all that.'

'You don't fool me, Verity. You are longing for it – the excitement . . .'

'No, Charlotte, you are quite wrong. I saw enough of it in Spain to know that war destroys everything it touches. I hate it.'

'I'm sorry,' Charlotte said, realizing that she had upset her friend. 'I shouldn't have joked about it. You're right of course. The truth is we're all terrified of what's to come but we have to put on a brave face.'

Virginia and Leonard had bought Monk's House in the summer of 1919 for seven hundred pounds. It was a modest brick and flint two-storey building – little more than a cottage – weather-boarded on the street side. As she and Edward strolled the short distance from the Old Vicarage, Verity wondered if their hosts would resent them buying a much grander house than theirs.

They were let in by Leonard himself, although Verity caught sight of a maid bobbing around behind him. He was a gaunt, monkey-faced man with sharp intelligent eyes and a thin mouth, but his smile was attractive and she knew immediately that she liked him without his having said more than a word of welcome. He ushered them into a low-ceilinged, oak-beamed drawing-room apologizing for Sally, his cocker spaniel, who jumped up at them. Virginia rose to greet them and, holding out her hand to Verity, said how very much she had been looking forward to meeting her.

'I read your reports from Spain and I was about to ask you to write a book for us when I was beaten to it by Gollancz.'

The Woolves had started a small publishing firm called the Hogarth Press and Verity was flattered that she had even been considered as a possible author.

'It was so kind of you to have sent me books when I was ill, Mrs Woolf,' she replied. 'Although, I have to confess, I would always rather be "doing" than reading. Still, being laid up for so long, I was able to do something about my education – or lack of it.'

Verity found it almost impossible to take her eyes off Virginia. She thought she had never seen such a remarkable

13

face, full of pain, lovely and remote. She became aware that she was being introduced to a handsome man in his early forties whose face she recognized.

'Miss Browne – sorry, I mean Lady Edward – you won't remember but we met at the BBC two years ago – Byron Gates. You were being interviewed about the war in Spain.'

'Of course I remember. I didn't know you lived near here until Charlotte – Mrs Hassel – mentioned it this afternoon.'

'We're just across the road from the pub – Ivy Cottage. Mrs Woolf was kind enough to find somewhere for me, my wife and daughters to take refuge. You must have come to the same decision, to leave London to the mercy of the Luftwaffe.'

'I wouldn't put it quite like that,' Verity said, frowning. She did not like to be accused of running away. 'My husband and I need a home – we never had one in London – but we shall both be away a lot.'

'You are still hoping to be "in the thick of it"?' Byron inquired a little patronizingly. 'I thought you had been ill.'

'I had a very light case of TB but am fully recovered. Your wife . . . she's not here?' Verity said to change the subject.

'No, Mary's in Hollywood making one of those pictures where they take our history and turn it into Technicolor tosh. Nelson and Lady Hamilton, Queen Bess and the Earl of Essex – you know the sort of thing.'

'I saw *Fire over England*. Is that the kind of picture you mean? I rather enjoyed it.'

'Yes, but it was tosh, wasn't it?'

'It wasn't realistic but it carried one along. And your daughters . . . ?'

'Ada and Jean, my stepdaughter – they're at home with a sitter-in Virginia found me. I really don't know what I would do without her.' Again there was that patronizing tone of voice with the implication that the distinguished novelist had nothing better to do than sort out his domestic affairs.

14

'You mustn't mind Byron,' Virginia said, smiling indulgently. 'He's an intellectual and despises we "toilers-in-the-field". You know, he not only sets the crossword in *The Listener*, which I find impenetrable, but he actually completes the monthly Greek or Latin puzzle.'

Byron smiled smugly.

At dinner, Virginia served a brown vegetable soup from a huge tureen, decorated she said by her friend, the artist, Duncan Grant. She was silent but watchful as she drank her soup – sizing up the new arrivals, or so Verity presumed. There was nothing luxurious about Monk's House. The dining-room was small, the table narrow and unprepossessing, but the chairs, designed and decorated by Virginia's sister, Vanessa, were comfortable. Verity found that she was trying hard to impress Virginia. She told herself not to be so silly. She must be herself – take it or leave it.

Leonard and Edward seemed to be getting on well. Byron, rather rudely, Verity thought, broke in on their conversation to ask Edward whether it was true he was a private detective. 'I ask because, as you may know, I write detective stories and it would be useful to study a real amateur detective at work.'

Edward, attempting to hide his irritation, admitted that he had been involved in one or two murder investigations but absolutely denied being a private detective. 'My wife is much more astute than I am about discovering "who did it",' he joked. 'I have quite determined never to investigate another crime.'

'And if there's a war . . .?' Byron inquired. 'Will there still be anything for you to detect?'

'There can be no doubt about it,' Edward replied sombrely, ignoring Byron's attempt to needle him, 'war is coming. It's only a question of when. As for murder, I should have thought that, by definition, there will be many thousands of murders but, as I said, I won't be investigating them.'

Verity was looking at Virginia when Edward said that war was inevitable and saw her rather sallow face go very pale and wished he would change the subject. Virginia must have seen that she had been observed and seemed called upon to explain her feelings.

'You know about war, Lady Edward. It is terrible, is it not? I am by instinct a pacifist but I'm not a politician, thank God. I leave politics to Leonard. He spends hours with dirty, unkempt, impractical philanthropists at whom I'd throw the coal scuttle after ten minutes if I were in his place. I know he's happy when I hear the drone of a committee meeting in the next room. Politics is Leonard's hobby, his passion. Mind you, in my experience, nothing advocated by well-meaning literary men ever happens.'

She spoke vehemently and Leonard looked rather surprised and not a little hurt.

Edward, trying to change the subject, said, 'At Eton, you know, some of us played a ludicrous medieval football on St Andrew's Day called the Wall Game. On St Andrew's Eve, we feasted and passed around a loving cup. As we drank from it, we chanted "*In priam memoriam* JKS."'

'So I have been told,' Virginia said more cheerfully. As Verity looked blank, she added, 'J.K. Stephen was my cousin – a great classical scholar and footballer.'

'And what happened to him?' Verity inquired.

'He went mad and died aged just thirty-three,' Virginia said flatly.

Verity wished she had not asked and her discomfort was made more acute by Byron's next sally.

'You are a Communist, aren't you, Lady Edward?' He spoke aggressively, emphasizing her title.

'I was. I still feel a Communist at heart but I grew to dislike the Party's slavish obedience to Moscow so I decided

16

to hand in my card. In fact, I have just written an article for *Revolt!* on the Party's destruction of the Anarchists in Spain. My Communism is, I suppose, closer to the socialism Mr Woolf preaches in the *Political Quarterly*.'

'Please,' Leonard interjected, 'now we are friends and neighbours, I hope you will call me Leonard and, if I may, I shall call you Verity and Edward.'

'Please do,' Verity said smiling. She knew she would have no difficulty calling him by his first name but doubted she could ever call Mrs Woolf 'Virginia' – not that she had as yet been invited to do so.

'*Revolt!* – what's that?' Adrian inquired. 'It sounds sanguinary.'

'It's a magazine edited by George Orwell and Vernon Richards which discusses the Spanish Civil War from an anti-Stalinist point of view.'

'I hope you get paid,' Leonard said with a laugh. 'I heard yesterday that it has folded.'

'Yes, I know. I wasn't paid, as it happened, but I didn't expect to be. I much admire Mr Orwell and was glad to do what I could to help. I'm only sorry my offering didn't make a difference.'

'Did you read Orwell in *Tribune*?' Byron asked. 'In the "As I Please" column he called English intellectuals "boot-licking propagandists of the Soviet regime". A bit unnecessary, I thought.'

'Orwell was a contemporary of mine at Eton when he was called Eric Blair,' Edward put in. 'I didn't know him well and I never guessed he would turn into such a remarkable journalist. I find I share his views on most things.'

Leonard nodded in agreement. 'I'm sorry, Byron, but I do agree with him that we were too quick to excuse Stalin's political trials. One can see now that it was just state murder.'

Byron growled a protest.

17

As he carved a boiled chicken, Leonard said to Verity, 'When you were recovering from TB, did I send you John Strachey's *The Coming Struggle for Power*?'

'No, but I mean to read it.'

'I have a copy, if I can find it, which I shall be glad to lend you. Though it was written from a Marxist perspective as long ago as 1932, I think it still relevant.'

'You did send me Iris Origo's novel about Byron's daughter, Allegra, which you published. Have you read it, Mr Gates?'

'I have, as a matter of fact. Byron's behaviour was quite inexcusable. He took her away from her mother out of spite and left her to rot in an Italian convent. I called my daughter Ada after Byron's first legitimate daughter. She fared better. She was taken from him by his wife when she left him in 1816. Ada was only a month old and never met her half-sister. Unexpectedly, Ada became an accomplished mathematician.'

'I didn't know that. Is your Ada a mathematician, Mr Gates?' Verity asked.

'She's a good girl but no one could ever call her intelligent,' he replied dismissively.

Verity was shocked. If she ever had a child, unlikely as it was, she knew she would never talk about her with such contempt.

Leonard and Verity went on to discuss Lady Carter's recently published book about women in prison – *A Living Soul in Holloway* – Leonard's work towards disarmament and the failure of the League of Nations.

Inevitably, Verity was soon talking of the Spanish Civil War which – as they spoke – was ending in victory for General Franco and the Fascists, or Phalange Party, as it was called in Spain.

'You know my nephew, Julian, was killed in Spain?' Virginia broke in. 'And now it's going to happen again. It depresses me so much to think of all our young friends caught up in something unutterably worse than what we went through in 1914.'

Verity saw Leonard look at his wife with concern.

'Yes, I met your nephew once and much admired him,' Verity replied gravely. 'Of course war is horrible but, like Lord Byron, I think Julian knew he was doing the right thing. It's the same today. Any sane person hates the idea of another war with Germany but Hitler has to be withstood. Surely it is better to fight than be made a slave?'

'You're so like him – like Julian.' Virginia put out a hand as if she would touch her but withdrew it. 'Despite what you say, I still don't understand what made him do it. I suppose it's the fever in the blood of your generation which we can't possibly understand. We were all conscientious objectors in the Great War. I was a great admirer of Senator La Follette, a much misunderstood patriot, and, though I understand the war in Spain was a "just cause", my natural reaction would be to write against it.'

'As I did,' Verity interjected.

'The moment force is used, it becomes meaningless to me,' Virginia continued. 'I'm sometimes angry with Julian but his feelings were fine, as you say . . . fine but wrong.'

'His feelings were fine and right,' Verity said firmly but, she hoped, not rudely. 'And we must now fight again until Hitler is destroyed. It is the same war.'

'But the bombing . . .?' Virginia said faintly. 'I'm so terrified of gas attacks . . . We're giving up our house in Tavistock Square.'

'To live here at Monk's House, permanently?' Verity asked.

'No, a few months ago we bought a house in Mecklenberg Square and we are in the process of moving our things. We must have been mad to buy another house in London but, when we decided to move, we didn't think war was coming so soon. In fact, in my more optimistic moments I still don't think there will be war.'

19

Verity could not believe that this highly intelligent woman could so delude herself but she said nothing.

'London is a huge city spread over a vast area,' Edward said, in an effort to calm her. 'In my view, if war does come and I fear it must, the Luftwaffe will not be able to reduce it to rubble as quickly as people seem to think. Mr Churchill . . .'

'You're a friend of his, I believe?' Byron interrupted. 'I don't trust him. He brought on this war by his posturing. There's still time to make our peace with Germany. I don't believe war solves anything.'

'Your namesake fought for freedom,' Edward couldn't resist saying.

'And died for it,' Byron agreed. 'What a waste! Great poets . . . great artists, great scientists are too precious to be wasted. Look at Archimedes – killed by a common soldier.' He shook his head in sorrow.

Edward wondered if he considered himself to be a great poet and rather thought he did. Unwisely, he was unable to restrain himself from quoting from Lord Byron's last poem.

"'If thou regret'st thy youth, why live?
The land of honourable death
Is here: up to the field, and give
Away thy breath.'"

Verity was embarrassed, fearing that Virginia would be upset, and said quickly, 'Edward, how often have I asked you not to show off? Poets – with the exception of Wilfred Owen and Sassoon – have very little idea of the reality of war.'

Unabashed, Edward again addressed Byron. 'I have a rather odd link with Lord Byron. When I was at Trinity, I had the privilege of being lodged in his set of rooms. I'm told he kept a bear which he would take out walking with him. Then, when I moved into Albany, I discovered that my set also once belonged to him.'

'Byron had a fine time at Cambridge,' Leonard put in. 'In fact, I gather he lived a life of what must be called dissipation.'

'He fell in love with a choirboy,' his namesake said with a smirk. 'He had wanted to go to Oxford – Christ Church, my college as it happens – but there were no rooms vacant so Trinity was second best.'

'I think the only living creature he truly loved was his dog, Boatswain, a Newfoundland. It's said that, when admirers asked Byron for a lock of his hair, he used to send them a curl or two of Boatswain's fur.'

'But what is important,' Virginia said, as though she found the tone of the conversation distasteful, 'is that he wrote wonderful poetry. "Fain would I fly the haunts of men. I seek to shun, not hate mankind. My breast requires the sullen glen, whose gloom may suit a darkened mind."'

There was a silence when she finished speaking. Her deep, melodious voice put an end to trivial gossip.

When dinner was over, they moved into the drawing-room. The maid brought in a pot of coffee. Leonard put a record on the gramophone and, when they had sat down on an odd assortment of chairs, he lit a pipe while Virginia rolled a cigarette – a blend known as My Mixture. Adrian, who had said little at dinner, preferring to watch Verity and Virginia take each other's measure, asked Leonard how he had enjoyed his French holiday. In June, he and Virginia had driven through Brittany and Normandy.

'We very much enjoyed ourselves. Virginia is a great admirer of Madame de Sévigné and we thought we should visit Les Rochers and pay our respects while we still could.'

'Oh, I do wish we could forget about the war for a moment,' Charlotte protested. 'We'll soon have our fill of it. While we are still at peace can we not talk of peaceful things?'

'Indeed,' Leonard agreed. 'Now, who of our neighbours have you met, Lord Edward?'

'Please, I thought we had agreed that you would call me Edward. One of the things that made Verity hesitate before agreeing to marry me was the idea of being saddled with a title.'

'Lady Corinth I could have lived with,' Verity explained, 'but Lady Edward . . .' She threw up her hands in mock despair. 'When people call me that I feel I'm just an appendage.'

'Well, to answer your question,' Edward continued, smiling, 'we've only spent one night here so we haven't had much time to meet people, but Colonel Heron came by to give us advice on the blackout. Apparently, our curtains show too much light and will have to be lined with what I believe is black felt.'

'Heron is a busybody,' Byron said. 'He tried to tell me how to black out Ivy Cottage but I'm afraid I told him to go to hell. The worst thing about this war is going to be the little home-grown Hitlers who'll try to regulate every minute of our daily lives.'

'Didn't I hear that Heron attacked you in the pub a few nights back?' Leonard asked him.

'He was drunk,' Byron said dismissively. 'He apologized the next day and we agreed to forget about it.'

'Can I ask what he was accusing you of?' Leonard persisted.

'Apparently he knew my first wife – this was some time before we married – and he had the gall to accuse me of mistreating her. I've no idea how he would know as he was in India during the time we were married. It was all some fantasy of his. I believe he may have had a thing about Marion and went off to India when she rejected him. I don't know for certain and I don't care but we agreed to keep clear of one another. That's why I don't want him telling me how to black out my cottage.'

'I'm so sorry,' Virginia said. 'Rodmell's too small a village for quarrels.'

'Don't concern yourself, Virginia,' Byron replied. 'It was just a silly misunderstanding and it's all over now. Let's forget it, shall we?'

'He says he's going to drop off some gas masks for us to try on,' Virginia added, 'as though one were trying on a hat.'

'Well, it's no good if they are too small or too large,' Leonard said gently.

'I refuse to wear a gas mask. The thing disgusts me. If there is a gas attack, I shall just die. I'd rather die than wear one. The very sight of a gas mask with its hateful snout and tiny eyepiece terrifies me.' Virginia's eyes were wide, her pupils dilated.

'I agree,' Verity said, hoping to soothe her. 'It's certainly not a fashion accessory.'

Virginia smiled weakly and the hysteria that had seemed about to bubble over subsided.

'Colonel Heron is one of our churchwardens,' Leonard told them. 'He's very active in the village.'

'Too active, if you ask me,' Byron grumbled. 'You won't catch me in church. I get the feeling our dear vicar doesn't approve of me at all.'

'I want you to meet Mark Redel, the painter,' Leonard went on as though Byron had not spoken. 'He lives in the little cottage just down the road. We invited him tonight but he absolutely refuses to come out to dinner when he's in the middle of a picture. You've got to know him well, haven't you, Adrian?'

'Yes. He's difficult – no point in pretending he's a social animal – but he's a great painter, in a different league from me.' Verity smiled at her friend. Adrian was always so modest about his work but when she chided him he joked that he had a lot to be modest about. 'He's racked with guilt about being safe in England and hate for the Nazis. He gets terrible depressions but . . .'

'I get the impression, Leonard,' Edward interjected, 'that you have gathered quite an artistic colony around here?'

'We have done our best, particularly for our Jewish friends. I'm a Jew, of course, but Virginia feels just as strongly that we have to do what we can, though it's little enough.'

'And you must meet The Ladies, as we call them,' Virginia said with a smile. 'Miss Bron and Miss Fairweather have lived together for thirty or more years just outside the village.'

'Miss Fairweather? Is she the writer?' Edward asked.

'Yes, she's a wonderful woman. Quite formidable, though. I have to admit, she frightens me sometimes. She reminds me rather of Rebecca West. Her novels are acute, sensitive, and I believe they will last but she, like Redel, can be impossible. She bullies her friend unmercifully, which I don't like.' She hesitated and, as though something had just occurred to her, added, 'Or at least I think she does. Maybe in reality . . . I don't know – it's odd that someone who writes as well as Miss Fairweather can be so unfeeling, but who knows how friendships work? I have spent what seems like a lifetime trying to make sense of human relationships but I still know nothing.'

'You're coming to the fête, I hope, Edward? You'll meet them there. In fact you'll meet everyone there,' Leonard said.

'Miss Fairweather writes a pageant which the children perform,' Virginia explained. 'It's slightly absurd but one can't not be moved to watch them, dressed by their mothers as Queen Elizabeth or Cromwell or whatever, and so proud to be taking part.'

'Do they act out scenes from history?' Edward inquired with a smile.

'The children are arranged in tableaux – you know the sort of thing, St George with his dragon, Alfred burning the cakes, Canute ordering the tide to turn. Miss Bron, who has a remarkable speaking voice and was, I believe, an actress at one time, recites Miss Fairweather's description of what each tableau illustrates. There are prizes of course. The fête wouldn't be the same without the pageant.'

'It sounds splendid,' Edward said. 'It's tomorrow week, isn't it? We shall certainly be there.'

As long as I'm not on my way to France, Verity thought to herself. Aloud, she asked Leonard what he meant by 'everyone' coming to the fête. 'How many is "everyone"?'

'You remember the census the government carried out earlier in the year when it was preparing plans to evacuate children from town to country? The population of Rodmell and Southease was put at three hundred and fifty nine though with incomers like you we must be almost four hundred now.'

Shortly after ten thirty, Edward and Verity pleaded fatigue and asked to be forgiven for breaking up the party.

'How is the house?' Leonard asked as they rose to leave. 'The Paxtons, who had it before you, loved it – particularly the garden. Did you know it has a ghost?'

'The Old Vicarage? How exciting!' Verity replied. 'When we were sent the sale particulars, I never saw anything about a ghost.'

'You don't have to worry. The Paxtons said it's a friendly ghost. Apparently, it walks from room to room in the night. These old houses crack and creak like any arthritic old man.'

As they walked back with Charlotte and Adrian, Verity reprimanded her husband. 'It was so tactless of you, Edward, to quote that depressing poem about dying. Couldn't you see Mrs Woolf was upset?'

'What about you going on and on about Spain?' he riposted. 'I believe her nephew's death really upset her, as of course it would.'

'She's very close to her sister, Vanessa,' Charlotte nodded.

Adrian, always the peacemaker, said, 'They both liked you, I could see. The way Leonard opened up to you about politics . . . social conditions, everything. He loves to have someone to argue with and Virginia likes anyone who keeps Leonard happy.'

'So you think we will be asked back?' Verity inquired.

'Of course! What did you think of Monk's House?'

'I loved it,' Verity replied, 'though I'm not sure about all that green paint.'

'It's smaller than I imagined,' Edward added. 'I can't think where Mrs Woolf writes.'

'There's an upstairs sitting-room which you didn't see, and she's converted a tool shed at the end of the garden into a writing-room,' Charlotte told them. 'I love the house. It's a house in which books are all-important. You usually can't see the floor for books but they tidied up for us.'

'And did you like Byron?' Adrian asked.

'He's very good-looking,' Verity said, sneaking a glance at Edward to see if he would rise.

'I didn't like him,' he responded predictably. 'His hair's too long and he smelt. I'm not surprised he seems to have made so many enemies in the village.'

'I hear on the grapevine that he has a mistress in London. While his wife's in Hollywood . . .' Adrian told them with a smirk in his voice.

'Just what I would have suspected,' Edward commented loftily.

'I wonder what the children are like?' Verity mused.

'You'll see them at the fête if not before,' Charlotte pointed out.

26

2

The following morning was spent trying to put the house to rights. Verity flapped about, surprisingly indecisive, agreeing gratefully with any suggestion Mrs Brendel made about what furniture should go where. Edward quickly got bored and irritated and left with Basil for a walk on the downs, which he was already beginning to love. He felt he could breathe when he was up above the hurly-burly and he enjoyed a kind of peace striding along with Basil bounding in front of him chasing after hares, rabbits and pheasants, none of which he managed to catch. Much as he loved Verity, Edward found that he needed to be alone sometimes to think and contemplate the future. He knew this was the calm that comes before a storm and he wanted to make the most of it.

Verity was not a natural home-maker. She had always lived out of a suitcase and, although she liked the idea of a nest to which she could return from foreign trips, she had no belief in the reality of her new home. It was partly because so little of the furniture was hers. It mostly came from Mersham and she felt rather hopeless when – appealing to Edward for advice on, say, curtain material – he shrugged his shoulders and told her to ask Charlotte. She knew, too, that in just three or four weeks she would receive her marching orders from Lord Weaver at the *New Gazette* and have to drop everything to travel to some war-torn capital to report on another scene of misery and chaos. This was just playing, and she felt a slight chill in her bones. Was this marriage going to work? Would they be able to make the necessary compromises?

At lunchtime Adrian appeared and she welcomed the excuse to stop pretending she was being useful and leave everything to the housekeeper and the gardener's boy. Adrian wanted to introduce her to his friend, the painter Mark Redel.

'I'm afraid he's not an easy man to get on with. He says what he thinks, however hurtful. He hates my paintings! But he's a great painter – completely undervalued. In May he had an exhibition at the Lefèvre galleries but it wasn't a success. People were shocked by the nudes – he likes large ladies – but there were some wonderful still lifes and landscapes. You ought to make Edward buy one.'

'Of course. He's Jewish, isn't he?'

'Very,' Adrian responded.

'Is he married?'

'His wife left him about a year ago and took their son, Luke, with her.'

'Left him!' Verity suddenly felt panicky as though someone had said Edward had left her.

'Yes, she's in Paris with an Austrian refugee. Another painter, I believe. Oh dear, I make it sound all doom and gloom but really he can be very good company when he's not drunk or depressed.'

As they approached Redel's house – a small cottage on the main street –Verity wondered if she would be able to cope with him, but she was pleasantly surprised. He was in his studio, which was little more than a hut in the garden, and welcomed her with a smile.

'Please don't let us interrupt you,' she said nervously.

'Not at all,' Redel replied, putting down his brush. 'I've done enough for today.'

'May I see?' she inquired, expecting to be snubbed.

Redel lifted the painting off the easel and showed it to her. It was a self-portrait – quite small – but even Verity, who knew little about art, could feel the power and vigour of each brush stroke.

'It's magnificent!' she exclaimed.

'You really think so?' Redel sounded shy but pleased.

'I do. It quite takes my breath away. You know we have just moved into the Old Vicarage? We have no pictures – neither my husband nor I have ever had a house fit to hang pictures in. Will it be for sale – the self-portrait? Oh dear, I'm so sorry. I'm probably being rude. We've hardly met and here I go . . . '

'Don't apologize. You can't imagine how heartening it is for a painter to have his work praised. Adrian knows what it feels like.'

'Not often,' Adrian said ruefully, 'but I agree with Verity. It's magnificent.'

'Have you eaten?' Redel asked. 'We could walk down to the pub for a pint of the local brew and bread and cheese. Charlotte is always telling me I'm too thin but I don't eat much when I'm working. When I'm idle, I put on weight – it's very odd.'

'What a good idea,' Adrian said. 'Charlotte's trying to finish off a book and has banned me from the house, and Verity, you said Edward has abandoned you.'

'Not abandoned me, I hope,' she said nervously, 'but he's taken the dog for a walk. Mrs Brendel will tell him where I've gone.'

'Bread and cheese is about all I live on,' Redel said gloomily.

'That's nonsense, Mark. You are always being invited out to dinner. You just don't choose to accept. The Woolves invited you last night – they told us.'

'Yes, but I couldn't go. Virginia said she'd invited Byron Gates. I really can't stand the man. He has nothing to say and he says it at great length.'

'You don't like his poetry?' Verity inquired.

'Do you?'

'I have to admit I have never read any. When we go to Lewes I'll buy some. There is a bookshop, isn't there?'

'Yes, but really you don't need to bother,' Redel said viciously. 'It's rotten. If you want to read real poetry – there's a fellow I know, Dylan Thomas. Now, he's a real poet.'

'You know Byron well, Mark?' Adrian inquired.

'When I used to live in Highgate our paths crossed, but we were never friends. If I'd known Virginia had got him a cottage down here, I might not have come myself.'

'Oh, I see, Mrs Woolf found you this cottage?' Verity asked.

'Yes,' Redel responded shortly. 'She's very kind. She heard I was on my uppers after Marjorie left and said I ought to come to Rodmell.'

'How long have you been here?'

'Just six months. I like it here. I've done some good work even if nobody agrees with me. I was really hoping to sell two or three to the Tate. Rothenstein came to the exhibition but bought nothing. In fact, I only sold two pictures. I think the Lefèvre will drop me.'

'Don't be so pessimistic, Mark,' Adrian chided. 'Virginia and Vanessa loved the exhibition and Roger Fry said – how did he put it? – that you retained your "clear vision of youth and were still an uncompromising rebel".'

'Yes, I know but I'm still broke. Did I tell you that I'm thinking of writing my autobiography? Gollancz has offered me a hundred pounds.'

Verity looked at Redel with interest. She thought that, if he ever did write it, it was a book she would like to read. He wasn't good-looking. His face was pouched and creased as though fate had thrown too many blows at him which he had been unable to absorb. His nose was red and she guessed he drank too much. His eyes, though small and black, were attractive – very bright and intelligent – and his hair was thick and almost lustrous. She found herself wondering what sort of lover he would make and decided he would be exciting but selfish and probably violent.

In the Abergavenny Arms, Redel was welcomed as a regular and he and Adrian each ordered a pint of the thick local stout. There didn't seem anything for Verity to drink so she asked for cider. It was strong and rough and her head began to swim. She hoped Edward wouldn't be cross with her. He had rather an odd attitude to public houses. He never went in the pub at Mersham – something to do with it not being proper for the Duke or his brother to be seen drinking with the peasantry, she supposed. All nonsense, of course, but what could you do? As for women, she was quite sure the Duchess would never have entered it and she herself had never been allowed in. Yet, at the annual Mersham Show, the Duke would drink a pint or two in the tent with the local worthies and think nothing of it.

When Verity got home, a little unsteady on her feet, she found Edward pacing the drawing-room.

'There you are, V! I couldn't think where you had got to. Mrs Brendel told me you had gone out with Adrian to see Redel but no one was there. I suppose you all went to the pub.'

'We did. Why didn't you join us?'

'I don't like pubs,' he said, sulkily, 'and I didn't want to interrupt anything. I had to have lunch on my own.'

'Don't be absurd. I wish you had come with us. Mark is a remarkable painter and a most interesting man. His stuff is really amazing. You must see it. I told him we needed paintings for the house. There's a self-portrait . . .'

Edward spluttered. 'If you think . . .' He restrained himself from saying something he might regret. He didn't want a row. 'Well, anyway, now you're back I want to tell

31

you who I met on my walk. You remember Paul Fisher? We met him with Tommie Fox.'

Tommie was one of Edward's oldest friends, now a north London vicar. They had not seen him since their marriage which Verity guiltily attributed to her refusal to let him bless their union. Tommie had been badly hurt but she had insisted that it would be hypocritical to introduce a Christian element into the ceremony. She wondered if it had been selfish to deny an old friend a gesture which would surely not have affected her one way or the other and would have given him pleasure, but it was too late to do anything about it now.

'Paul was up at Trinity with us,' Edward went on, 'though he's a couple of years younger than me and we never got to know one another. Anyway, it turns out he's the vicar down here. Since St Peter's is practically in our garden, I thought I would show interest. I've asked him to supper after evensong tomorrow. I hope you don't mind.'

'Paul Fisher? Yes, I do remember him. Short and thin with not very much hair. Rather earnest and weedy-looking with a feeble attempt at a beard.'

'That's right, only he's got rid of the beard and I'd call him wiry rather than weedy. And he was – is – very clever in a theoretical sort of way. I suppose you'd call him a caricature intellectual. Anyway, he got a first. He's a bit of a climber too, rather surprisingly.'

'Social climber?'

'No! The other kind. I seem to remember that he did the Fourth Court climb.'

'What on earth is that?'

'Didn't I ever tell you about the night climbers of Cambridge?'

'No. One of your drinking clubs?' Verity suggested.

'On the contrary. Drink could be fatal. Some of us – I wasn't a regular, you understand – used to climb buildings in Cambridge – mostly the colleges but also some of the town buildings. I almost killed myself on King's College Chapel. I got stuck on the north-east pinnacle.'

'It all sounds rather silly,' Verity said, sounding superior.

'Maybe, but the exaltation when one reached the top of the Chapel was something else. No surprise that many of the great climbers went on to climb in the Himalayas.'

'Well, I'd be delighted to have Mr Fisher dine with us tomorrow but I hope you warned him that I can't accompany you to evensong.'

'Not even out of politeness?'

'I couldn't. I'm sorry.'

'Well, you're a heathen.'

'You have always known that. Is he married?'

'No, not as far as I know.'

'And you met him on the downs?'

'Yes, he tells me there are dozens of wonderful walks from the village. You walk up Mill Lane to the top of Mill Hill, turn right through the twitten . . .'

'What's that?'

'Paul says it's a narrow path between two hedges. Then, you continue along the ridge to Northease Farm. Basil would love it. He just failed to catch a hare this morning. We saw all sorts of wildlife – swallows and skylarks . . . You must come with us next time.'

'I had work to do,' Verity said virtuously, trying to forget how much she had left to Mrs Brendel. 'I was just thinking, why don't we ask Tommie down? We haven't seen him since the wedding.'

'*Our* wedding, you mean?' Edward responded, not liking the way she had distanced the event in her mind, as though it was a theatrical performance they had happened to attend. 'I said we'd get together with him in London. He's still rather upset about you-know-what.'

'But that's absurd!'

'Maybe, but didn't someone say that friendship is the first casualty of marriage?'

'Tell me more about Paul Fisher,' Verity said, ignoring his quip. 'It's coming back to me. I thought he was rather a stick.'

'Not at all. I liked him – a bit austere perhaps. He said it clears his head walking on the downs and he can think better at the top of a hill. He says he can hear God's voice when the birds swirl and skirr above him and I know exactly how he feels. He composes his sermons as he walks. He says the downs put all our human problems into perspective.'

Verity was surprised but pleased by Edward's enthusiasm. She wanted him to have friends in the neighbourhood to keep him company when she was away, and a bachelor vicar, clever enough to argue with him, sounded just the ticket. She thought she had better make sure the shoulder of mutton Mrs Brendel had mentioned would last until tomorrow and stretch to three.

She was a little annoyed to find that Edward had forestalled her and had already mentioned to the housekeeper that there would be three for dinner the following evening. She wondered if she should say to him that, if she were to have any authority in domestic matters, *she* must be allowed to instruct the servants. Then she realized she was being petty and probably bourgeois and decided to say nothing. It was hardly realistic for her to forbid Edward to give Mrs Brendel orders when she expected to be away so much.

She sensed that Edward was not completely relaxed despite what he had said about walking on the downs. In fact, they were both on edge. Too much hung over them for either to be convinced that their time in Rodmell was anything more than a brief interlude before 'real life' resumed.

Later that day, when a telegram arrived for Edward summoning him to town, he was visibly relieved.

'I was beginning to think that Vansittart might have

forgotten me,' he confessed, 'but I'm to present myself at the FO on Monday at eleven. I can take the eight ten and be at Victoria with time to spare. Will you be all right here, V?'

'If you don't mind,' Verity said, 'I'll come with you. I think it would do no harm for me to be seen at the paper. Weaver said he would telegraph me when he and the editor had decided where to send me but, as you say, it's better to show one's face if one doesn't want to be overlooked.'

'What a good idea! We might spend the night in Albany. Since Fenton was called up, I haven't done much in the way of cleaning but it should be all right just for a night. We might go to the Embassy and have a last whirl on the dance floor before it's all bombed to smithereens. No, I don't mean that,' he added, seeing her face fall, 'but we won't have much time for nightclubs when the balloon goes up.'

When they woke the next morning it was not yet seven but, when Edward threw back the curtains, he declared that it was going to be another beautiful day and they must get up. Basil seemed to agree because he burst through the door, put his front legs on the bed and barked. Verity would have preferred to stay in bed and make love but Edward had started shaving before she had time to protest.

Edward made breakfast – it was agreed that Mrs Brendel must have Sunday mornings off – and, after they had eaten eggs and bacon washed down with large cups of milky coffee, they decided not to go up on the downs but instead explore the river that wound its way through the valley on the edge of which Rodmell stood. Leonard had lent Edward an Ordnance Survey map of the area and he worked out what looked like a fairly easy walk of about three miles.

35

It was a mile to the Ouse and when they reached it – Basil panting in ecstasy at the surprising and unfamiliar smells – they followed the river to a bridge which, Edward was interested to see, pivoted to allow boats to continue upriver to Lewes. At Southease, they admired the ancient church, crossed the stile on the edge of Telscombe village and then followed the South Downs Way to Cricketing Bottom. They hardly met a soul but, as they made their way back to Rodmell, they ran into Leonard walking his dog. Basil sniffed at Sally appreciatively and embarked on a complicated flirting ritual which their owners watched, ready to intervene if necessary. Basil sometimes forgot he was twice or even three times the size of most other dogs.

'Walk back with me to Monk's House,' Leonard said abruptly. 'You must be dry after your exercise. I can offer you lemonade or the local cider.'

'Won't we interrupt your wife?' Verity said, not knowing whether to call her 'Virginia' or 'Mrs Woolf'.

'No, she is researching a biography of our friend Roger Fry. It's hard work but it doesn't drain her in the same way as writing a novel. The paradox is that Virginia says that the novelist is free but the biographer is tied. By which I believe she means that she relishes the challenge that writing a novel presents.'

When they had expressed their gratitude for the evening at Monk's House, Verity said, 'I felt bad about mentioning the Spanish Civil War. I did not mean to upset . . .' She hesitated and then decided on 'Virginia'.

Leonard frowned. 'It's not a subject that can be avoided but Julian's death was a terrible shock. Virginia's despair was almost as great as his mother's. For six months she all but gave up her work to share Vanessa's grief. Julian's death made no sense to her. She said to me only the other day that, when she's out walking, she often argues with him and abuses him for his selfishness in dying. She sees war as the ultimate evil and pacifism as the only possible response.'

'How will she cope when war breaks out?' Edward asked diffidently.

Leonard shrugged his shoulders. 'You must read *Three Guineas* if you haven't already. In the book she asks if it would not be better to jump into the river and end it all. I think she feels war makes all her work seem pointless.'

'Is there any way in which we can help?'

'It is very good of you – only by providing her with intelligent company when she needs it and being as optimistic as one can be in these terrible times.'

'Are you a pacifist, Leonard?' Verity asked.

'I sympathize and understand why one might be, but I'm not. Like you, I think one has to fight evil. Virginia had a lot of letters after *Three Guineas* was published last year. Not all her friends liked the book – some called her defeatist – but she had to say what she said. What did you think of Byron?'

Seeing Verity's face, he laughed. 'He's not as bad as all that. He behaved badly the other night but I think he was jealous.'

'Jealous? What of?'

'You have achieved something . . . You proved yourself in Spain. Byron's not a man of action but in his dreams he'd like to be.'

They had by this time arrived back at the church which stood just beyond both their gardens. Walking through the churchyard, sleepy with history in the heat of the midday sun, they stopped to admire the stone sundial.

Edward peered at it and asked how it had come to be there.

'It's not so old,' Leonard replied. 'It was erected by the rector, Pierre de Putron, in 1876. It's thought to have come from the garden of a house nearby. Do you see?' He pointed to the inscription. 'John Saxby and Richard Saxby. John farmed round here and was a local benefactor. Virginia has an affection for it and, when she was writing

The Years which is about the passing of time, she liked to come here and meditate.'

'I thought I'd go to evensong tonight,' Edward said.

'I might come with you. Virginia won't but I like to go occasionally out of respect for our vicar. I suppose, if anything, I'm a Jew but I'm not religious.'

'I'm afraid I won't come,' Verity said. 'I can't believe in it and I don't want to pretend.'

'Paul Fisher is a friend of a friend of ours,' Edward explained. 'What do you make of him, Leonard?'

'I like him. He's an old-fashioned, moral young man with strict views on good and evil. We argue a lot because I think his attitude does not make allowances for the complication of real life. He calls me a Laodicean which I think in his eyes is the severest of criticisms.'

'What's a Lao-what-do-you-call-it?' Verity inquired.

'Someone lukewarm or half-hearted about morality and religion. He's been looking ill – much too thin. I suppose it's just the war. It makes everyone nervy.'

They found Virginia sitting in a deckchair outside her writing-room. She greeted them warmly.

'We're not disturbing you, I hope?' Edward said.

'Not at all. Leonard, ask Louie to bring us lemonade, unless you would prefer cider, Edward?' He assured her that lemonade was just what he needed. 'I have decided I am going to take up knitting,' Virginia said unexpectedly. 'I need something soothing to help me think.'

When Mrs Everest came out with a jug of lemonade and glasses on a tray, Edward recognized her from when they had dined at Monk's House.

'Thank you for the excellent dinner we had the other night,' he said. She beamed and Leonard looked pleased.

When she had gone, he said, 'I don't think we could survive without Louie. She's an excellent cook and also an active member of the local Labour Party. In fact, she's secretary of the Rodmell branch which meets here.'

Verity felt at peace as she sat beside Virginia in the sunshine, sipping lemonade and watching Edward and Leonard talking earnestly about politics. The peace was shattered by Mark Redel who came striding on to the lawn without any apology for intruding.

'I'd like to kill that man,' he fumed.

'Which man, Mark?' Virginia asked.

'Byron, of course.'

'Do sit down and cool off with a glass of lemonade, Mark. You look as though you are about to explode.'

'I'm sorry but it really is the limit. He came round to my studio to ask if I would do a portrait of that girl of his, Frieda Burrowes. She's a pretty thing but too thin – not really my type. Anyway, I said I wouldn't do it and that he ought to be ashamed for carrying on with her behind his wife's back. Then we had a row and he accused me of all sorts of absurd things – about Marjorie and Luke. He said she was right to leave me and that I was a failed artist . . . lots of silly stuff. I shouldn't have done it but I called him a goat and a versifier, not a patch on Auden. I suppose I'd been thinking I wasn't much good but it hurt to have it said by that man.'

'I didn't know you knew Frieda Burrowes,' Leonard said.

'In Highgate – we were a sort of group, I suppose. I was keen on her myself to tell the truth but she was hitched to another man – Lewis Cathcart – and I still had Marjorie. Frieda modelled for me and I think everyone, including Marjorie, thought I'd slept with her but I hadn't. Oh God, why am I telling you all this?'

'So what happened – I mean after your row? Is he still in your studio?' Leonard asked.

'No, he stormed out but not before he'd called me a lot of names, some of which I expect I deserve.'

'How silly you boys are,' Virginia said. 'Now Mark, have you met our new neighbours, Edward and Verity Corinth?'

'I have met Verity.' Redel noticed Edward scowl. 'Forgive me but your wife said I could call her that. I hope you don't mind.' He shook Edward's hand energetically.

Edward thought him rather bumptious but smiled and said that he didn't mind and that Verity had been extolling his work. 'She wants to buy one of your paintings – a self-portrait?' he finished.

'Only if *you* like it. You can't live with a painting you don't like. I have plenty of others. My last show wasn't a success as I'm sure Adrian will have told you. Come over tomorrow and have a look if you'd like. As usual, I have no money but at least I've no longer got a wife and son to support,' he added bitterly.

He looked so miserable as he said this that Edward felt quite sorry for him but then wondered whether he was being manipulated. He had an idea that Redel was often sorry for himself and liked others to sympathize and make allowances for his erratic behaviour.

'Now, what about a game of bowls?' Leonard said. 'Don't look so surprised, Edward. Hasn't anyone told you? I'm a demon bowls player and Virginia is quite good.'

He laughed and looked at his wife affectionately. He went into the writing-room and came out with a box. 'All right, everybody?'

Evensong in the cool, quiet church was a moment of peace in a world in turmoil. Edward savoured the Englishness of it – the badly sung hymns, the wheezing organ and even Paul Fisher's lengthy, hell-and-damnation sermon during which Edward studied the marble plaque on the wall listing the villagers killed in the Great War. He thought of the first time he had walked under School Arch into School Yard and seen the names of the dead in black bronze stretching along the arcade and into the cloisters. He remembered how he had wept for the first and last time as an Eton schoolboy as he read the words from Milton's *Samson Agonistes*. 'Nothing is here for tears, nothing to wail or knock the breast, no weakness, no contempt, dispraise or blame; nothing but well and fair, and what may quiet us in a death so noble.'

There were a dozen people seated on the narrow pews. According to Leonard, this was a few more than usual – no doubt as a result of the terrifying reports on the wireless. The Nazis were threatening the Baltic port of Danzig, the Poles' access to the sea. To add to the fear, the IRA were planting bombs in London and for security reasons the public were being denied access to the House of Commons. The Chancellor, Sir John Simon, had just announced new defence borrowings of five hundred million pounds, and at the Ideal Home Exhibition luxuriously fitted-out bomb shelters were being offered for sale.

Edward wondered whether it was sentimentality that made him pray that this village and its ancient church, which had survived so much bloodshed in its long history, would be spared the tide of destruction relentlessly sweeping over Europe.

As the little congregation left the church, Paul took Edward by the hand and asked to be excused from joining them for dinner. He gave no clear reason beyond a need to pray and a general disinclination, as he put it, to make merry at such a time. Edward was surprised and annoyed but did not press him. He knew that Verity would take his change of mind as a snub but, if Paul had decided not to come, there was nothing to be done about it.

'Another time,' Edward said, trying to sound undisturbed.

'Of course. Please convey my apologies to your wife. I hope she will understand.'

Leonard had overheard the exchange and said, 'Our vicar's a rum cove but I respect him. Tell Verity not to take it personally. We are all anxious and out of sorts and will

41

be until this war has really begun. Then I believe we will buckle down and do what has to be done.'

As they strolled through the churchyard out past the village school, he added, 'The news is very bad. It can't be long now. Both of us have cyanide pills. If the Nazis do invade, we shall not wait to be rounded up and sent to a concentration camp.'

'We have withstood invaders before now,' Edward tried to reassure him.

'Not ones with powerful flying machines to transform the Channel into a simple ditch. But I do not despair,' he said, hunching his shoulders. 'Not yet, at any rate.'

3

Waiting on the platform at Lewes the following morning, they literally bumped into Byron Gates. Edward was effusive. Verity had noticed before that, when he did not like someone, he tended to hide his distaste by being extra-friendly. Byron explained that he was on his way to Broadcasting House to plan the next series of talks he was due to give on why Britain had to stand up to Hitler.

'Better late than never,' he added ruefully. 'Reith backed the Prime Minister all the way. Now even he has to accept that appeasement has failed and that war is inevitable. I knew from the first that it was better to defy Hitler,' he lied.

Sir John Reith, the BBC's first Director General, had recently resigned to become Chairman of Imperial Airways but his shadow still hung over the BBC.

'Churchill can't abide him,' Edward commented.

'That's because, during the General Strike, he refused to let the government take over the BBC. Quite right too,' Byron said. 'He set the precedent and it's a good one. The BBC must remain independent of government. Even in wartime, though we may have to censor the news-papers and wireless broadcasts, the government must not be allowed to take them over and dictate what they print or broadcast. If it did, the public would never again believe what they heard on the wireless or read in the newspapers.'

Edward had to agree. 'What are you doing tonight?' he found himself saying. 'Verity and I thought we might have dinner and go on to the Embassy. It'll probably be the last time before war breaks out, but I expect that sounds rather frivolous to you.'

'Not at all. As it happens, I was thinking of doing something similar. I quite often go to the Embassy when I'm in London and I thought of taking my friend, Miss Burrowes – Frieda. Did I tell you about her?' He was all eagerness – evidently not at all hesitant about introducing them to his girlfriend.

'Well, why not join us?'

Verity wanted to kick Edward for spoiling their last romantic evening in London.

'Oh, no – I'm sure you want to be on your own,' she said rather too quickly. 'We wouldn't want to butt in on a romantic evening . . .' She smiled and wondered if Byron would be indignant with her for making it clear that she knew Frieda was his mistress. He gave no sign of it and said he particularly wanted her to meet Frieda. Edward, instead of taking the hint she had dropped about not wanting to ruin *their* romantic evening, insisted that they would be welcome if he and Frieda would like to join them.

In a black mood, Verity sank back in her seat and attempted to read her book – Arthur Koestler's *Spanish Testament*. To do Byron justice, he did not continue to make conversation but took out *The Times* and *The Listener* in which he buried himself until they reached London.

It was odd, Verity thought, but in Sussex where there was no visible sign of the approaching war Edward had seemed restless and on edge. In London, with trenches in the parks and sandbags outside public buildings, he seemed more relaxed. His long nose seemed to sniff the air like a hunting dog catching the scent of a fox or badger. Most of the men under forty wore uniforms of one sort

44

or another and, from the taxi, they saw a barrage balloon being hoisted up by a winch. In the sunshine it looked strangely beautiful, even innocent, like a child's toy, but it sent a shiver down Verity's spine.

Edward paid off the taxi at the Foreign Office. Verity said that, as it was such a lovely day, she would walk to Fleet Street. They agreed to meet in his rooms in Albany at about six.

'The porters will let you in if you get there before me, V.'

'No need to be furtive now we're married?' she teased him. 'Rather spoils the fun. It'll be odd being there without Fenton, "yes, my lording" all over the place. How long are you going to manage without a valet?'

'Mrs Brendel seems to fit the bill. To be honest, I got the feeling that Fenton decided to give notice as soon as we announced we were going to be married. Much as he liked you, V, he was used to living with a bachelor so it was perhaps a relief to both of us when he got his call-up papers.'

As he entered the Foreign Office, Edward could not help but think of the many times he had walked up that imposing staircase. Always there had been some sort of 'flap' on, to use a phrase his nephew had taught him. Frank was a junior lieutenant aboard the destroyer HMS *Kelly* commanded by Lord Louis Mountbatten and was constantly in his uncle's thoughts. Would there be a great naval battle like Jutland in 1915 or would it be a war of attrition, ship against ship? Edward could only guess but he knew, whatever kind of war it turned out to be, that Frank would be in great danger.

Oddly enough, *Kelly* came up in the conversation when, having kicked his heels for half an hour, he was shown into the office of Sir Alexander Cadogan who had taken over from Sir Robert Vansittart as Permanent Under Secretary at the Foreign Office. Edward had only met him once before but had been impressed by his no-nonsense approach. He might be brusque, even rude, but Edward understood and forgave. He did not envy Cadogan the immense burden he carried and was only grateful if, in some humble way, he could be useful.

'Corinth – good to see you. How's marriage treating you?' Without waiting for a response, Cadogan went on, 'You know the Duke of Windsor, do you not?'

'I haven't seen him since the Abdication,' Edward replied in surprise.

'Well, the fact is the Duke has appealed to us for help.'

'He's still at his villa in the south of France?'

'He is,' Cadogan confirmed, 'but as soon as war breaks out we must bring him home. I think you also know Lord Louis Mountbatten?'

'Yes, my nephew is serving on the *Kelly*.'

'Very good! When I give the word, you will go aboard the *Kelly*, sail to the south of France and pick up the Duke and Duchess and escort them back to England. You are not to leave the Duke's side until I tell you. The fact is, we don't yet know what we are going to do with him. He can't stay in England so he'll have to go to Canada or Australia – somewhere conveniently far away, you understand me? You'll get your orders but Van says you can be trusted to keep him out of trouble.'

Edward was aghast. The Duke was going to be an embarrassment for his brother, the King, and for the British government wherever he went. He was patriotic in his own way but, as a fervent admirer of Hitler and bitter at the way he had been treated by the Royal Family, he was never going to sit tight and obey orders.

Edward gulped. 'I'll do my best,' was all he could say.

'Good man! Well, that's all for now. Expect to receive your orders sometime in the next month – maybe sooner. Now I must be off. I've got a meeting with the PM and Winston. You're a friend of his too, I hear. Amazing man but untrustworthy and he doesn't like the FO – thinks we're all defeatists. You may be useful as a go-between. We'll have to see.'

They shook hands and Edward found himself back in Whitehall hardly knowing how he got there. Pulling himself together, he went off to see Guy Liddell, the head of MI5. Whatever job he might have for him, it could hardly be more demanding than nursemaiding the Duke of Windsor.

Verity took a deep breath as she entered the modern glass building on Fleet Street that housed the *New Gazette*. She greeted Fred on the door who touched his cap and hoped she was quite recovered. She felt as though it was her first day at a new school. Everyone else was rushing about, busy with their daily routine – only she had no particular purpose. She had not worked since she had caught TB over a year ago. There was a new editor whom she did not know and she had no idea whether or not she would be welcomed back into the fold. She was well aware how quickly one could be forgotten.

She had always been the special pet of the newspaper's proprietor, Lord Weaver, which hadn't made her popular. It had annoyed the editor at the time to find that he had no control over her and could not even sack her. It also annoyed her colleagues, who thought she got special treatment and probably a higher salary than they did. It hadn't mattered so much when she was in Spain covering the Spanish Civil War but, if she were to be in London for any length of time, she knew she would get into trouble and end up having a row with the editor, even if he proved to be much more tolerant than the previous incumbent.

Verity knew herself to be a first-class foreign correspondent despite, or even because of, her sex and she longed to be at the centre of things once more. This was one of those moments in history when the fate of England and her

Empire hung in the balance, and she wanted above all else to be a privileged witness to the momentous events of the next few weeks and months and record what she saw in the newspaper she loved.

Jutting out her chin, she asked Fred if Lord Weaver was in the building and was told he was. She decided to risk going straight up to his floor – there was a private lift that only went to Lord Weaver's suite at the top of the building – and see if she could wangle an interview with her boss. His secretary was a friend of hers and she knew it could be managed if he wasn't rushing out to some high-powered meeting. There was a rumour that, when war broke out and if Churchill became Prime Minister, Lord Weaver would join the government. He had been a great friend and supporter of Churchill's while always taking care to keep channels of communication open with the Chamberlain government. He knew Churchill valued his 'get-up-and-go' approach and fancied he could serve his adopted country – he was Canadian by birth – at the head of a department tasked with producing war materials. He hated 'red tape' and would breathe fresh air into a moribund ministry. Like Churchill, he had complained time and time again at Britain's failure to rearm in the face of the Nazi threat.

Miss Landon was delighted to see Verity and asked if she were fully recovered and whether she was coming back to work. Verity said she was, in answer to both questions, and reminded her that Lord Weaver had promised her a posting. As they were talking, the door burst open and the great man himself appeared. He was a bear-like figure at the best of times and Verity thought he had put on weight since she had last seen him. His colour was bad, too, but his energy seemed undiminished.

'I thought I heard a familiar squawk. What are you doing here, Verity? I thought I had made it plain that you were to take a month off to get used to marriage and all

48

that sort of thing before I sent you anywhere. Don't say you are already bored with the domestic life. By the way, how *is* Benedick, the married man?'

'Benedick . . .? Oh, you mean Edward. He's not too bad – a bit restless perhaps but that's only to be expected. We all are. Everyone's on tenterhooks waiting to be told we are at war at last.'

'And I suppose that pleases you?'

'Not at all, Joe. I've seen enough of it to last a lifetime but there are times when one has to . . .' She suddenly remembered a favourite quotation of Edward's, '"stiffen the sinews and summon up the blood".'

Weaver harrumphed. 'I haven't forgotten you, if that was what you were worried about. It's either Paris or Madrid. I haven't quite decided.'

'Gosh! Thank you, Joe. I won't let you down.'

Weaver looked at his watch. 'Look, I'm having lunch with Jock Reith. To be honest, I find him hard work. It might annoy him but amuse me if you came along.'

'Oh, I say, I don't want to gatecrash . . .'

'It could do you some good. The Prime Minister has asked him to head a new Ministry of Information. Top secret at the moment, you understand.'

Weaver smiled. He loved gossip and delighted to be 'in the know'. He found Reith's earnest morality irritating and he knew Reith considered him a rascal but they needed each other. Both men lived for the powerful institutions they had created – the *New Gazette* and the BBC.

Reith had created the British Broadcasting Corporation in his image. It was principled, independent and directed according to strong public service principles. A Scot, and the son of a United Free Church minister, Reith carried with him into adult life the strict religious principles of the Kirk. During the General Strike, the Labour Party had criticized the BBC for taking the government side while the government accused it of being unpatriotic and threatened to take it over if it did not broadcast the official line. It was Reith's finest hour. He resisted the pressure from both sides and succeeded in retaining the BBC's independence.

Reith hated Communists, disliked the idea of women taking jobs which, in his view, were unsuited to their femininity, and believed they should play no part in public life. It amused Weaver to think that, if he took Verity with him to lunch, she would tell Reith that his views were outdated and insulting to women and he would be indignant and either sulk or lecture her. In either eventuality, he would sit back and enjoy the fireworks.

'Joe, I thought we were going to . . . you did not tell me . . .' Reith struggled to his feet, letting his napkin drop to the floor.

'Waiter, bring another chair, will you? Jock, I wanted you to meet one of my most talented correspondents – Verity Browne, now Lady Edward Corinth.'

Verity smiled her sweetest smile and watched Reith struggle to control himself. He was immensely tall with a high-domed forehead and shaggy eyebrows. She remembered Edward telling her that Churchill, who did not like him, called him Wuthering Height.

'Very nice to meet you, Miss Browne . . . Lady Edward. I met your husband when I was at the BBC. I have admired your work though I can't approve . . . you are a Communist, I believe?'

'Not any more, Sir John. The Party I joined has long gone. I'm afraid it is now a tool of the Soviet Union. I saw it happen in Spain. Good men betrayed by unscrupulous apparatchiks.'

Reith's face cleared. 'I'm glad to hear you say that. The Prime Minister would have us ally ourselves with Stalin against Hitler but I have tried to persuade him that we can't be in league with the devil.'

'Mr Churchill says that our enemy's enemy is our friend,' Verity remarked meekly.

'That is cynicism at its worst. But please sit. Waiter . . . what will you have to drink?'

'Just water, thank you. I never drink at lunch,' Verity replied primly but truthfully.

Reith smiled broadly and said to Weaver, 'You were right, Joe. You have done very well to secure Miss Browne's services. I think I shall call you "Miss Browne" if that is all right with you?'

Verity nodded and smiled and Weaver sighed. He had been done out of his fireworks – though not entirely. Verity did not hesitate to launch an attack on the BBC for employing women only to read stories on Children's Hour or talk about cooking or clothes. Reith defended himself vigorously but without rancour, pointing out that women read the news as early as 1926 during the General Strike.

'I'd say another thing,' he went on with a seriousness that impressed Verity. 'No one can deny we have lived in a Britain of two nations, rich and poor. The BBC has begun to bring the two together. Three-quarters of British homes now have a wireless set. You can buy one for as little as two pounds. Now, the Durham coal miner, after a day down the pit, can listen to a top dance band playing in a smart London hotel – Lew Stone on Tuesday, Roy Fox on Wednesday, Harry Roy on Friday . . . And when war comes, the BBC will bring the nation even more closely together to forge a patriotic alliance of rich and poor.'

'There's something in what you say, Sir John,' Verity admitted, 'but if you were a miner working in a danger-ous pit, coming home dirty because the pit owner failed to provide showers at the pithead, squatting in a tin tub in front of the fire with water from a primitive boiler, no cooker, just a gas ring, the house verminous, the children ill-fed and diseased – you could not afford the five shil-lings to call out the doctor, remember – would it not make

51

you bitter to hear the clink of champagne glasses and the smooth sounds of a dance band playing in some swanky hotel? It would me.'

'I don't think so. I agree that the conditions in which many people live are intolerable but things are already changing for the better. In the past year, we have built thirty thousand new houses, many in the suburbs of our cities – healthy, new homes – and after the war the government will use the powers it has taken to build a better society.'

'The first thing will be to nationalize the coal mines,' Verity grumbled, feeling quite uncomfortable as Reith propounded a vision of a just society to which any Communist would have to subscribe.

'And as for class envy,' he went on, disregarding her interjection, 'I do not believe that working people enjoying dance-band music on the wireless want to be in one of those – as you put it – swanky hotels dancing and drinking champagne. It is like the cinema. Twenty million people go the pictures every week usually to watch worthless rubbish but they don't believe they could dance like Fred Astaire or Ginger Rogers or live the life they see on the screen. It is pure escapism and we all need that. I won't deny that I would rather they wanted less trivial entertainment and more instruction to help them live better and more useful lives, but at least we can make ordinary people aware of what there is out there and appreciate the England for which they are going to be asked to fight.'

As she watched Reith's eyebrows waggle with excitement, Verity realized what an extraordinary man he was. He had a vision, and if it wasn't one she shared in its entirety, it certainly had its appeal.

'Well, Sir John, I am impressed but when I am next in 6 Stanhope Gate,' this was Gunter's restaurant in which debutantes gathered in the season to drink champagne and spend a working man's wage on a single meal, 'and see the noses of the unemployed pressed against the plate-glass window, I will think of you and not be embarrassed.'

Reith smiled, knowing he had won.

'This is all too worthy for me,' Weaver grumbled, though he was secretly intrigued to find that these two, who on the surface had so little in common, shared similar views on the state of the nation. 'Jock, did you know, Lord Edward has recently bought a house in Sussex, near Virginia and Leonard Woolf?'

Weaver knew this seemingly innocent remark would precipitate another lecture from Reith on the loose morals of the 'artistic' set and so it did. He did not hesitate to label them immoral, free thinkers – unpatriotic and corrupters of the young. It was apparent that the morality he had learnt as a child brooked no challenge from the modern, post-war materialistic world.

'During the Great War, those people – long-haired lay-abouts living in Bloomsbury – were conscientious objectors and should have been put up against a wall,' he said indignantly. 'My time in the trenches was the making of me. I'd go so far as to say they were the happiest years of my life, even though I was wounded.'

'I know what you mean,' Verity agreed, to Weaver's surprise. 'There is something about the sheer excitement of war – the feeling of being alive *because* so near to death that makes life doubly valuable.'

'Wait a moment,' Weaver interjected. 'I thought you said, Verity, that you didn't want war.'

'Of course I don't. You'd have to be mad to want death and destruction. I'm simply saying that, once you're in it, there can be a kind of satisfaction in seeing how one measures up to it.'

Her eyes shone and Reith looked at her with surprise and approval. Joe sighed again. All this mutual admiration was getting on his nerves. Lighting a cigar, he said, 'Were you sad to leave the BBC, Jock?'

'I admit I was, Joe. I created it and I think I did a good job but I have learnt in life that there's no point in looking back. The Prime Minister – I speak in complete confidence – has asked me to set up a Ministry of Information to control the media in the event of war so I'll once again –' his eyes twinkled mischievously – 'regain some authority over the organization I created. Ogilvie's a good fellow but, between ourselves, he isn't up to the job of Director General.'

Verity wondered at how indiscreet these great men could be, talking in front of journalists they neither knew nor trusted. Reith could not resist denigrating the man who had usurped him, whatever the consequences.

'These foreign broadcasts are a good idea,' she said.

'Yes, I'm glad you think so. My friend Dr Wanner, who was head of the South German Broadcasting Organization until the Nazis took over, is doing a very good job, so much so that the Germans try to "jam" his broadcasts. The PM told me the other day that he was unhappy at the tone of the BBC's foreign broadcasts, that they were too gloomy. I pointed out that the news *was* gloomy and that the best way of making sure the BBC was listened to and trusted in Europe was to tell the truth however gloomy. Then, when there was good news to report, it would be believed.'

'And the talks by Harold Nicolson and Byron Gates – they are very popular but serious, too,' Weaver put in. 'Gates, in particular, strikes just the right tone – serious but not pompous, cultured but not patronizing.'

'Ugh! That man Gates. I can't stick him,' Reith said vehemently. 'He's immoral and irreligious – a damned hypocrite. According to one of my people, he almost got himself kicked out of the building just before I left. I would have done so myself but Ogilvie has kept him on.'

'What had he done?' Verity inquired with interest.

'Women! What else. Someone's wife – it's all too sordid to go into, my dear. Saving your presence, when I was in charge I tried to do without them. It's bad enough having them as secretaries. They flirt with the men and . . .' Seeing the twinkle in Weaver's eye, he stopped himself. 'Well, don't get me on my hobby horse.'

Verity stifled a protest. She looked at Weaver and saw that he was surprised and even a little disappointed that she had been able to control herself.

On their way back to the *New Gazette,* Weaver said, 'I hope you enjoyed that, Verity.'

'I was very interested to meet Sir John but I still don't understand why you took me along with you. Was it just to rile him? He really wanted to see you on your own.'

'He's going to be Minister of Information, as he said, and I want him to use you, if possible. I need someone who can stand up to him and who knows about newspapers, which he doesn't.'

'But . . . I'll be abroad, won't I?'

'I hope so, I very much hope so. I don't want to sound defeatist but, a year from now, will there be anywhere in Europe for you to report from?'

'Paris – there'll always be Paris.'

'I hope so, Verity,' he repeated. 'It was almost lost in the last war and that was before the Germans had Panzers . . .'

Verity, suddenly aware of the very real possibility that Britain would be defeated, lapsed into silence.

4

That evening, Verity didn't altogether feel like going out but Edward had got it into his head that these were the last moments of peace and that they would look back with nostalgia on a London of bright lights and innocent pleasure. However, once she was dressed in a shimmering gown she had bought from Schiaparelli and had straightened Edward's white tie, she felt she would, after all, enjoy herself.

The West End was crowded with people intent on having a good time, determined to put out of their minds the imminent catastrophe. It would come but, until it did, they would party. Edward and Verity dined at Gennaro's and then, as it was a warm evening, strolled down to the Embassy at the Piccadilly end of Bond Street. Verity felt her spirits lift and tunelessly – she was not musical – hummed the lines from a popular song. 'There's film stars, peers and peeresses, all crowded on the floor. There's the Prince of Wales and Lady F and every crashing bore I know in the dear old Embassy.'

The nightclub was reached down a wide, low-ceilinged tunnel. The entrance at the far end was guarded by a tall, impressive-looking commissionaire who greeted Edward as though he had been in just a few days before, though it was at least a year since he had been 'out on the tiles', as he put it. He bought a buttonhole from the one-legged man at the door and they made their way through a throng of dancers to a table well back from the dance floor.

Verity went off to 'powder her nose'. The ladies' cloak-room was fitted out with marble basins and gold taps. Looking at herself in the mirror, she thought Edward had no need to be ashamed of his wife. Her new dress, sensuous blue silk that hugged her body, made her feel desirable. Maybe she wasn't as smart as the expensively dressed women making up their faces on either side of her – and talking across her as though she did not exist in harsh, high-pitched voices – but she did not envy them. Their air of extreme boredom and consequent discontent, though possibly adopted to convey worldly wisdom, made their eyes hard. The powder with which they cov-ered their faces turned their skin a deathly white so that, in the bright artificial light, they appeared to be wearing masks. She thought she recognized one or two of them but they belonged to a world of which she had never been part. She might be Lady Edward Corinth but she knew – or thought she knew – that these idle, wealthy women would despise her as a *parvenue* if they ever deigned to notice her.

Her ears pricked as she heard the name Byron Gates. She would hardly have imagined that – being neither rich nor titled – he would be known to such women but it appeared she was wrong. One of the women was saying that her sister worked at the BBC – '*too* amusing, my dear, but if the war comes we'll all be expected to do our bit, I suppose.'

'I wouldn't mind having a job,' the woman on Verity's left put in. 'It might be rather exciting driving officers round London. Men look so much more manly in uniform, don't you think, Babs?'

'Not my Reggie. He's a dear but not even a field mar-shal's uniform would make him – how did you put it? – manly. As for Byron dressing up to look like Oscar Wilde, it might have been amusing in the twenties but how he manages to look louche without being attractive, I can't think. And he hasn't got any money.'

'You don't really think that, do you, darling?' one of the other women said. 'I think he's so handsome and he dances divinely.'

'Well, why don't you ditch him, Babs? Reggie, I mean,' the woman on Verity's right suggested.

'But how would I support myself without Reggie's millions? There seem to be so many fewer unattached rich men in London nowadays.'

'But, Babs, you promised to tell us about Merry,' another woman said.

It appeared that Byron had taken 'Merry'– who, Verity deduced, was Babs's younger sister – to the Embassy and then abandoned her for 'some tart', leaving her without the money to get a taxi home. 'I mean, what a cad! Luigi had to sub her a pound,' Babs finished.

'How perfectly frightful! Well, of course he's not a gentleman,' one of the women said, powdering her nose with ferocity.

'No, but he's a poet and jolly good-looking,' another of Babs's friends said with a giggle.

'Still, Merry's learnt her lesson,' her sister added, painting her lips a deeper shade of red. 'She told me she's thinking of becoming a lesbian – *so* amusing. Apparently the BBC is full of queers.'

'If he did that to my sister, I'd get Ronald to give him a thrashing,' her friend said, blotting her crimson lips on a paper towel.

Edward rose as Verity reappeared at the table. She apologized for being so long. 'I just couldn't drag myself away. I was eavesdropping on a conversation about Byron Gates. I gather he brought a girl here and left her without a sou while he went off with another girl. You men!'

She sank on to the banquette beside Edward and sipped at her champagne. Harry Roy's band was playing dance music and a few couples were already on the floor.

'Edward, look! That's the woman who was talking about Byron.'

'I know her. She's Lady Gore-Bell. When I went out more often she and I used to "trip the light fantastic".'

'Well, introduce me to her. I want to see her face when she realizes she lost you to an unimportant journalist.'

'Jealous, my own one?' Edward said, taking her hand. 'No need to be. I wouldn't want to be anywhere else tonight with anyone else. Let's dance and we can "bump into" Barbara and I'll introduce you.'

'You know I can't dance but I suppose no one will notice.'

'Babs! Haven't see you in ages,' Edward said as he engineered the 'bump'. 'Do come and have a drink at our table. I don't think you know my wife. Verity, this is Barbara Gore-Bell.'

Verity tried to look pleased.

'Edward, darling – how absolutely lovely! I heard you were married and to a famous foreign correspondent.' She offered Verity a limp hand. 'I thought I recognized you downstairs. Oh help, I hope I wasn't being indiscreet. I didn't say anything about Edward, did I? The moment I saw your picture in *Tatler* – or was it the *Illustrated London News*? – anyway, the moment I saw it I said to Reggie, trust Edward to marry someone different. We debs bored him silly, didn't we, Edward? By the way – this is Reggie, my husband. I absolutely adore him, don't I, darling? And he's heavenly rich.'

Reggie, a balding man some twenty years older than his wife, looked tickled to be adored for his wealth and smiled at her indulgently.

'Lady Edward,' he said taking Verity's hand. 'I say, beautiful and brainy! Not really fair, what!'

Edward saw Barbara wince but Verity held her smile which had become, he thought, roguish if insincere.

'Sir Reginald . . .' Verity allowed him to kiss her hand.

'Reggie, you must call me Reggie. Everyone does, you know.'

'And Verity – I may call you Verity, mayn't I?' his wife echoed. 'You must call me Babs. I feel we are going to be great friends.'

'Babs, I couldn't help overhearing your conversation when we were powdering our noses.' Verity took pleasure in the lady-like euphemism. She tried not to sound arch. 'You mentioned the name Byron Gates. We've just bought a house in Sussex and he happens to live in the same village.'

'Oh Lord, was I talking ill of him?'

'No need to apologize. We have met him but he's not a friend. In fact, I have to confess that I didn't take to him and it doesn't surprise me to hear he behaved badly to your sister. I hope I am not being impertinent but the coincidence . . .'

'Not at all. Edward knows I have the sweetest nature and never normally say anything bad about anyone but, really, he's a rat.' Barbara looked towards the stairs. 'Good heavens, talk of the devil. Here he is now.'

'Yes,' Edward explained, 'we came up to town on the same train and we sort of agreed to meet here. How embarrassing!'

'We'll leave you to him, won't we, Reggie? I really can't talk to him. I might have to douse him with champagne. Who's the woman with him? It's not his wife. She's the actress, Mary Brand. I've met her. Don't say he's brought his mistress! When you are the Aga Khan, you can get away with having a string of mistresses but not when you are plain Mr Gates. Well, goodbye, both of you. Telephone me, Edward – Sloane 247. We must meet and talk over old times. Come, Reggie – it's time we went home.'

She swept off haughtily, leaving Verity and Edward to greet Byron.

'Wasn't that Barbara Gore-Bell?' Byron asked, sounding puzzled. 'I wonder why she made off like that?'

'She said you had abandoned her sister here one evening and gone off with some other girl.' Verity thought it would be interesting to see how he reacted to being told the truth. Edward looked pained.

'Oh really!' Byron was indignant. 'I brought Merry here, yes, but it was she who abandoned me. I had a dance or two with an old chum and, when I got back to the table, I found she had vanished. It was all a silly misunderstanding. She's not still holding a grudge, is she?'

Edward had risen when Byron had come over to their table and now gently reminded him that he had not introduced them to his friend.

'I do apologize. May I introduce you to Frieda Burrowes? Frieda, Lord and Lady Edward Corinth. Verity, I wanted you and Frieda to meet because I thought you would have so much in common.'

'Really?' Verity said, raising an eyebrow.

'Yes, Frieda's a journalist too. She works at the BBC.'

'Oh, don't be ridiculous, Byron. Miss Browne – I mean Lady Edward – is a real journalist. I merely interview women of note, that sort of thing. I interviewed Charlotte Hassel – she's a friend of yours, I believe?'

'One of my oldest friends,' Verity said, warming to the girl.

'She's one of my favourite novelists. I say, Lady Edward . . . or do you prefer to be called Miss Browne?'

'Miss Browne is the name I work under, but please call me Verity.'

'Gosh! That's very nice of you. I say, do you think I might interview *you* one day? You have had such an interesting life.'

'I suppose so, but it'll have to be soon. I am expecting to be posted abroad in the next few weeks.'

'Of course. I'll talk to my producer . . . Mr Barnes.'

'Have you always been a journalist?' Verity asked.

'Well, I was an actress but I wasn't getting on too well. Then I was lucky enough to be introduced to Val Gielgud. Do you know him?'

'I'm afraid not but I've heard of him, of course. His brother is the actor?'

'That's right. Anyway, Val said I had a good voice for the wireless and he offered me a trial. So here I am at the BBC and, I must say, I really enjoy it. It's true we women are rather kept in our place but we're gradually being allowed to do more – like this interviewing.'

'Are you allowed to interview men?' Verity asked genuinely interested.

'Not politicians or anyone important. It's usually writers, artists – those sort of people.'

'Unimportant men,' Byron commented acidly.

'Oh no, Byron. You are important but just not . . .'

'Have you interviewed Byron yet?' Verity asked to help Frieda out.

'That's how we met, actually. I engineered it! I thought he was gorgeous and I loved his poetry. Don't you think he's a great poet?'

'I'm afraid I haven't read any yet,' Verity admitted, turning to Byron, 'but I'm going to buy one of your books while I'm in London.' She added in excuse, 'I don't read much poetry but I do like W. H. Auden.'

Byron frowned. No one likes to hear a friend praised.

'I'm surprised to see you in a place like this, Verity,' Byron said, displeased. 'With your left-wing principles, I mean.'

'I could say the same about you,' Verity responded, smiling until her face hurt.

'*Touché*, but we have to have some pleasures, don't we? The band's very good.'

'I'm told you're a good dancer,' Verity teased, and was taken aback when he seemed gratified by her compliment.

'You are very kind but I just do what I can to avoid step-
ping on my partner's toes. Will you . . . if your husband
permits?' he said, holding out his hand.

Verity had no option but to take his hand and get up.
She had to admit after a minute or two that it wasn't a
penance. Byron *was* a good dancer and, even better, he
made her feel she too could dance well. They moved
some distance from their table and she began to relax
as the music and Byron's instinctive grace gave her
confidence.

'I'm afraid I'm not much of a dancer,' she said. 'I never
did the Season and there wasn't much dancing in Spain.'

She wished she had not made the excuse. It sounded as
if she was trying to claim the moral high ground but Byron
did not seem to notice.

'You dance beautifully. Your partner has very little to do
except try not to trip over his feet,' he said with a smile.

'Where did you learn to dance so well?'

'You'll laugh, but when I was young and very short of
money, I used to spend what little I had going to dance
halls. I don't suppose you think of poets as being social
animals but I always liked company, particularly female.
No starving in a garret if I could possibly avoid it.'

'Presumably there isn't a vast amount of money in
poetry, or am I wrong?'

'You are not wrong. I worked in a preparatory school
for some time – oh dear, you can't imagine how awful that
was – and then I hit lucky with these detective stories. In
fact, there's talk of turning one of them into a film. My
wife, Mary, is in Hollywood, as I think I told you, and she
has a certain amount of influence with some of the producers over there.'

'How exciting! I didn't know you wrote detective stories
as well. I'll buy one of those too. I'll dash round to Bumpus
tomorrow straight after breakfast. I wonder if they'll give
me a discount if I say you are a friend?'

'I doubt it,' Byron said, not seeming to notice he was being teased.

Verity thought he might offer to give her a copy but he didn't. He sounded a little too pleased with himself and she wanted very much to prick his self-esteem but she could hardly blame him for bragging. *She* might be tempted to brag if she had had the same success with her writing as he had enjoyed.

'And your wife doesn't mind you dancing the night away with your charming friend?' She hadn't been able to stop herself. 'Oh sorry, how rude of me!'

'My wife doesn't mind. We have a sort of understanding. What she does in Hollywood is her business and while she's away . . . Well, she doesn't expect me to be celibate. Are you shocked?'

'No, of course not!' Verity *was* shocked even if she couldn't admit it. She wouldn't want to think Edward was 'dancing' with other women when she was abroad. 'I like detective stories,' she said, trying to recover herself. 'They're an escape from the reality of death. Which do you think is your best?'

'I really wouldn't know. I always think my most recent book is my best.'

'What's it called?'

'*The Unkindest Cut*.'

'What's it about?'

'Oh, the usual thing – a man hears something he shouldn't and gets murdered.'

'*The Unkindest Cut* – that's a quotation, isn't it? I'm sure I've heard Edward say it when he cuts himself shaving. You know, he maddens me by seeming to know the whole of Shakespeare off by heart. Is it Shakespeare, by the way?'

'It is, as a matter of fact – *Julius Caesar.* "Judge, O you gods, how dearly Caesar lov'd him! This was the most unkindest cut of all . . ."'

'Yes, it's usually Shakespeare when the grammar's wonky. Even I know not to write "most unkindest". So, in your book the victim was stabbed?'

'He had his head cut off, but in the play Brutus stabbed Caesar, as I expect you remember. I would have called it *Cut off his Head* but I'd already used it as a title. It's from *Henry VI*, you know – all my titles come from Shakespeare.'

'Not Byron?'

'I'll tell you a secret.' He leant forward and whispered in her ear. 'I prefer Shelley. In fact, my detective is called Shelley. "I met Murder on the way – he had a mask like Castlereagh – very smooth he looked, yet grim; seven bloodhounds followed him . . .".' he quoted.

'Gosh! I'm quite confused,' Verity said, trying not to sound sarcastic. 'So you're Shelley, not Byron after all!'

When they returned to the table, Byron swept up Frieda for a foxtrot and Edward suggested Verity might like to dance with him.

'I doubt I'm up to Byron's standard but . . .'

'Don't fish for compliments. You know very well you are an excellent dancer.'

After they had been round the floor a couple of times, she said, 'Could we sit out the next dance? In fact, I feel rather tired suddenly. Couldn't we go home to bed? You know, this really isn't my sort of thing.'

'Certainly not,' Edward replied sharply. 'You are going to enjoy yourself whether you like it or not. You certainly seemed to enjoy being in Byron's arms.'

'Edward! You can't really be jealous? I loathe the man, if you must know, and it's he who has ruined our evening.'

Edward was immediately contrite. 'Sorry, V. I'm a brute. Yes, let's go back to Albany.'

She finished her champagne and felt better. They waved goodbye to Byron and Frieda who were still dancing and went to get their coats.

As they walked into Piccadilly, Verity said, 'I've just

remembered. At the lunch today with Sir John Reith, he mentioned that Byron had almost got himself thrown out of the BBC over some woman. Was that Barbara's sister, do you think, or Frieda?'

'Neither. I rather gathered from Frieda while you were cuddling up to Byron – she was very candid – that it was someone else altogether, the wife of a BBC executive.'

'What do these women see in him? I think he's positively repulsive.'

'Oh, I don't know. I remember you saying you thought him good-looking. Most women seem to find him charming.'

'Well, I don't. He says he can do what he likes when his wife's in Hollywood and she doesn't mind. I hope that's not what you think, Edward – I mean, if I'm away.'

'Of course it isn't. I'm quite hurt that you could think such a thing.' He took his arm out of hers.

It was Verity's turn to be contrite. 'I'm sorry. That was a horrible thing to say. I apologize.' She took his arm. 'Tell me I'm forgiven.'

'You're forgiven,' he said but there was still a touch of reserve in his voice.

'How can Byron afford to wine and dine his girlfriend at the Embassy?' Verity asked, trying to get back on neutral ground.

'His books, I suppose, and I imagine his wife earns a good deal in Hollywood. Perhaps she gives him an allowance.'

Verity sniffed. 'Would you accept an allowance from me? It's demeaning.'

'I wish you wouldn't keep on comparing me with Byron Gates. He's a . . . well, he's a shit, if you'll forgive my language. What my brother would call a cad and a bounder. And I didn't like the way he was holding you on the dance floor. I thought of coming over and giving him a punch in the eye.'

'What fun if you had! I was merely trying to find out about him.'

'Why? Have I missed something? Are we investigating a crime? What's he suspected of doing?'

'There is always a crime,' Verity said sententiously, 'whether we know about it or not. He's a womanizer and a philanderer – or are they the same thing? He needs to be taken down a peg or two. Anyway, don't rile at me. I thought I saw you getting very friendly with Miss Burrowes. I see her as a furry little mouse burrowing into her men before they know it and nibbling them. Yes, look – you are frayed at the edges.' She touched his cheek.

'What a disgusting image.' Edward yawned theatrically. 'I'm getting old. These late nights . . . But it was worth it, wasn't it, V? Who's to say when we'll dance at the Embassy again? Listen! Was that the song of the mythical nightingale? If we do not hear it on a night like this, when shall we?'

'It was the squawk of a taxi,' she replied unromantically but squeezed his arm so that he would know she wasn't snubbing him.

As they entered Albany, the night porter smiled and said, 'Good evening Lady Edward, my lord . . . A gentleman left this for you, my lord,' he added, handing him an envelope.

'Thank you. Goodnight, Rogers.'

'I'll look at it in the morning. It can't be important,' Edward said when he had shut the door of his rooms behind them.

'No, look at it now. It's not in my nature to get a letter and not open it.'

'You open it if you want,' he called out, going into the bathroom. 'I'm for bed.'

Verity tore open the envelope and drew out a sheet of paper. She read it, read it again, turned it over and gave a snort of disgust. She had received anonymous letters in

67

her time when she had been seen as the scarlet woman but nothing like this. She reminded herself that it had been addressed to Edward and not to her.

'What is it, V?'

'I don't know. Read it for yourself.'

Edward took the paper and read it aloud. '"Your wife is a whore. You mix with whores and sinners in dens of wickedness. He was cut off out of the land of the living." Good Lord! Where on earth did this spring from? It's quite bizarre. It's in block capitals but it's clearly written by someone educated.'

'Why? Because they spell "whore" correctly?' Verity said bitterly.

'V, I'm sorry. It is upsetting but you really can't take it seriously. It's quite mad.'

'Is the last bit a quotation?' Verity inquired, pulling herself together. It was ridiculous to be upset by such a thing but it had been a shock. It was the last thing she had expected to find in the envelope. Her guard was down when it came to being insulted. She had thought that, now she was married, she was safe from calumny but apparently that wasn't the case.

'I'm sure it's from the Bible but I'd have to ask Tommie to be sure. Hey, come on,' Edward said, seeing she was on the verge of tears. 'Don't let it get to you, V. There's so much malice in the world but what does it matter when we have each other?' He took her in his arms and held her to him.

'I'm sorry,' she said, sniffling into his shoulder. 'I know I'm stupid but it was such a shock and we had such a happy evening, despite Byron. Now it's spoilt.'

He held her away from him so he could look into her eyes. 'Now, come on. Don't you see? I think this is aimed at Byron and his girlfriend – not at us, except by association. Someone must have seen us together.'

'You think so?'

'I do, and we must find out if Byron received one too.'
He still had the sheet of paper in his hand. He let go of
Verity and read it again.

'Hm, ordinary Basildon Bond you could buy in any
stationer. A cheap pen – look how the nib has spread and
the ink blotted.'

Verity felt herself becoming more interested as the shock
wore off. 'Yes, the writer must have been almost stabbing
the paper as he wrote. Or aren't these sort of letters normally written by women?'

'Wait there while I go and talk to Rogers. I'm sure he
said it had been delivered by a man. Though, of course,
that doesn't mean a man wrote it.'

While Edward was out of the room, Verity took off her
dress and slipped on a dressing-gown. Now she no longer
had her flat in Cranmer Court, she kept a change of clothing
and night things in Albany. Edward had made some inquiries and discovered that, though Albany was mainly bachelor
apartments, there was no objection to a married gentleman
having his wife to stay for a night or two, provided she
did not call attention to herself. As she went back into the
drawing-room, Edward returned from quizzing the porter.

'All Rogers could say was that it was a man with a
moustache, rather shorter than me, but he doubted he
would recognize him again.'

'A stick-on moustache, no doubt.'

'Quite possibly. One thing did strike him as odd.
Although it was such a warm night, the man was wearing
a coat – a Burberry, he thought – and a bowler.'

'When was this?' Verity asked.

'About eleven thirty.'

'So someone watched us go into the Embassy . . .'

'And saw Byron and his girl . . .'

'But why would they think we and Byron were together
if we entered the Embassy separately? Doesn't that suggest
it has to be someone who knew we knew Byron?'

'Or who saw us in the club together. We are assuming "whores and sinners" refers to Byron and Frieda. I may be wrong. I could have spoken to Byron tonight if I had his telephone number.'

'Well, surely Frieda's number will be in the telephone book?'

'True, but . . .' Edward looked at his watch. 'It's almost one fifteen. I think we must wait till the morning. Let's try and forget about it, shall we? It would be just what the writer wanted, to spoil our evening.'

When they were in bed, Edward tried to stroke away the tension he sensed in Verity but it wasn't until he had made gentle love to her that he felt her relax. As she slept in his arms, he lay awake wondering who had taken the trouble to attack them and why. Rack his brains as he might, he could not think of anyone. He slept fitfully and was glad when it was morning.

5

They returned to Sussex the following morning without telephoning Byron Gates. On reflection, Edward had thought it might be better to wait until they saw him before raising the anonymous letter. To talk about it on the telephone might be to make too much of a malicious prank. It would be easier face-to-face either to make light of it or take it more seriously, depending on whether Byron had received a similar letter.

Edward had, however, rung Tommie Fox who had immediately identified the quotation.

'"He was cut off out of the land of the living"? It's Isaiah – a famous chapter about Christ. "He is despised and rejected of men, a man of sorrows, and acquainted with grief" – you remember it?'

'Yes, of course, from Handel's *Messiah*.'

'That's right. Hold on a minute and let me get the exact words. Ah! Here we are. "He is brought as a lamb to the slaughter . . . he was cut off out of the land of the living. For the transgression of my people was he stricken. And he made his grave with the wicked, and with the rich in his death." Why do you want to know?'

'No special reason, Tommie.' Edward had no desire to tell anyone – even a close friend – that he was getting threatening letters.

'Well, if you need religious instruction, you know where to come.'

'We're getting quite a lot of that already. You remember Paul Fisher? It turns out he's our vicar.'

'Paul! I haven't seen him for some time. I heard he'd been ill – had a breakdown or something. But being vicar of Rodmell should be quiet enough to heal the most unquiet mind.'

'You'd think so, wouldn't you? The fact is he preaches like some Old Testament prophet reprimanding us for our sins. I went to evensong on Sunday and he implied that, if we get war, it's no more than we deserve. A trifle unsettling, to say the least.'

'I'm sorry to hear that. Paul was always rather a strange bird. I felt he hated our weak Church of England huffing and puffing and would be happier with Calvin or someone like that.'

'I say, Tommie, I'd be really grateful if you could come down to Rodmell for a day or two, or are you still cross about us not getting married in a church? I tell you, Verity is very unhappy about you dropping us.'

'I haven't dropped you,' Tommie said defensively, 'but I have a lot to do in my parish.'

'Will you visit us?' Edward asked bluntly.

'Yes, I'd like that,' Tommie responded with genuine warmth, relieved that an obstacle to their friendship had been removed like a rotten tooth. 'At a time like this, one can't afford to lose touch with old friends. Not this weekend but soon. I'll send you a wire. Funny about Paul . . .'

On the day of the fête the sun chose to shine as though it never did anything else. The bunting flapped idly when the breeze stirred but the Union flag above the tea tent remained somnolent. The villagers congregated on the green, the children dressed in their best, the men wearing Sunday suits and the women brightly coloured summer frocks and hats. The festivities were opened by Leonard who, rather to Edward's surprise, proved to have a commanding voice and was listened to with respect and attention. Colonel Heron, standing beside Edward smoking and coughing, noted his surprise and reminded him that, as a young man, Leonard had ruled much of Ceylon.

'Ours is the last generation trained from birth to rule an empire,' Heron remarked when Leonard had finished. 'As a child, my nanny used to read me G.A. Henty's stories of derring-do and how the British Empire was made. I attribute my decision to join the Indian Army directly to Henty's *With Clive in India*. Did you ever read it?'

Edward shook his head. 'Not that one, but I too enjoyed Henty. It was a less complicated time, was it not? Britain's God-given destiny was to rule the world and anything or anyone who opposed it were His enemies.'

Heron sighed. 'I do not believe that the Empire can survive this war. For a century or more we have ruled India by bluff.'

'By bluff?'

'Yes, Corinth. What is it other than bluff when under a million white men rule a country, or to be more accurate a collection of countries, of many millions? This chap Gandhi . . .' Heron shook his head sorrowfully. 'This weedy little man dressed in rags, leaning on a stick and peering at the world through absurd-looking spectacles, is going to destroy the British Empire as surely as Christ destroyed the Roman.'

'It's an interesting thought,' Edward murmured. 'I don't disagree with you.'

'I say,' Heron said heartily, 'I mustn't maunder on. This isn't the moment to contemplate the end of empire. We must enjoy ourselves at this particularly English event. I

73

must introduce you to people. Everyone's dying to meet you. Now, who don't you know?'

'I'd like to meet Miss Bron and Miss Fairweather.'

'Nothing could be easier. However, you may have to buy some jam.'

Verity watched Leonard and Virginia walking around the green talking to stallholders and buying a sponge cake from Mrs Craddock, the baker's wife, and plants from Mrs Smith, the wife of the farmer who owned much of the land around the village. Virginia even bowled for the pig, and the grace with which she flung down the wooden ball and toppled half-a-dozen skittles made the little audience applaud.

Verity could not decide whether the fête was a cele-bration of democracy – the sort of social gathering which had prevented the revolution that had engulfed France in the eighteenth century – or whether it actually *celebrated* the class system. True, the gentry mixed with the 'lower orders' but it was at such a superficial level as to be almost insulting. However, she had to admit, everyone seemed to be having a good time and if the villagers felt any resent-ment at being patronized by their so-called betters, it was not evident.

She walked over to one corner of the green where excited shouts indicated that a race was in progress and arrived in time to see an attractive-looking girl of about fifteen – lanky, freckled, large-eyed and wide-mouthed – winning the egg and spoon race comfortably ahead of a younger girl with spectacles slipping off her rather large nose.

'Well done, Jean,' the younger girl panted. 'What next? Shall we do the three-legged race together?'

'I don't mind.'

'Jean, well done! Come over here, will you? I want to introduce you to Lady Edward.'

Verity looked round to find Byron Gates standing beside her. Despite the heat, he wore his black cape and, round his neck, a highly coloured bow-tie.

'Jean? That must be your stepdaughter? She's very pretty. Is Ada here too?'

'Yes, that's Ada, with the spectacles,' Byron said dismissively.

'Well, I'd like to meet her too, if I may.'

'If you want to, of course, but she's terribly dull. Ada, Lady Edward wants to meet you, though I can't think why,' he added in a low voice but Verity feared that his daughter had heard him.

She shook hands with both girls and congratulated them on their athleticism.

'Oh, I'm hopeless,' Ada said immediately, 'but Jean's amazing.'

Verity looked at her pensively. 'Ada, if you'll forgive me for speaking frankly, you mustn't feel that it matters just because you aren't as fast as your sister. It's not how fast you run that counts in the end. Don't let your father hear this but it's not even how well you do at school. I was hopeless at everything at school. In fact, I got expelled more times than I can count but, when I left school and was able to do what I really wanted, I was all right.' She was aware that she must sound sententious but Ada didn't seem to mind.

'I know all about you,' she beamed. 'My father says you are a famous foreign correspondent. You were in Spain, weren't you? Was it very frightening? Daddy says I can't say boo to a goose so I don't suppose I could do what you do.'

'I always had butterflies in my tummy before anything happened,' Verity said gently, 'but when you are in the thick of things you forget to be frightened. When it's all over I shake like a leaf but . . .'

'You're just trying to be kind. I don't believe . . .'

She was interrupted by Jean who had been hugged and kissed by her stepfather. Breaking away from his embrace, she turned to Verity.

'Why are you called Lady Edward? That's a boy's name.'

'Don't be impertinent, Jean,' Byron reprimanded her.

'You're not being impertinent. I think it's a very good question. It's one of the stupid things about being married to my husband. He's Lord Edward so apparently I have to be Lady Edward.'

'Better to marry than to burn,' Byron murmured inconsequentially.

'But what's your real name?' Jean persisted.

'Verity – Verity Browne. At least that's the name I work under and I hope you will call me by it.'

'Miss Browne – I mean Verity – can I come and talk to you when you have time? I want to be a journalist but I don't know if I can. My stepfather wants me to be an actress, like my mother, but I really don't want to be. I'm no good at performing. Now, Ada . . . she's brilliant. She can take off anybody. Ada, do the vicar. It's so funny.'

'Not now, Ada,' Byron said quickly. 'We don't want to bore Lady Edward.'

'You won't at all . . .' Verity began but it was too late. Ada went off looking crushed.

'Now the girl's sulking. I really don't know what to do with her.'

'You should be more understanding, for a start,' Verity said sharply. 'She's sensitive and needs her confidence building.' Byron shrugged and wandered off.

'Where do you go to school, Jean?' Verity asked.

'We've both started at Pilbeams – it's a boarding school the other side of Lewes.'

'What's it like?'

'It's all right but it's not easy starting at a new school halfway through a term. Everyone already has their friends and it's difficult to . . . you know, break in. It's not too bad for me because I'm good at games – lax and hockey, even cricket – but it's not so easy for Ada.' She looked round to make sure that Ada was out of earshot.

'To be honest, I think she's lonely. I do my best but she finds it hard to make friends, and my stepfather – well, he's not very sympathetic. Oh gosh, why am I telling you all this?'

'I expect because you sense that I had the same sort of problem. My mother died just after I was born and, though I love my father and he loves me, he's a busy lawyer and I seldom see him. I had a string of nannies when I was little to whom I was perfectly foul. I was sent to boarding school as soon as I was old enough but I hated it – all those rules and regulations. I couldn't wait to be grown up.'

'I say,' Jean looked at her with interest, 'I've had an idea. I know it's not your business . . . I mean, you've got so much else to do but, if you had time, do you think you could have a talk with Ada? She'd take it from you if you told her that it doesn't matter not being good at school. She's floundering around at the moment. She's unhappy even if she doesn't know it. She hasn't got a mother . . .'

'I've just been telling her exactly that, but I don't think she believed me. She worships you, which I expect can be a bit of a burden . . .' Jean made a moue of distaste and Verity added quickly, 'Of course, I'll do what I can but I don't want your stepfather to think I'm interfering or, worse, setting Ada against him.' Jean look rather crestfallen so Verity tried to reassure her. 'But it was a good idea of yours to tell me about her. I'll see what I can do to encourage her to have confidence in herself. There's always something we can do better than anyone else, if one can just work out what it is.'

She rejoined Edward and they wandered round the green buying things they did not want and meeting everyone. Although they attracted some curious stares, Edward was pleased to find that their notoriety had not percolated through to deepest Sussex. It was enough that he was a lord to make the women simper and the men touch their hats. He could see Verity would have preferred a little healthy disrespect but it's a fact that there is no one more conservative than the average English villager.

Edward also bowled for the pig. He was relieved not to win it and then attempted to knock a coconut off its perch with equal lack of success. However, he absolutely refused to bob for an apple despite Jean's urging. He watched with admiration as she dipped her head in the tin bath full of water to retrieve a maddeningly elusive apple with her teeth. While she managed to look like a mermaid as she resurfaced, the water pouring off her head, he knew he would only look ridiculous.

Seeking other ways to spend money, he discovered 'roll a penny' which involved sliding pennies down little chutes on to a board marked with the amount one might win – not more than sixpence – but in the end, to general amusement, all his pennies were lost. Other ancient games, featuring straw 'dollies', 'whacking the rat' and pinning the tail on a donkey while blindfolded, made everyone thirsty. The children drank 'pop' or lemonade. The grown-ups had a cup of tea and a slice of cake in the tea tent and there was also 'scrumpy' – a rough cider – which Edward muttered to Verity must be at least a hundred per cent proof. Then, at five o'clock, Edward and Verity trooped off with Leonard and Virginia to watch the children's pageant, which Virginia was to judge.

There were nine tableaux in all, each illustrating a famous moment in British history. As each tableau was revealed, Miss Bron declaimed a brief account, written by Miss Fairweather, of the story being portrayed. Two or three children, dressed by their mothers with magnificent inventiveness and inaccuracy, evoked a scene from 'our island story', as Miss Fairweather called it: Canute addressing the waves – rolled-up newspaper painted blue – Alfred burning the cakes, Harold with an arrow in his eye, then a big leap in time to the Princes in the Tower.

Henry VIII – impersonated, Verity was surprised to see, by Ada – was shown personally beheading Anne Boleyn with a sword – presumably an axe was considered too heavy for a child to wield safely. Charles I suffered the same fate – decapitated by, it looked to Edward, the same sword. Finally, a loyal tableau was revealed comprising Britannia – Jean waving the sword and obviously enjoying her moment – draped in a Union Jack protecting the two little Princesses, Elizabeth and Margaret Rose. Edward was moved by Miss Fairweather's appeal, barked out by Miss Bron, for every Englishman to do his duty and defend his beloved country from an unnamed foe. He noticed several of the onlookers dabbing their eyes. Miss Bron had an actor's ability to discard her normal self and inhabit a quite different persona when the occasion demanded.

When the pageant was over, the children gathered on the little stage to take their bows and everyone joined in a spirited singing of the national anthem – or at least the first verse, which was all that most people could remember. There was much applause as Virginia handed out bags of sweets to each child and a half-crown to the boy who had impersonated Admiral Nelson with another to 'Lady Hamilton'.

Edward whispered to Verity that it was only right that they should have won first prize as Lady Hamilton had often amused Nelson with similar tableaux which she called 'attitudes'.

'I wonder where they got that sword?' Verity asked of no one in particular.

'It belongs to me,' replied Colonel Heron who happened to be standing behind her. 'An ancestor of mine brought it back from Ramillies. It hangs over the mantelpiece in my library but I always lend it for the pageant. Rather splendid, isn't it? I'd better go and rescue it before someone cuts themselves.'

'Yes, it looks quite lethal,' Edward remarked.

'Who's Ramillies when he's at home?' Verity demanded when Heron had gone.

'I've just been reading about it, as a matter of fact. You remember? I showed you Mr Churchill's biography of the Duke of Marlborough. He sent it to me with that very kind inscription. There was a picture in it of the Duke on his horse pointing at the enemy.'

'Oh, so it was a battle?'

'Ramillies? Yes, 1706 – fought on a Sunday. One of "Corporal John's" greatest victories. Did you know the Duke suffered from very bad migraines during or after the battle?' A thought struck Edward. 'I wonder if that could be Paul's problem? He seems to have that white, strained look . . .'

'Hold on a minute, I think Paul's going to make a speech.'

The vicar clambered on to the stage and thanked Mrs Woolf for judging the pageant and God for the good weather, and then the fête was over. Stallholders started packing up and the pig was led off squealing by its proud owner.

'Come back with me and have a chota peg,' Colonel Heron commanded Edward. 'It's hardly out of your way.'

Edward would have given a lot to be able to go straight home but he saw that the Colonel would take mortal offence if they refused.

'Delighted, but we mustn't be long. Mrs Brendel, our housekeeper, promised something special for dinner and we mustn't be late.'

Heron looked at him like a hungry dog but Edward absolutely refused to ask him to join them.

His house – Seringapatam – was a ten-minute walk away. It was a mid-Victorian monstrosity and much too large, Edward thought, for a single man.

'You called your house Seringapatam after the battle, I suppose?' he said, to make conversation.

'Yes, the last battle of the Mysore War. It was either that or Dhundia Wagh,' Heron laughed, 'and that would have been a bit of a mouthful.'

'Now remind me – who or what was he?'

'He was a robber chief who escaped from prison in Seringapatam and raised an army. Wellington defeated him but, in the battle, he fell off his horse and one of my ancestors defended him until he was able to get up and remount. Of course, he wasn't the Duke then, just plain Arthur Wellesley or Wesley, I can't quite remember.'

'Gosh!' Verity said. 'Wasn't he – I mean your ancestor – made a duke or something?'

''Fraid not, but he ended up a general.'

'Good heavens!' Edward exclaimed. 'How interesting – worth a tableau, I should have thought. So your family have always had this connection with India?'

'Indeed. In fact, I was born in Calcutta where my father was stationed. I served in the Indian Army at the beginning of the last shindig. I was with the India Corps on the Western Front in 1914. They coped magnificently with the rain and mud – a continual monsoon, it seemed – but the butcher's bill was terrible. Khudadad Khan, who was awarded one of the first Victoria Crosses in the war, was one of my chaps. He remained with his machine-gun despite very heavy bombardment and was bayoneted at his post. A very gallant soldier. We had nine Indian Victoria Crosses awarded on the Western Front and, in the war as a whole, over forty thousand Indians lost their lives in the service of this country. People forget the part played in our victory by troops from every corner of the Empire and of every kind of creed and colour. I was a proud man, I can tell you, when I led my boys "over the top". And now we've got it all to do again.' Heron shook his head in despair.

'Brave men, indeed. They make me feel very humble,' Edward responded.

'You never married, Colonel Heron?' Verity inquired.

'No, Lady Edward. Never had the time. Never met the right woman, I suppose. So I retired here – bought this house and I suppose I'll die here.'

'But why here?'

'I met Mr Woolf in Ceylon many years ago when we were both young men. Then I bumped into him again when I was back in England – at the Travellers' Club. He was kind enough to suggest coming down here. I had no links with anywhere in particular so I thought, why not?'

'Mr Woolf seems to be responsible for a lot of people coming to live round here,' Verity remarked. 'We are in Rodmell because our friends, the Hassels, suggested it and they came because Charlotte Hassel is a friend of Mrs Woolf's. Do you know the Hassels, Colonel?'

'Met them, of course. The husband is that painter fellow, isn't he?'

'Yes, Adrian's a painter – a rather good one I believe, but I'm no judge myself.'

Heron looked unconvinced. 'Those orange and yellow things and the stick men . . .? Modern art – can't make head or tail of it. To my mind, Munnings is our only great painter. To look at one of his horse paintings, you just know you are looking at the work of a master. In fact, I managed to buy one myself. Come into the dining-room and I'll show it to you.'

After they had admired the Munnings, which Edward thought very dull, they were able to make their excuses and depart, promising – when they had their house in order – to ask Heron over to dinner.

'God bless my soul,' he said suddenly. 'What with the vicar making his speech, I forgot to pick up my sword. I think I'll just walk back to the green and see if I can find it. I wouldn't like to lose it. Bit of an heirloom, if you understand me.'

'Of course, but I'm sure someone will have put it some-where safe. "Keep up your bright swords, for the dew will rust them".' Edward could not prevent himself quoting Othello. Verity rebuked him with a look but Heron did not seem to have heard.

'He must have made a bit of money to have been able to buy that house,' Edward observed as they walked home.

'But wasn't it cold, and I thought it smelt horrid.'

'Yes, I noticed that too – as though his char had spilt the cleaning liquid.'

Verity shivered. 'If it's cold in midsummer, I shudder to think what it must be like in winter.'

They were just sitting down to eat Mrs Brendel's Austrian ragout when there was a loud knocking on the door. Mrs Brendel went to open it and they heard a panicky-sounding Colonel Heron ask for Edward. As they rose from the table, Heron broke into the dining-room and, without apology and almost incoherent, urged them to come with him to look at something he had found.

'For goodness sake, calm down and tell us what's the matter,' Edward ordered.

With a visible effort, Heron moderated his voice from an unintelligible gabble to something they could understand.

'On the green . . . It's Byron Gates – he's dead.'

'Dead!' Verity exclaimed. 'Has he had a heart attack? Have you telephoned the doctor?'

'He doesn't need a doctor, I tell you. He's dead! PC Watt has just telephoned Lewes police station.'

'The police?' Edward's heart sank. 'Why the police?'

'Someone's cut off his head.'

6

'Someone's cut off his head! I don't believe it. How . . . was it an accident . . .?'

Edward looked at her pityingly. 'I don't see how it could be an accident.' Grabbing his coat and a torch he said, 'I'll go with Heron. You stay here, V. I won't be long.'

'Of course I won't stay here. What do you take me for? Colonel, how did he lose his head?'

'You'll soon see,' Heron replied grimly, beginning to recover himself. 'I went to find my sword, you remember? I wanted to take Velvet, my retriever, out too. I don't bother with a lead and when he disappeared I didn't worry. I thought he had just gone off into the bushes to do his business. When he didn't return, I whistled – I was just on the edge of the green – and he appeared with something in his mouth. I had a torch with me and when I shone it on Velvet I just couldn't believe what he had in his mouth.'

'What was it?' Verity asked, feeling slightly sick. It was a relief to be out in the fresh night air.

'It was a human head. Velvet had it by the hair. Of course, I made him drop it immediately and that's when I saw it was Gates. I grabbed hold of Velvet's collar and tried to see where he had found it. I couldn't see anything at first. Then I spotted something dark in the middle of the green. When I got nearer, I saw it was a body – or rather a torso. Then I saw the sword and then, I'm afraid, I was sick.'

'Did you see anyone – alive, I mean?' Edward asked.

'No, the green was deserted. The head must have rolled away from the rest of the body and Velvet retrieved it.' Heron was panting now, partly because they were walking fast and partly, Edward thought, from the shock. Heron coughed from deep in his chest and Edward thought he was going to be sick again but he managed to pull himself together. 'It was disgusting. I never saw anything like it, not even in India.'

'The rest of the body . . . was it lying on the ground?'

'No, you'll see in a moment. It's kneeling against a block. I think it's the one the children used in the pageant. You know, when Charles I was executed. His legs have been tied at the ankle and his hands roped together behind his back. Look! Over there!'

They had reached the green and walked gingerly towards the dark shadow in the middle where the stage had been. They stared at the torso in fascinated horror.

'Where's the head?'

Heron pointed to the edge of the green. 'He's been beheaded with my sword just like in the tableau. It's horrible. I'll never get the image out of my mind.'

Edward saw that he was shaking. 'After you were sick – what did you do?' he asked.

'I panicked. I ran to PC Watt's cottage and banged on his door. He didn't believe me at first when I told him what I had found but I made him come with me to the green. As soon as he saw I was telling the truth, he went back to ring headquarters. He told me to stay on guard but then I thought of you, Lord Edward. I remembered that you had investigated murders . . . I hope you didn't mind my breaking in on you like that.'

In the light of the torch, he looked white and haggard.

'No, of course not, but you probably shouldn't have left your post. Ah, Constable,' Edward continued as he saw a figure approaching them across the green, 'my name is

Corinth and we've recently moved into the village. Colonel Heron came to get me. I was just telling him that he ought to have stayed by the body as you'd instructed, but no harm done, I hope. You have telephoned Lewes?'

'Yes, my lord,' Watt responded, clearly well aware to whom he was talking. 'Will you stand guard here? I must make sure no one disturbs the head until the Inspector arrives.'

'Verity, take the Colonel back to his house, will you? There's no point in him staying here. Make sure he has a tot of brandy. You too, V. This isn't a pretty sight.'

For once she did not argue, glad to have an excuse for leaving the grisly scene.

How the news of the atrocity had spread, no one could say, but there was already a little crowd gathering on the edge of the green, staring at the severed head. PC Watt was having difficulty holding people back and preventing them from poking at it ghoulishly. 'Keep back, keep back,' he shouted angrily, 'and put that dog on a lead. Keep back there, I say. Stay off the green. This is the scene of a crime.'

Alone with the torso, Edward knelt to examine it more closely in the light of his torch. Byron's bow-tie had fallen off and lay on the grass, a bloody ribbon. His hands had been tied behind his back with what looked like fishing twine and his ankles were also bound. Edward looked for the cape he normally wore and saw it some distance away. The murderer must have made him take it off before he tied him up. Edward had a horrible feeling that the killer cut off Byron's head while he was still alive. The terror he must have felt in those last few minutes didn't bear thinking about. On the other hand, it was a clean cut. If Byron had struggled, there was no evidence of it.

Edward looked at the sword and then at the neck. The sword was covered in blood but it suddenly came to him that it was unlikely to have been the murder weapon. A sword, so he had read, was not an easy weapon with which to behead someone, particularly if they weren't 'cooperating'. Anne Boleyn was executed using a sword, he remembered – in that respect Miss Fairweather's tableau had been accurate. Heron's sword – none too sharp by the look of it – would have left a ragged wound but this was a neat execution. It was much more likely that an axe or something similar had been used to behead Byron.

Edward leant back on his heels and thought about it. Even an axe could be awkward. He had read, only that morning as it happened, in Churchill's biography of his great forebear, that the unfortunate Duke of Monmouth, captured after his ill-fated rebellion, had been beheaded in the Tower of London. Although the Duke had tipped Jack Ketch six guineas, his executioner had botched the job. Having failed to kill him with three hacks, Ketch threw down his axe in disgust and refused to continue until the angry crowd had made him. Another two blows failed to sever the Duke's head and, in the end, Ketch had had to worry it off with his knife.

This seemed a much more professional job. Edward shone his torch around but there was no sign of any other weapon. He examined the twine used to bind the dead man. It looked unremarkable to him but perhaps the police might discover its origin. He wondered why Byron had been on the green after everything had been cleared away. Perhaps he had been composing another deathless ode – no, 'deathless' was the wrong word in the circumstances. Had the murderer known he would be on the green? Had he perhaps arranged to meet Byron, or had the attack been opportunistic?

His train of thought was broken by the sound of a bell, shrill in the night air. He stood up, wondering whether or not to make himself scarce. 'I go, and it is done – the bell invites me,' he muttered to himself. In truth, he had no wish to be involved in this murder investigation. On the other hand, if he left the scene now he would have some explaining to do. He watched as the police car came to a halt at the edge of the green. Two large policemen in plain clothes got out, followed by a constable in uniform. Watt pointed his torch at the head and then towards Edward standing over the torso.

The two burly policemen strode towards him while the constable set about helping Watt push the little crowd of gawpers back off the green.

'Who are you,' one of the policemen asked, striding up to Edward, 'and what are you doing here?'

'My name is Lord Edward Corinth. Colonel Heron fetched me after he had discovered the body. He thought I might be able to help.'

'Yes, I have heard of you,' the policeman said with something like disgust. 'You live . . .?'

'Just over there, at the Old Vicarage. And you are?'

'Inspector Trewen. Now, sir, please will you go back to your house. I may need to ask you a few questions in the morning. And the man who found the corpse – Colonel Heron, you said – where is he?'

'He was very shocked. I sent him home.'

'You sent him home! Very well. Now, if you don't mind . . .'

The other policeman intervened. 'Sir, the murder weapon . . .' He pointed his torch at the bloodied sword.

'Actually,' Edward began, 'I don't think . . .'

'Please, sir – do what I ask and go home. You may already have destroyed evidence – footprints . . .'

'It's too dry for footprints,' Edward pointed out. Then, seeing the Inspector's face, he added, 'but I shall leave you with the greatest pleasure.'

'Before you go – do you know who this man is?'

'Constable Watt will tell you,' Edward said, turning away.

He chided himself for being petty but the Inspector obviously had no need of him to solve the crime, for which he was heartily grateful.

When he got home he found Verity, white-faced and overwrought.

'Is the Colonel all right?' he asked.

'Yes, I think so. I must say, he looked awfully ill but he wouldn't let me stay with him. Do you think he murdered Byron? I don't,' she added before Edward could answer. 'He was very shocked and upset.'

'No, I don't, but it's nothing to do with us, thank God. An Inspector Trewen arrived and sent me about my business. He made it clear he needed no help in solving the crime.'

'I've been thinking, Edward, about the children. Ada and Jean may not know what has happened. I don't know who is looking after them but they need to be told now before they hear it from the police.'

'Must we be the ones to tell them?' he groaned, feeling quite weak at the thought. 'Won't they be asleep? It's very late.'

'Probably, but they should still be told,' Verity said firmly. 'I know I won't be able to sleep if we don't go over to Ivy Cottage. It's our duty to try and comfort them. I mean – what a terrible thing for Ada to lose her father in this way and even Jean . . . We must do what we can.'

'But is it our business?' Edward protested, knowing in his heart that she was right.

'Whose else is it? Until Mrs Gates gets back – and that may not be for ages – they are quite alone.'

Edward straightened his back. 'You're quite right, V. It's not our responsibility but we should do what we can to soften the blow. There is something particularly gruesome about this murder. It wasn't an act of unpremeditated violence – a sudden quarrel or something. This was coldly planned to be as theatrical as possible – an execution in a public place. The killer must have seen the children's tableaux and thought it would be amusing to echo the execution of Charles I. The murderer is mad – quite mad.'

'And – I've just remembered – Byron told me his most recent book is called *The Unkindest Cut*. Someone has their head cut off. Was it a cruel joke, do you think?'

'I really don't know.' Edward felt exhausted and longed to be able to go to bed and forget all about Byron's ugly death but Verity wasn't going to allow it.

'In someone's eyes, he must have committed a heinous crime,' she continued.

'Treason?' Edward suggested, thinking of Anne Boleyn.

'Worse, but what, I can't begin to imagine. We hardly knew him, although we did know he was vain, possibly cowardly and not very kind to his daughter. But none of those are motives for murder.'

'He was a philanderer,' Edward pointed out. 'After money, isn't love, or the loss of it, the strongest motive for murder? But V, I'm determined that we shouldn't get involved in investigating this case. This is *our* time together – perhaps the last we shall have before you're sent off to some far-away place and I won't see you again for months. These few weeks are very precious to us. We mustn't let this awful murder spoil things. I won't let it happen.'

Verity said nothing. There was nothing to say. She knew that, whether they liked it or not, they would be drawn into the investigation. Their only hope was that the policeman in charge of the case would not want anything to do with them.

They set out for Ivy Cottage with heavy hearts. Was there was any kind way of telling Ada that her father had been brutally murdered? Edward knocked at the front door. It was answered by a girl, hardly older than Jean, whom Verity vaguely remembered seeing behind the cake stall at the fête.

'I'm so sorry to disturb you, Miss . . .?'

'Mary Tallent.'

'Well, Mary, my name's Corinth.'

'I thought you must be Mr Gates,' she said peevishly.

'He said he'd be back hours ago. It's almost one o'clock. I need to get home. My mother will be worried. I was supposed to leave at eleven.'

The girl, pretty enough in a sluttish way, looked almost ugly as her mouth puckered in complaint.

'Hold on a minute,' Edward broke in. 'A terrible thing has happened. The fact is, Mr Gates has been killed.'

'Killed? How do you mean?' Mary looked at them, stupefied.

'It's rather horrible but I'm afraid he has been murdered,' Verity said. 'We have to break it to the children.'

'Murdered! Oh my God! I didn't think . . . Murdered? How can he . . .?'

Verity looked at her with sympathy tinged with contempt. 'May we come in?'

Still dumb-struck, Mary opened the door and they followed her into a small but pleasant sitting-room. There were piles of books on every flat surface and a bookcase bulging with them. There were some roses in a vase and, on a desk, several exercise books which, Edward thought, must be the children's school work.

Their dilemma as to whether or not to wake the girls was solved by their appearance on the stairs. They were in their dressing-gowns and looked very young.

'Daddy – is that you?' Ada called, rubbing her eyes.

'No, I'm afraid it's not,' Verity said, her heart cold with fear. She was not good with children at the best of times and no one would find it easy to tell a child her only parent had died – had been murdered. 'I'm so sorry but we have something very horrible to tell you.' Jean went very white and took her half-sister in her arms.

'What is it?' she demanded. 'Has Dad had an accident?' Verity was interested to note that she called her stepfather "Dad".

'Yes, and I'm very sorry to be the person who has to tell you that . . .'

Ada made an unpleasant snorting sound as though she had been punched in the stomach. 'He shouldn't have done it . . .' she cried out and then put her hand to her mouth as though to stifle her words.

'Dad's dead?' Jean asked.

'I'm afraid so.'

'What . . . what happened?'

Verity wished she were a hundred miles away. Seeing her distress, Edward went over to the girls. 'You must be very brave. We think your father was killed by someone – an enemy.'

'Where is he?' Jean's voice trembled but she did not cry. 'Can we see him?'

'I'm afraid not,' Edward said, 'not now. The police have taken him away.'

Still neither girl was in tears. Ada was shivering uncontrollably in Jean's arms while Jean was trying with all her might not to burst into tears and frighten her sister even more.

'Jean,' Verity said softly, 'can you help me get Ada up to bed? I'm going to ask the doctor to come over and give her something to calm her. I'll stay with you tonight and tomorrow we'll send for your mother. Until she is able to get here, we will look after you,' she found herself saying. The two girls – particularly Ada – looked so bereft that it was impossible for her to leave them. Mary Tallent was in such a state that – even if she agreed to stay – she would be worse than useless and simply frighten the girls even more.

Mary at last found words. 'Oh, my! How can I get home in the dark? I might be murdered too.'

'How did he die?' Jean asked, ignoring her.

'We'll talk about it in the morning,' Verity said, her courage failing her. 'We can't tell you anything more now. Mary, where's the kettle and the hot water bottles?' Mary, pulling herself together under Verity's firm gaze, took two stone bottles out of a cupboard and put the kettle on the hob. 'Now, while the kettle is boiling, help me get the children back to bed, will you?'

As Mary and the children went upstairs, Edward said, 'V, I'm going back to the house. I'll telephone the doctor from there. Mrs Brendel will know who I should call and I'll ask her if she would mind coming over to help you.'

'Yes, do that, and escort Mary home on your way. She's not much use here. Oh, and ask Mrs Brendel to bring over some warm clothes for me. I'll sleep in the armchair, if I can.'

There was a knock at the door. It was PC Watt and the vicar.

'Paul, I'm so glad you've come,' Edward said. 'We have just been telling Ada and Jean about Byron. They've been very brave but if you could . . .'

The police constable looked relieved. 'So you've already told them, have you? The Inspector asked me to fetch the vicar and come round but if . . .'

'Thank you, Constable, but there's nothing you can do for the moment except take Miss Tallent back to her mother. She's in rather a state, as you can imagine.'

'It's a dreadful business. Never come across anything like it in all the years I've been here,' Watt remarked, inanely, Edward thought.

'Yes,' he agreed, 'it's a dreadful business.'

7

The following morning Verity was relieved by Charlotte Hassel, who had finished her book. Tired and depressed, she walked home in time to join Edward at the breakfast table. Mrs Brendel, who had insisted on getting breakfast even though Sunday was her morning off, poured her a cup of coffee and asked after the children. She said she would go to Ivy Cottage later to see what she could do to help Charlotte.

'You look terrible, V,' Edward said, unhelpfully.

'I'm not surprised! I hardly slept while I suppose you were snoring happily. This morning I decided to tell the girls exactly how Byron had died. I didn't want them to catch sight of lurid headlines in a newspaper and find out we hadn't been honest with them. I hated having to do it and I'll never forget Ada's face. She was stricken – that's the only word for it.'

'Can't we prevent them seeing the newspapers, V?'

'We can try but they can't be protected from the truth forever. That's why I decided to tell them the facts as gently as I could. Jean seemed to accept it and was remarkably calm – almost unnaturally so. Ada has – only temporarily, I hope – lost the power of speech. She hasn't said a word since I told her. She just smiles sweetly and then stares into space. As I say, she's stricken – it's the first time I understood what the word means. I can hardly bear to think about it. I hope I did right to tell her. I remember how children in Spain were traumatized by seeing their parents killed.'

'Well, thank God, they didn't *see* him killed,' Edward said. 'I've telephoned the Foreign Office and explained the situation. They said they'll ask our consul in Los Angeles to speak to Mrs Gates, or rather Mary Brand. She's filming somewhere in Hollywood. I wonder whether we should have Ada and Jean to stay until she gets back?'

'What do you think, Mrs Brendel? Could we cope if we had them here?' Verity asked.

'Yes, mam. If I get a girl in from the village to help, I'm sure we could.'

'No, that wouldn't be fair on you, Mrs Brendel,' Edward said firmly. 'We'll find someone qualified – a nanny or a governess – to look after them until Jean's mother gets back from America.'

'I suppose so,' Verity agreed. 'There don't seem to be any grandparents or uncles and aunts. What about asking Frieda Burrowes to come down?'

'It's a bit awkward, isn't it? How would Ada feel about her father's mistress looking after her? And when Jean's mother returns, do you think she'll want to find Frieda in her house?'

'No, you're right. It was a bad idea,' Verity admitted. 'I say, I suppose Frieda knows about Byron?'

'She must do. Anyway, it'll be splashed over all the papers tomorrow. Still, maybe I ought to telephone her. It'll be a terrible shock.'

'Excuse me, sir,' Mrs Brendel broke in, 'but did you know that Colonel Heron has been arrested? He seemed such a gentleman – I can hardly believe him to be a murderer. When I left Vienna to the Nazis, I thought such horrors were behind me but even here in England . . . to cut off his head! And Mr Gates was such a charming man.'

Edward looked at Verity. 'They've arrested Heron? I call that precipitate. He didn't do it, Mrs Brendel,' he added flatly. 'I'm almost sure of it.'

Verity agreed. 'What motive could he have had?'

'He did have a motive,' Edward reminded her. 'Do you remember Byron saying that evening at Monk's House that Heron had accused him of mistreating his first wife?'

'But why would he "find" the body unless it was some bizarre double bluff? Should we go and talk to the Inspector, Edward?'

'But what do we know? We would just look like interfering busybodies.'

'We have to do something. We can't let the Colonel be hanged for a murder he didn't commit. Someone set him up, I feel it in my bones. I can hardly believe that yesterday was the fête and Byron was alive,' Verity said, rubbing her eyes. 'So much has happened in just a few hours. Our nice, peaceful village has been soiled.'

'I wonder what this chap is like – Inspector Trewen, I mean? I can't say I took to him last night.'

'I can tell you a little about him, sir,' Mrs Brendel put in. 'When Mr Woolf brought me to live here, he introduced me to the Inspector to make sure I was not . . . troubled. He said some refugees had been suspected of spying and he wanted the police to know that I was respectable.'

Mrs Brendel was as comfortable-looking as an apple strudel and more respectable, but Edward knew that – just as she said – many innocent people, who had fled their country to escape Nazi persecution, faced prejudice and hostility in their new home. Suspicious neighbours and heavy-handed authorities obsessed by the notion of spies and 'fifth columnists' tended to see all foreigners as enemies. The police force was a reserved occupation but, even so, a young man with spirit preferred to fight for his country than stay at home to deal with petty crime. Many of the best police had joined the armed forces and some of those who remained were not up to much – either past retirement age or young, ill trained and inclined to be unsympathetic, if not brutal, in their dealings with people who had sought refuge in England. Although Edward would never say so in public, he thought that the force had suffered as a result.

'So what's he like, Mrs Brendel?' Verity asked.

'He was very polite to me, mam, but that may have been because I was with Mr Woolf. If I may say so, I thought him rather arrogant and . . .'

'And what?'

'Not very clever, mam.'

'I still think we ought to go and talk to the Inspector. I'd hate Colonel Heron to think that we assumed he was guilty.'

'As long as that's all it is, V. We swore we wouldn't get involved in any investigation. The Inspector wouldn't welcome it and he'd be right.'

'No, of course not, but still . . .'

As soon as they had finished breakfast, they drove to Lewes in Edward's Lagonda.

'What do you think Ada meant last night when she said, "He shouldn't have done it"?' Verity asked.

'I don't know. Someone's got to ask her – but not until she has recovered from the shock. I'm worried about her, V. You said that you thought she was very insecure when you talked to her at the fête. God knows what this will do to her. Thank goodness Jean is such a sensible girl. She's probably in the best position to help Ada come to terms with her loss.'

'Yes, I agree, but of course Byron wasn't Jean's father. Poor Ada is all alone in the world now. Whoever killed him may also have dealt Ada a blow from which she may never recover.'

The police station proved to be a poky little building in the town centre and was already under siege by the press. Edward groaned when he saw the cameras and the notebooks.

'Oh, my God. I didn't think there would be this much interest, but I suppose it's only to be expected. Byron was almost famous.'

'And not many people are beheaded in this day and age,' Verity added grimly.

As soon as Edward and Verity were recognized, they were surrounded by reporters who immediately made the assumption that Edward was investigating the murder.

'My lord,' Ken Hines, the *News Chronicle* crime reporter called out, 'is it true that you were a friend of the murdered man?'

'Please, let me through. I'm sorry, Ken, but I can't tell you anything.' Edward had had dealings with the reporter once or twice before and liked him.

'But you are investigating the killing?'

'I am not investigating anything. Now please make way. Thank you, Constable.'

A burly constable opened the door of the police station and put out an arm to hold back the mob.

'I wonder if this is wise,' Edward muttered, his nerve weakening. 'Perhaps we should have telephoned the Inspector. You realize, V, that your beastly rag will be on to you for a piece about the murder?'

'Well, I shan't oblige,' she replied unconvincingly. 'I'm a foreign correspondent not a crime reporter.'

The trouble was that, whatever she might say, she was a newspaper reporter through and through and, even though it wasn't strictly in her remit, she could not ignore a good story when it was served up to her gift-wrapped. She told herself that she could at least be accurate and protect the girls if she were to write the story, but wouldn't she be betraying both them and also Colonel Heron?

'The Inspector cannot see anyone,' the constable at the desk informed them when they had given their names.

'We are friends of Colonel Heron,' Edward said firmly, stretching the truth, 'and we have some information relating to the murder.'

'I'm sorry, sir, but I have my orders. I will, of course, tell the Inspector . . .'

At that moment, Inspector Trewen himself appeared.

'Oh, it's you, is it?' he growled. 'The amateur detective. You have no doubt already discovered the murderer?' The contempt in his voice was almost palpable.

'I am not a detective, amateur or otherwise,' Edward replied icily. 'I merely wanted to help the police in their inquiries but I see you are not interested in any information I might have so I shall leave. Here is my card if you wish to see me at any time.'

'Well, now you are here, I suppose I might as well see you, but I can only give you five minutes,' Trewen said grudgingly.

'Verity, will you wait for me here?' Edward was worried she might lose her temper and say something she would regret if the Inspector proved to be as hostile as he expected. She started to protest but, seeing Edward's face, reluctantly nodded her head.

The Inspector plumped his large frame down in the chair behind his desk. There was a metal chair in front of the desk but Edward was not invited to sit on it. He did so anyway.

'Well, what is it you have to tell me?' the Inspector rasped, lighting a foul-smelling pipe.

Edward kept a check on his temper. 'I understand you have arrested Colonel Heron for the murder of Byron Gates. Is that correct?'

'It is. The Colonel's sword was used to behead Mr Gates. His fingerprints were on the sword and it was bloody. His hands also had blood on them, as did his clothes. I arrested him at his house last night.' The Inspector looked pleased with himself.

'What motive did he have, Inspector?'

99

'That's not something I can discuss with a member of the public.'

'Very well but, since it was Colonel Heron's sword, it's hardly surprising that his prints were found on it,' Edward retorted.

The Inspector grunted.

Edward tried again. 'One thing occurs to me, Inspector. I've never tried it myself but I seem to remember from the history books that it is quite difficult to cut off a man's head with a sword. You have to saw away at the neck – particularly if the sword is blunt. I assume that, if this sword was last used in 1706 at the Battle of Ramillies, as the Colonel told me it was, it is hardly likely to be sharp.'

Edward was purposely trying to shock the Inspector and believed he was succeeding. Trewen took his pipe out of his mouth and looked rather queasy.

'Of course, it was dark when I saw the body,' Edward went on remorselessly, 'but I have a powerful torch and I noted that the head seemed to have been quite neatly severed from the trunk. Have you considered that Mr Gates may not have been killed by the sword but by an axe or some other sharp, heavy instrument? It's only a suggestion, mind you, but worth exploring before you assume you have arrested the right man. As for the blood, Colonel Heron could easily have got blood on his hands and clothes without actually having killed Mr Gates. For one thing, he removed the bloody head from the mouth of his dog who had found it. Furthermore, he reported finding the body to Constable Watt – hardly the action of a guilty man, I would have thought. What is more, I am quite convinced that, when he came to our house afterwards, his shock and horror were genuine.'

'Why did he come to see you?' the Inspector asked suspiciously.

'Because he knew that in the past I have been involved

in a number of criminal investigations though, as I hope I have made clear, I will not be getting involved in this case.'

'I'm glad to hear it. Amateur Sherlocks always make it harder for the professionals to get at the truth,' Trewen said rudely. 'Well, Lord Edward,' he added, making an effort to be polite, 'I appreciate you taking the time to come and see me but, really, I think you can put the whole thing out of your mind. The murder is gruesome but the murderer made no effort to disguise what he had done and there's an end of it.'

'Has Colonel Heron admitted to murdering Gates?'

'Not exactly but we have witnesses to the fact that he had threatened him.' The Inspector realized he was giving this meddling aristocrat more information than he needed to and stopped. 'Be that as it may, Lord Edward, you can safely leave the matter in our hands. We are not all the bumbling bobbies you like to paint us.' He laughed mirthlessly.

'"You can safely leave the matter in our hands"– is that what he said?' Verity was indignant. 'We're certainly not going to.'

Edward looked at her quizzically but said nothing. Verity, as a long-time Communist, had a suspicion of the police which had not been allayed by finding one or two policemen who she had grudgingly to admit *were* honest and competent. In her experience, the police wasted too much time monitoring the Communist Party and not enough on frustrating the dark designs of the Fascists.

'And there was no question of you being allowed to see Heron?' she continued.

'Absolutely not.'

'He has a solicitor, I presume.'

'Apparently so. The constable on the desk told me before I left that he's a local man called Murchison who will, I am sure, know that he's completely out of his depth with a case like this and pass the whole thing over to a London firm with experience in criminal matters. I'll try and see Murchison tomorrow. I'm going to suggest he consults Tom Hutchinson. He's a partner in Tenbury and Cootes and a pal of mine from way back. One of the best.'

'You're not going to leave it at that, are you?'

'What do you mean? No, V, you can't be serious. I thought we'd agreed last night that there would be no more investigating. We're going to have these last few weeks together to rest and enjoy country life.'

'I can't help noticing, Edward, that – even in the short time we've been down here – you have sometimes looked bored. When you got that summons to go to London, your eyes lit up. I'm afraid we are just not the sort of people who can sit back and do nothing in a crisis. And, what's more, your conscience won't allow it. You can't let Heron be hanged because you're too idle to find the real murderer.'

'I say, V,' Edward began weakly, 'that isn't fair. . .'

'Who said life was ever fair? It certainly hasn't been fair to Ada.'

'Oh, God, why are there no good coppers around?' Edward demanded. 'My instinct tells me that Inspector Trewen is one of the worst.'

'We have to find the murderer for Ada's sake,' Verity went on remorselessly. 'And for Jean – but mainly for Ada. She's not in good shape and, if she ever found out that her father's murderer had got off and someone else had been hanged in his place, it might destroy her.'

'Stop, V! Stop, I beg you. I always knew this was what marriage would be like. You tell me what to do and I do it.'

'*We* do it,' Verity said, giving him a kiss.

'Lord Edward, this is a very great pleasure. Do sit down.'

It was Monday morning and Edward was ensconced in an armchair in Mr Murchison's comfortable office in

Lewes. He was a country solicitor of the old school. There was nothing brash, nothing flash about Mr Murchison and he reminded Edward of his brother, the Duke's, solicitor. Generation after generation, these men had looked after the landed gentry and the aristocracy, piling up in tin deed boxes family secrets – financial embarrassments, unsuitable marriages, sudden deaths and necessary confinements of the mentally unstable or the criminal. Discreet until and beyond the grave, they very occasionally defrauded their clients but were, for the most part, society's gatekeepers and the acme of respectability. The complete trust their clients had in their integrity ensured that, if they did sometimes fall below the standards of rectitude they had set themselves, it might take several generations before anything was proved against them.

In the main, they deserved their reputation as the glue that kept the social order in place, the buttresses of a society that put land above money and old money above new money, and measured respectability in acres owned. The Great War had perhaps loosened the glue but the landowners great and small still retained their power and position despite the loss of sons and heirs, the coming of universal suffrage and the tide of democracy lapping at the castle gates.

'It is very good of you to see me.' Edward was at his most affable and aristocratic. He knew how these men loved a lord. 'I won't beat about the bush, Mr Murchison. I've come about this horrible business of Mr Gates's death. I understand Colonel Heron has been arrested. It seems to me quite ludicrous that just because he found the body and his fingerprints were on his sword – the sword which the police think, wrongly in my view, was used to kill Mr Gates – he should be accused of murder. I wondered if there was anything I could do to help?'

Mr Murchison beamed and then, feeling perhaps that smiles were inappropriate, rearranged his face to look shocked and saddened.

'That is very kind of you, Lord Edward. Of course, I am aware of your reputation as an investigator but I really think there is very little that can be done, at least until Colonel Heron is charged. The police have, as you say, arrested him on suspicion of murder and they must decide whether or not to charge him in the next forty-eight hours.'

Edward was genuinely shocked. 'Surely you believe him to be innocent? I don't know him well – my wife and I have only just moved to Rodmell – but he seems to me a most respectable man. I would have said he was the last person to go around beheading people – even if it were possible to do so with a sword, which I'm inclined to doubt. In any case, what possible motive could he have?'

'Well, there we are. He *did* have a motive. He tells me that the first Mrs Gates – Marion – was a close friend of his. Between ourselves, I believe there may have been something between them. That must have been before she married Mr Gates,' Mr Murchison added hurriedly. 'I am only guessing, you understand, but Colonel Heron has very strong feelings on the subject of Gates's behaviour. In fact, there are witnesses to an incident in the local pub who say they heard him threaten Mr Gates. He was heard to say that he intended to "mete out justice" and that Mr Gates deserved to have his head chopped off.'

'Yes, Mr Gates mentioned the incident the first time I met him. However, he said the Colonel had come round and apologized the following day and they had agreed to forget about it. Heron had a motive for hating Mr Gates, I grant you, but not for murdering him.'

'I hope you are right, Lord Edward, and that the police share your view.'

Edward hesitated before asking, 'What exactly did Colonel Heron tell you was his reason for threatening Gates?'

'Well, it's very delicate but since you are ... I presume I can count on your absolute discretion?' Edward nodded and Mr Murchison seemed satisfied. 'The Colonel seems to believe that Marion died of what the poets used to call a broken heart on account of Gates's philandering.'

'I thought she died of cancer.'

'That was what was on the death certificate but the Colonel decided not to believe it, and it is true that, as a document of record, they often prove erroneous. To spare a relative grief, a doctor may choose to attribute death to a chill or a fever rather than some unpleasant disease carrying a social stigma.'

'You mean, like syphilis,' Edward said bluntly.

'Yes, but . . .'

'You are not suggesting that in this case . . .?'

'No, no . . . I was merely making a general point. I have no reason to doubt that Marion Gates died of cancer. I am simply saying that it is not totally unreasonable for my client to question it. Grief may well have been a contributory factor, but no doctor can say that it was a cause of death.'

'I accept Marion could have been Heron's motive, though not a very strong one unless she really was the love of his life.'

'I agree, of course, Lord Edward, but would a jury share our opinion? I fear they might not.'

'I don't doubt that Gates was a philanderer – unprincipled where women were concerned . . .' Edward conceded.

'A priapic – I understand it is a medical condition,' Mr Murchison said, looking down his nose.

'"Alas! The love of women! It is known to be a lovely and fearful thing."'

'*Don Juan*, I think.' Mr Murchison looked pleased with himself. 'I might add, "Sweet is revenge – especially to women." Mr Gates's namesake had much to say about women and death, did he not?'

'Indeed, Mr Murchison, and much of it quotable, which I fear is more than can be said about Mr Gates's published work. He seems to have shared Lord Byron's disregard for morality, particularly in regard to women, but behaviour tolerable in a genius looks merely shoddy in a lesser man. Do you not agree?'

'I do, Lord Edward.'

'I don't wish to be impertinent, Murchison, but I imagine that not many of your clients are accused of murder. Have you considered involving a London firm with more experience of criminal matters? Because of who Mr Gates was and the nature of his murder, public interest will be immense and a jury may be affected as much by public opinion as the facts of the case.'

'I am very much aware of that,' Mr Murchison said stiffly. 'I was considering going to Tenbury and Cootes but the Colonel isn't a wealthy man so I hesitate to . . .'

'A very good firm. One of the partners – Mr Hutchinson – is a friend of mine. And if it is a question of money, I will be happy to guarantee payment of their fees although I am surprised to hear you say that the Colonel could not afford the very best legal representation. He has a large house . . .'

'A most generous offer, yes indeed,' the solicitor said, his face once again wreathed in smiles. 'If you are quite serious, I shall telephone Mr Hutchinson immediately. The Colonel does indeed own his house but it is mortgaged to the hilt. He has no other significant assets. He was, as you probably know, in the Indian Army and that is not a profession in which to make a large sum of money. In the eighteenth and nineteenth centuries it was quite different and many an officer came home with a considerable fortune, but not these days, I fear.'

'I would very much like to talk to the Colonel. Can that be arranged? I had the impression that Inspector Trewen would refuse me but . . .'

'Of course, Lord Edward. Now that you are part of the defence team . . .'

'If the Colonel is charged, he will not be given bail, I imagine?'

'I very much doubt it. It would be most unusual in a murder case, as you well know.'

'Colonel Heron *may* be guilty of murder. It is possible, but I am certainly not yet ready to accept that he killed Mr Gates despite what you have told me. Would you broadcast your intention to "mete out justice" before actually doing so? I wouldn't.'

These remarks were meant as a reproach to the solicitor for assuming that his client was guilty, but Mr Murchison seemed unaware of it as he ushered Edward out of his office, bowing and smiling with all the unctuousness of Uriah Heep.

As he got into the Lagonda, Edward murmured to himself,

'"Yes, Leila sleeps beneath the wave,
But his shall be a redder grave;
Her spirit pointed well the steel
Which taught that felon heart to feel."'

He felt momentary guilt for quoting Byron facetiously when the matter was so grave. Could Colonel Heron have pointed the steel? 'There's blood upon that dinted sword'! He wondered if 'dinted' was the same as dented. He sighed. Damn and blast! Could he never be allowed to watch a murder case from the sidelines without getting involved? It seemed not.

Edward arrived home to be told by Mrs Brendel that Verity was at Ivy Cottage with Jean and Ada. As he was finishing lunch, Mr Murchison telephoned to say that the police had, after all, decided not to charge Colonel Heron.

'Apparently it was something you said, Lord Edward, about the beheading not having been done by the sword.

The doctor has confirmed your suspicion and the police are now looking for an axe or something similar.'

'Very good! By the way, did you telephone Mr Hutchinson?'

'I did. He will come down from London if he is needed.'

'And where is the Colonel now?'

'I think he's on his way to see you. I hope you didn't mind but I told him of your very kind offer to fund his defence which, of course, we now hope may not be necessary.'

'I see. I rather wish you hadn't told him but there we are.' He heard someone knocking on the front door. 'That may be the Colonel now. Goodbye, Mr Murchison, and please keep me in touch with any developments.'

Edward went into the hall to find Mrs Brendel opening the door to a harassed-looking Colonel Heron.

'They've released me,' he said, grasping Edward by the hand, 'and I believe I owe it to you, Lord Edward. I can't tell you how grateful I am. When you are cooped up in a cell accused of murder, you do have time to think. I've got no relatives and precious few friends here in England and I felt very alone. Then to hear that you had been working on my behalf – well, it lifted my spirits no end.'

'Don't mention it, Colonel. I merely pointed out to Inspector Trewen that, from the brief glimpse I had of poor Byron's body, it didn't look as if his head had been cut off with your sword. Mr Murchison tells me that the doctor who examined the body came to the same conclusion.'

'I feel very embarrassed. I gather you heard from Mr Murchison that I'd made some silly threats against Gates. I meant nothing by them, I assure you, but he did treat his first wife despicably. Murchison probably mentioned that she and I were close at one time – it might be called an engagement, informal, you understand – but I had my career. Marion did not fancy accompanying a chap to the subcontinent and who can blame her? It wouldn't have been an easy life for a white woman. Instead, she married Gates and lived to regret it.'

'I heard Gates say that the quarrel had been made up the following day when you went to apologize.'

'I am glad to hear it. I was in India when Marion married and when she died, and I suppose I felt guilty about not being there when she needed me. When I got back to Blighty, I discovered that the bloody man had been fooling about with other women while Marion was lying in a cancer ward, and I saw red. I wrote him a couple of letters calling him names but he never answered and after a bit I let it drop. When I heard he was moving into the neighbourhood with his new wife, I'm afraid my anger reignited.'

'I see.' Edward hesitated before continuing, 'I imagine there may be others he hurt by his philandering, but no one deserves to be executed – especially when there are two children who are probably going to be badly scarred by it.'

'That's right. The girls – I can hardly bear to imagine what they must be going through. Ada particularly . . . Who is looking after them?'

'My wife is with them now. She is bringing them back here. We decided it would be easier and better for the children if they stayed with us until Jean's mother can get back from America.'

'But that's a burden . . .'

'We think we may have found someone to help look after them. The vicar knows a girl – a teacher staying with her parents in Lewes – who sounds suitable.'

'That's very generous of you. Dear, dear! Even though I had nothing to do with Gates's murder, I do feel guilty about the girls . . . Ada in particular. She's an orphan now. If I can help . . .'

'There's no reason why you should blame yourself if, as you say, you didn't kill him.'

'I say, old man, I'm telling you the truth. You do believe me, don't you?'

Edward grunted, not yet ready to declare his faith in Heron's innocence. 'By the way, I suppose you don't know who did kill Byron, if it wasn't you?' he asked.

'I think I do,' Heron answered, to Edward's surprise. 'I suspect it was a man called Lewis Cathcart – one of those long-haired poet chaps who works at the BBC. I happened to meet him in a pub nearby. We got talking – you know how you do when you are drinking at the bar. I must have had a drop too much because I told him about Marion. Anyway, he said Gates had stolen *his* girl – an actress called Frieda Burrowes. He said he was going to get him even if it was the last thing he did.'

'And you think he meant he was going to kill him?'

'Well, it seemed on the cards at the time but it may have been like me in my cups – just words.'

'Quite a coincidence meeting this man Cathcart. Do you mind me asking what you were doing in a pub near Broadcasting House? Not your usual stamping ground, surely?'

'I was on my way to the Travellers' to meet a chap I know who I thought might offer me a job. To tell the truth, I'm a bit hard up at the moment as Murchison may have told you.'

'But the Travellers' is in Pall Mall?'

'I know, the BBC wasn't exactly on my route, but I was a bit early for lunch and, anyway, I felt I needed a drink before meeting this chap.'

'Did you get the job?' Edward asked mildly.

'Never made it to the club, I'm afraid. I just stayed in the pub till closing time. Cathcart poured me into a cab and I came back here – tail between my legs. I doubt it would have come to anything,' Heron finished sheepishly, coughing heavily.

Edward looked at him closely. He wasn't sure if Heron

was telling him the truth. On balance, he thought he probably was, or at least part of it.

'That's a nasty cough, Heron. Let me get you a drink. I expect you need it. Whisky and soda?'

'Please. And it's Mike – you must call me Mike. What do you think I should do now?'

'Nothing. There's a London lawyer Mr Murchison will want you to talk to if Inspector Trewen changes his mind and rearrests you.'

'But I can't let you pay for that,' Heron protested.

'Don't worry about it. He's a friend of mine called Tom Hutchinson. He won't be sending any bills, at least not for the moment, but you must see him. It is very important that you are properly advised. I don't think you killed Byron, but there's a case against you and it's a strong one.'

'Ought I go and see the girls? I'd like to tell Ada that I didn't kill her father.'

'In a day or so, perhaps – this isn't the right moment. Go home and get some rest. We'll talk again tomorrow. In fact, come and have dinner.'

'I don't know what I've done to find such a good friend in a comparative stranger. Why are you helping me?'

'I don't like seeing the law get it wrong. And I don't like Inspector Trewen jumping to conclusions. Mind you, if I find you've not been telling me the truth, I'll . . .'

'I'm telling you the gospel truth,' Heron insisted. Edward nodded, accepting his word, for the moment at least.

'Are you awake?' It was after midnight and Jean had been asleep for an hour or two but had been wakened by Ada sobbing. Sensing she had disturbed her stepsister, Ada tried to stifle her grief but could not do it. 'Would you like to get into my bed?' Jean offered.

Ada said nothing but put her feet on the cold floor and jumped into Jean's bed. She felt safe in the Old Vicarage. She liked Verity and was half in love with Lord Edward but her grief for her father could not be easily assuaged. She knew that he had never loved her and believed she had never been worthy of his love. Was she in some way guilty of his death? She puzzled over it but could come to no conclusion.

It had not been easy for Jean, either. Although she did not know her stepfather very well, what she did know she had not liked. When her mother was away, he had sometimes come and sat on her bed and stroked her foot and then her leg until she protested. It was one advantage of Ivy Cottage being so small and having to share a room with Ada – her stepfather had given up coming to say goodnight to her.

'Ada, dear,' she said as she held the girl in her arms, 'you must cry as much as you want. Don't try and be brave. I know I'd howl like a banshee if my mother had been . . . had died.'

'Daddy didn't love me, I know it,' Ada sobbed. It seemed easier to say these things with her head buried in Jean's shoulder.

'Yes, he did,' Jean whispered, not really believing it. 'Of course he loved you. He was very proud of you. He wanted you to become a writer like him.'

'Did he tell you that?' Ada said, sounding almost hopeful.

'He told me ages ago,' the other girl said firmly. In fact, it had been Jean who had said Ada would write novels and her father had pooh-poohed the idea but she couldn't admit that. Ada must be left with some fond memories of her father. Her self-confidence, always at a low ebb, had hit rock bottom, naturally enough, when she had been told she was an orphan and, worst of all, that her father had been murdered. However, Jean suspected that, behind the natural grief Ada was suffering, there was an added feeling that she had not been worthy of him.

'Ada, is there anything you want to tell me? I know how lonely you feel but I will always be here, I promise, and my mother will want to look after you as though you were her own daughter.'

'No she won't,' Ada said fiercely. 'Why should she? I'm a stranger. I'm not related to her. I'm . . .' She remembered a word her father had used once when she had asked to go with him to London. 'I'm an encumbrance. I'm not clever or beautiful like you. I wish . . . I wish I was dead.'

'That's a wicked thing to say,' Jean chided her.

'Well, I am wicked. I . . . He told me . . .'

'Who told you – your father? What did he tell you?'

'Nothing,' Ada said sullenly. 'It's a secret. I promised not to tell.'

'Can't you even tell me? I won't tell anyone.'

'No.' Ada shuddered as if she were battling with some demon. 'No, not you, not even you. I love you, Jean. You are the only person in the world I do love, so I won't kill myself unless you stop loving me. I promise.'

'Ada!' Jean said faintly. It was a burden she did not want to bear. 'Please don't talk about killing yourself,' she whispered but Ada had fallen into a deep sleep of exhaustion.

8

Verity had had an anguished trunk call from Frieda Burrowes earlier that day in response to a message she had left for her at the BBC. Frieda took no notice of the operator's three-minute reminders that the call was costing a small fortune. Should she come to Rodmell? Who had killed Byron? What was she to do now? Apparently a reporter called Ken Hines had been making her life a misery, wanting to know if she had been Byron's mistress.

'Look, Frieda,' Verity said, seizing on something she might be able to do to help, 'I think my husband knows Hines. I'll ask him if he can get him to stop persecuting you.'

'Will you, Verity? You are kind. I know you think I'm a sort of scarlet woman and I shouldn't be – have been – sleeping with Byron but, honestly, his wife doesn't mind. He told me she gets up to all sorts in Hollywood and the bloody thing is – or was – I did love him. I gave up someone else for him. Did you know that?'

Edward had told Verity what Heron had said about Cathcart threatening to kill Byron for taking Frieda from him. However, she didn't want to admit it to Frieda so she avoided giving her a straight answer.

'I really don't think it's a good idea for you to come down here. The press will latch on to you and the last thing anyone needs is more publicity. Anyway, best say no more, Frieda. These long-distance calls aren't secure and you don't know who might be listening.'

'Well, good luck to them,' Frieda said viciously. 'I had another reason for telephoning. Before all this happened, I talked to Mr Barnes, my boss, and he gave me the go-ahead to do an interview with you – if you still want to do it, that is.'

'Do *you* still want to do it?' Verity responded.

'I've got to go on working. What else can I do? You say I can't come down to Rodmell . . .'

'Yes, of course I'll do the interview if you're sure. It must be awful for you but I think you must be patient for a few days until the press move on to something else. The *New Gazette* has been pressing me to write about Byron's murder but I've refused.'

'Why don't you come to London and then we can talk properly? I feel so excluded. I'm worried about Jean and Ada, for one thing. Are you sure there's nothing I can do for them?'

'I don't think so. As a matter of fact, they've moved in with us until Mary Brand gets back from the States.'

'Goodness! That's really kind of you, Verity.'

'They're no trouble and it won't be for long but we couldn't leave them at Ivy Cottage. Ada's in deep shock and hardly speaking, but the vicar has found a competent woman to help look after them so I'm not tied to the house. When do you want me to come up to town to discuss the interview? I need to know what's involved.'

'What about tomorrow?'

'Tomorrow? That's rather short notice.'

'Well, I thought you were expecting to go abroad any day.'

'Yes, that's true. I'll speak to Edward and telephone you back.'

'That would be good. Thank you, Verity. I was afraid you might not want to have anything more to do with me.'

'You mean because of your relationship with Byron?'

'Yes.'

'I'm not one to talk about morals. I think marriage is an overrated institution but I suppose we have to live with it.'

When she had rung off, Verity went to look for Edward. She found him sound asleep in a deckchair on the lawn, his panama hat over his eyes, a book by Virginia Woolf lying on his lap unopened. She did not wake him.

At breakfast the following morning, Verity, smartly dressed for her day in London, poured Edward a second cup of coffee and milk for the girls. 'You are sure you don't mind me going up to town? I'll be back in time for dinner. I haven't forgotten that Colonel Heron is coming so I'm aiming to catch the six ten. Will you meet me, Edward?'

'Of course we don't mind being deserted, do we, girls?' He appealed to Ada and Jean in mock self-pity. Ada nodded solemnly. She was still hardly speaking but Edward thought she was weathering the shock. Her colour was better and she had stopped chewing the ear of the teddy bear she had brought with her from Ivy Cottage. 'You take off for the big city and leave us in our cabbage patch. We don't mind, do we, Jean?' Edward pressed his advantage and Jean giggled nervously. 'You've forgotten, haven't you, V? After I've dropped you at the station, I'm going to pick up the young woman Paul has found. She sounds just what we need. I'll bring her back here to meet the girls and, if we all like her, we'll take her on.'

'I hadn't forgotten,' Verity said guiltily because she had. 'Don't take her on unless you really like her,' she urged Jean and Ada.

'We won't,' Jean replied. 'I say, I hope I'm not being cheeky but do you think that next time you go to London you can take me with you? I so want to see inside a real newspaper office.'

'Of course I'll take you. I should have thought of it. And Ada, you'll come too, won't you?' Ada nodded and managed a smile. 'We'll go to the pictures and cheer ourselves up.'

'Don't worry about me,' Edward said, trying to sound aggrieved. 'I don't need cheering up. After we've seen Paul's young woman, I'm going to lunch with Leonard and Virginia.'

'I know. They are going to introduce you to The Ladies. You have got a busy day,' she said patting his cheek.

'Indeed! What could be more fun than having lunch with Miss Bron and Miss Fairweather? My pretensions to sounding well read will be seen through and I shall be jeered at for not having read James Joyce or Proust. I *have* read *The Waste Land* but I didn't understand a word of it.'

'And you've read that book of Virginia's. I saw you with it yesterday in the garden.'

'*Three Guineas*? Yes, I fell asleep over it. Even I can see she's a very good writer but I'm not sure I'm ready for a polemic on women's rights. I get enough of that from you. Now, you go off and get ready or you'll miss your train. I'm very proud to be married to such a famous person.'

'Oh, boo to you!' Verity said as she got up from the breakfast table to look for her handbag.

In the Lagonda on the way to the station, she said, 'While I'm at the BBC, I thought I would try and track down Lewis Cathcart – the man Colonel Heron says killed Byron.'

'Those were just wild words, V. From what I can see, if we lined up all the men Byron cuckolded, we'd have a regiment on our hands. Anyway, as we have agreed, we are not investigating the case. I couldn't let Heron languish in jail when it was quite obvious that he was no more of a suspect than anyone else who was in Rodmell on the day of the fête – but that's all I'm prepared to do.'

'That's the nub of it, isn't it? Byron must have been killed by someone at the fête – someone who saw the pageant. That narrows it down. If the Inspector was any good, he'd have whoever did it behind bars by now.'

'He won't catch anyone,' Edward said with feeling and Verity thought she detected a stirring of unrest in his voice as if, despite his protestations, he did want to find out 'who did it' and was frustrated by Trewen's obduracy in not taking him into his confidence.

'And I can tell Frieda you'll talk to Ken Hines?'

'I promise nothing. As you know better than anyone, we have a free press in this country and reporters don't like being warned off.' Edward saw her face cloud over and added quickly, 'But I'll talk to him and see what he's up to. That's all I'll promise.'

When he returned to the Old Vicarage with Joan Harries, the young woman whom Paul had suggested might help with the girls, Edward decided the best thing was to leave her alone with Jean and Ada for an hour or so and see if they liked one another. He retreated to the drawing-room and, for want of anything better to do, put in a call to the *News Chronicle*. To his surprise, he was through to Ken Hines before he had time to think what he was going to say.

'Lord Edward! To what do I owe this honour? You want to brief me on the progress of your investigations?'

'I'm not investigating anything, Ken. I just wondered what you were doing harassing Frieda Burrowes.'

'Who said I was harassing the delectable Frieda? And, more to the point, why should you mind? I didn't even realize you knew her.'

'I've met her once but I don't *know* her. I thought she was a perfectly nice girl who doesn't deserve what I believe is called "the third degree".'

'Has she been complaining?'

'Can you blame her?'

Hines did not answer but, after a few seconds, volunteered, 'I've been doing some digging. I mean it's a sensational story – famous poet and broadcaster beheaded like Anne Boleyn at a village fête . . .'

'After the village fête,' Edward corrected him.

'There's your presence at the fête and the famous novelist, Virginia Woolf. There's the film star mother in Hollywood, and a girl left fatherless and so on and so on. There's a lot of human interest in the story. Anyway, I've found out some interesting stuff.'

'You've told the police about this "interesting" stuff?'

'Are you kidding? That Inspector Trewen is a complete bozo.'

'So what are you proposing?'

'Let me fill you in on what I've found and you keep me posted. You can give me an exclusive when you've found the killer.'

'I've told you, I'm not involved in the investigation.'

Hines did not dignify this with a comment. 'Think about it. I'll tell you all about Miss Burrowes if you tell me who you suspect. I'll tell you this though for free. Frieda Burrowes may not be the "perfectly nice girl" you take her to be.'

Virginia, Edward thought, seemed even more ethereal than before. She was obviously badly shaken by the violence which had erupted in their quiet Sussex village. She said very little during lunch but this was scarcely noticeable as Miss Fairweather hardly drew breath and when she did, to drink the bottled beer for which she had asked Leonard, Miss Bron took the opportunity to have her say. Leonard made several attempts to lead the conversation in a different direction, obviously fearing that his wife was being upset by the tirade, but without success.

It was Miss Fairweather's view that Byron had been executed for his flagrant immorality.

'And whom do you suspect of taking it upon themselves to punish Mr Gates?' Edward asked mildly.

'I would think that was perfectly obvious,' Miss Fairweather barked. 'One of the men he cuckolded, of course. You merely have to make a list of all the women he seduced and go through it until you find the jilted man. One would suppose that even the egregious Inspector Trewen could manage that.'

Edward studied the two women. Miss Fairweather – who was in her early fifties, he guessed – was dressed entirely in black. She wore a black shirt, black trousers and a black bandanna round her head. She smoked incessantly, her long ivory cigarette holder clamped fiercely between scarlet lips. Miss Bron, the younger by five or six years, was rather mousy. Her hair was in tight ringlets, a fashion she had adopted, Edward imagined, when younger and never discarded. Her eyes were blue and her small hands quivered and pawed the air like a field mouse whenever she made a point. She wore a frilly blouse and tweed skirt and a jangle of jewellery on her wrists. And yet, despite appearances to the contrary, he thought it was Miss Bron who 'wore the trousers'.

'Did either of you see any strangers at the fête?' he inquired. 'As a stranger here myself, I would not have noticed.'

'I don't know that I did,' said Miss Fairweather. Miss Bron nodded, obviously content or resigned to having her friend answer for her.

'Did you have anyone particularly in mind?' Leonard asked.

'No,' Edward replied, 'but it's hard to believe that any-one in the village could have done such a thing.'

'I gather you have taken in Gates's children?' Leonard said. 'That is very good of you.'

'It was Verity who insisted we should do something,' Edward admitted, giving credit where it was due. 'They are good girls and bearing up well though poor little Ada is still very shocked, as one would expect. Paul Fisher has found a girl to come and help look after them until Jean's mother returns from America. I saw her this morning, as a matter of fact, and hired her on the spot. She's a teacher and is spending the school holidays with her parents in Lewes. Quite honestly, I think she was glad to have an excuse to get out of the house and earn a little money. She's not a great deal older than Jean and will be a companion for the girls and maybe even teach them something.'

'I suppose the police haven't yet found a bloodied axe, have they?' Miss Bron asked. 'They searched our cottage and the garden but the only thing they turned up was a set of my dentures in the cabbage patch. They fell out when I was gardening one day last week and I looked everywhere for them. I was glad to get them back though they were a trifle muddy.'

'They seem to have searched almost every house and garden in the village,' Leonard said, 'even the church, but apparently nothing has "turned up".'

'They haven't searched the Old Vicarage yet,' Edward mused. 'I wonder why.'

'How could anyone suspect you?' Miss Bron said, and Edward could not decide whether she was being sarcastic.

Virginia looked pained, perhaps at the idea of her beloved garden being trampled over by the police, and tried to change the subject. 'I'm worried about Mark. I saw him this morning and he was very depressed. His last exhibition was a disappointment – financially, I mean.'

'My wife tells me his paintings are very impressive,' Edward said. 'She wants me to buy one – a self-portrait, I think.'

'Well, you mustn't buy it out of pity. He couldn't bear that,' Leonard declared, 'but if you do like his work . . .'

'I was considering asking him to paint Verity's portrait but there won't be time for her to sit for him. The *New Gazette* is sending her to Paris or Madrid soon.'

'I admire her so much,' Virginia said. 'She's a woman of action while I remain at home squeezing out a few words a day trying to distil something true about life.'

'But your books will be read for as long as people read,' Edward told her tactfully.

Leonard smiled. He was always grateful when his wife's fragile confidence was bolstered by someone whose judgement she could take seriously. 'There you are, my dear, it's good for you to be told that now and again.' He turned back to Edward. 'My wife's only too ready to undervalue what she has achieved. As you say, when all the daily dirt of politics is swept under the carpet of history, people will read *The Years* and say, "That was how it was."'

When Edward got up to leave, Leonard walked to the gate with him. 'I gather you got Colonel Heron out of jail. He's very grateful and is telling everyone he meets what an excellent fellow you are.'

'It was nothing. I merely pointed out to the police that Byron could not have been killed with his sword.'

'I can't believe Heron is a killer,' Leonard said. 'He had a very good war, as they say, and is a distinguished soldier. The India Corps were on the Western Front before the end of 1914. They had a terrible time and I think by the end of it must have been in very bad shape. Most of the young officers who knew the men serving under them – understood their culture, religious beliefs and so on – were dead and their replacements were much less – what shall I say? – experienced. I gather Heron put down a mutiny in his regiment in 1918 which might have caused a lot of problems.

'The Germans did their best to stir up the separatist movement in India before the war but, as you know, in the event, India came to the aid of the Empire. Sadly, India has been badly mishandled since the war. I think most Indians expected to be rewarded for their loyalty with independence. Unfortunately, your friend Mr Churchill, among others, won't consider it. It's a policy which will cost us dear, I fear.'

9

Verity spent the morning at the *New Gazette*, lunched with the new editor, Matthew Long, whom she decided she liked, and then took a cab to Portland Place. Although she had been to Broadcasting House before, she had never looked at it properly. She was a little early for her appointment so she strolled past the Queen's Hall where a small queue was forming for the evening concert, and wondered idly if Edward had obtained a receiving licence for their new radiogram. Looking up at Broadcasting House, she appreciated why it was often likened to a great ship moored in Portland Place, about to cruise down Regent Street.

Parts of the building were being clad in protective concrete as though it was transforming itself from transatlantic liner to destroyer. As Verity passed through the massive swing doors – protected by sandbags against the bombs that were now expected daily – she passed under Eric Gill's Prospero and Ariel, the striking naked figure making no concession to modesty. She smiled as she recalled the controversy when it had been unveiled. The indignation of the moral majority had been fierce with the newspapers overwhelmed by letters of protest. Oddly enough, given Sir John Reith's strict Calvinist views, he had taken absolutely no notice and supported Gill against his detractors.

Inside, Broadcasting House resembled a liner even more closely. Verity had crossed the Atlantic on the *Queen Mary*, and the marble-clad pillars, mosaic floor and Eric Gill's sculpture of a half-naked 'sower', his decency preserved only by what looked like a bathing towel, inescapably brought to mind that great ship's swimming bath. She thought, irreverently, that she might demand a towel and a bathing dress at the huge mahogany desk which barred the way to the hallowed interior, guarded by uniformed commissionaires. Instead, she asked meekly for Miss Burrowes.

She sat down as directed on one of the uncomfortable benches and waited for Frieda to come and collect her. As she looked about her, she was reminded of the building she had just left – Lord Weaver's *New Gazette* in Fleet Street. The architects of both buildings had been influenced by the transatlantic liners which seemed to personify the modern age. Both the *New Gazette* and Broadcasting House set out to overwhelm the visitor and remind him of his insignificance. She tried to decipher the inscription over the lifts – it was in Latin but she recognized the date, 1931, and Sir John Reith's name, and guessed at the rest. No journalist, she thought wryly, would ever have their name set in stone in the foyer of a great building.

Just as Verity was beginning to wish Edward was with her to translate the Latin, Frieda appeared and, rather to her surprise, kissed her on both cheeks.

'Welcome to BH. We always call it that,' she added proprietorially. '"Talks" are on the third floor.' As they waited for the lift, Frieda told her that there used to be one lift for staff and one for 'artists'. 'But that soon went by the board. We're all terribly democratic now.'

Once they were alone in the lift, she burst out. 'It's too horrible about Byron. I didn't know what to do when I heard what had happened. I wanted to rush down to Sussex but, after what you said on the telephone about the publicity I would attract, I decided not to. I didn't want to make it worse for the children and, anyway, what would I have said to them? Tell me I was right – or was I just a coward?'

Fortunately, at that moment, the lift arrived on the third floor and Verity was spared having to answer.

'It's only ten to three. We've got five minutes before we see Mr Barnes. Would you like me to show you round?'

Verity said she would and followed Frieda through some offices to the heart of the building.

'The studios – "Talks" have three of them – are right at the centre so there's no noise from outside.'

Verity was amused to find that several of the studios had been furnished and decorated to resemble a study or library. Studio 3D had bookcases filled with fake books and a fake mantelpiece with, she supposed, a fake eighteenth-century portrait of George Washington hanging over it. A miniature bust of Sir John Reith stood on a fake windowsill.

'Do you see the chair?' Frieda said. 'It belonged to Arnold Bennett.' Verity was suitably impressed. 'And this is where Children's Hour is produced.'

Verity peeped into a large, rather austere, studio – empty apart from a few utilitarian metal chairs.

'It's hard to imagine it seething with people,' she commented. 'What's that big panel high up near the ceiling?'

'It's a window. Behind it is the Silence Room.'

'The Silence Room?'

'You can look down on the studios from it and see what's happening but not be seen, and you can talk on the telephone or to someone in the room with you without being heard and told to shut up by the programme producer,' Frieda explained.

'It feels very fresh – not stuffy at all.'

'Yes, the ventilation system is supposed to be the most modern in the world. Fresh refrigerated air is pumped up shafts right into the studios. Clever!'

'Indeed. And this is . . .?' She pushed at another door.

'That's 3E – the chapel – from which the Daily Service is broadcast.'

Again, Verity was amused by the effort which had been made to create an illusion. The studio was done up to resemble a church with tall windows – blank, of course, since they were deep inside the building – with flowers on the sills and a ceiling decorated with a huge cross surrounded by stars and clouds.

'Oh gosh, look at the time!' Frieda exclaimed, glancing at the clock on the wall. 'We mustn't keep Mr Barnes waiting.'

Reg Barnes proved to be a genial, red-faced man in his late fifties and his relationship with Frieda, Verity soon realized, was that of father and daughter.

'Miss Browne, or should I say Lady Corinth? – I'm not very good with titles – so pleased to meet you.'

'Please, call me Miss Browne. If I'm worth interviewing at all it's as a journalist and I write under my maiden name.'

'Very good! Now, down to business. Frieda suggested – and I think it's a good suggestion – that you might like to be interviewed on the significance of the final defeat of the Republicans in Spain.'

'You don't think it's a bit too political?'

'Not at all. It's ten years since Sir John Reith decided that politicians and politics could enter the BBC's hallowed portals. Since then, we have all shades of opinion in our studios. We are totally independent of government, remember. You know Guy Baron?'

Verity said she did.

'Well, he calls himself a Communist though I don't think he really is one. Anyway, in his *The Week in Westminster* he makes a point of having guests from every part of the House and the DG welcomes it. He is insistent – as was Sir John – that we must be balanced. We must be fair to all parties and represent all views.'

'Except the most extreme. I imagine you would draw the line at having a Nazi telling the country we'd be better off without the Jews.'

Barnes was shocked. 'That goes without saying. We do not allow anything to be broadcast which might incite hatred of any race or section of the community.'

'Then I'd be happy to be interviewed on the Spanish Civil War.' Verity wanted to ask if Frieda knew enough about it to ask her the right questions but Barnes preempted her.

'The idea is that Frieda represents the ordinary listener who may not know a lot about the war but wants to learn a bit about it without being drowned in detail, if you understand me. I suggest you send Frieda the questions you want her to ask. By the way, what will be the main thrust of your argument?'

'It would be that the Spanish Civil War was the first battle in the great European war which will shortly be upon us. Democracy lost that battle but it must win the war.'

'You won't be too depressing, will you?' Frieda put in.

'Don't worry! I'll end on a positive note. It may not be true but I'll argue that right wins out over wrong and dictators are, in the last resort, weaker than democracies. Will that do?'

'Perfectly!' Barnes exclaimed. 'And don't forget to include stories of courage and heroism and one or two humorous incidents . . .'

They went on to discuss details and it was agreed that the interview would be recorded on a Marconi-Stille direct disc machine on Wednesday week and broadcast a week or two later.

When they had finished, Frieda asked Verity if she had time for a cup of tea. The canteen was in the basement and, as they entered, Verity couldn't prevent herself looking round to see if there were any 'personalities'. She was rewarded by the sight of Henry Hall and most of his band tucking into Fullers cake and biscuits but, to her slight disappointment, there was no sign of the *Bandwaggon* stars, Arthur Askey and Richard Murdoch. She was about to mention her favourite show when Frieda once again raised the subject which was uppermost in her mind.

'It's just so awful . . . I can't imagine how Byron must have suffered waiting to be killed. And the children . . . Are they all right?'

'As I told you on the telephone, they're very shocked, and so Edward and I have arranged for them to stay with us until Jean's mother comes to claim them.'

'Oh dear, you are a true Samaritan. I feel so guilty, though I don't really know why. I was right not to come down, wasn't I, Verity? I wake up in the middle of the night and worry about it.'

'It would only have made things worse, especially as the press are hanging around Rodmell like wasps round a rotten apple. I say, Frieda, can I ask you something personal – something I have no right to ask you?'

'Are you going to ask me if Byron and I were in love?'

Verity was surprised at her acuity. 'Yes, I was. You told me on the telephone that *you* had been in love with *him*.'

'I thought I was, at least at the beginning. Byron didn't love me though and I had to accept that. In fact, I'm not sure if he even knew what the word meant. I quickly realized that to him I was just a "bit on the side". To be fair, he never pretended I was anything else. I think the only person he really loved was himself, but I suppose I ought not to speak ill of the dead.'

'What made you fall for him?'

'I like famous people. Isn't that an awful thing to say? And I was down in the dumps. My career was going nowhere. I had gone for so many auditions and been rejected. I was flattered when he made a pass at me and I suppose being with him was some kind of substitute

129

for having failed as an actress. I was always performing when we were together. You must have noticed when we met at that evening at the Embassy that I was playing a part – trying to give him what he needed. In a funny sort of way, he was very insecure. In return, he took me to nice places like the Embassy and Ciro's – he was a very good dancer – and introduced me to interesting and famous people. I suppose my dancing days are over,' she added sadly.

'That was it? Nothing else?' Verity wasn't normally judgemental – she'd lived too rackety a life to take the moral high ground – but Frieda's explanation sounded superficial to the point of triviality.

'He was a very good lover – sensitive and caring. I hate men my own age. My first experience of men was more like rape – he was a friend of my brother's and probably more frightened than I was. The more I said no, the more determined he became – I imagine so that he could brag to his friends he was no longer a virgin. I suppose it was all about his self-respect but it did nothing for mine. Anyway, to find that Byron knew what to do and how to do it was rather a relief. I discovered sex could be deeply satisfying. I expect you think I'm just a tart.'

'No, I don't,' Verity said, although she did think Frieda was naive and foolish. 'But, before Byron, they weren't all boys, were they?'

'What do you mean?' Frieda asked sharply.

It flashed through Verity's mind that Frieda thought she was accusing her of being a lesbian. She hurriedly made it clear that all she meant was that Frieda's previous lovers had been men rather than boys.

'Well, you know how people talk . . . Forgive me if I am being impertinent but I heard that you were with Lewis Cathcart before . . .'

'Who told you that?' Frieda sounded annoyed but also relieved. 'Do you know him?'

'No, but I thought I might see if he'll talk to me. He might have some idea about who hated Byron enough to kill him.'

'Well, I happen to know that you won't find him here today. He's gone off to make a programme in Wales with a poet friend of his, Dylan Thomas. Have you head of him?'

'Yes, I have. He's also a friend of the painter, Mark Redel. I gather you used to model for him in Highgate.'

'For Mark? Yes, I did. But that was all. We weren't lovers or anything.' Frieda was silent for a moment while she considered what Verity was implying. 'But surely you don't think that Lewis might have . . .? I mean, he had no reason to . . . Our affair had finished before I met Byron.'

'You were finished with him or did he finish with you?'

'I told him I had found someone else. He was very upset when we broke up,' she confessed, sounding very slightly smug. 'But he was getting on my wick. He patronized and stifled me. He didn't want me to get this job and, when I did, he tried to persuade Mr Barnes to sack me. I couldn't forgive him for that. Thank God, Reg – Mr Barnes – told him to go to hell. You don't really think Lewis could have killed Byron, do you?'

'I don't know. Do you?'

'No, I can't believe that.'

But Verity saw that Frieda *did* believe that Lewis was, at least, capable of it. She thought she would try one last question. 'By the way, Frieda, when we got back to Edward's rooms in Albany after our evening at the Embassy, the porter gave him an envelope which I opened. It was a horrible anonymous letter saying disgusting things about us . . . and about you and Byron. Did he get one too?'

'Not that he ever told me. What sort of things did it say?'

'Stupid, beastly things about us being immoral and . . . and worse.'

'Gosh! Do you think it was from the murderer?'

'It could have been.'

Frieda was rather less effusive when she said goodbye to Verity than when she had greeted her. There were no kisses – just a perfunctory handshake – and she seemed glad to see the back of her. Maybe, Verity thought, she felt she had revealed too much about herself. As a commissionaire opened the swing doors for her, a man wearing a clerical collar stepped back to let her pass. It was Paul Fisher, Rodmell's vicar – the last person she expected to see at the BBC. For a second or two she couldn't think who he was.

'Mr Fisher! What are you doing here?' she asked in surprise.

'Hello, Lady Edward. I might ask the same of you.' He seemed embarrassed and she was sure he would have pretended not to notice her had it been possible.

'What a coincidence!' she exclaimed. 'We were talking about you at breakfast. After he dropped me at the station, Edward was going to meet the girl you very kindly suggested might be able to help with Ada and Jean.'

'That was a very Christian act – taking in the Gates children.'

'Not Christian,' Verity could not resist correcting him. 'It was what anyone would do in the circumstances – even a Communist.'

Fisher looked as though he was about to start an argument but seemed to think better of it.

'So what are you doing at the BBC?' he asked.

'I'm being interviewed next week about the Spanish Civil War and I was talking through the arrangements. And you?'

'I'm taking the Daily Service tomorrow and some next week as well. My friend Pat M'Cormick, the vicar at St Martin-in-the-Fields, put my name forward. He took the very first service here.'

'Goodness. I'm impressed. I shall certainly listen even though I'm not one of the faithful.'

'I'm well aware of that, Lady Edward.' He sounded so disapproving that Verity recoiled as though he had hit her. She recovered herself and tried to be friendly. He was Edward's friend, she reminded herself, and she had no wish to quarrel with him.

'Please call me Verity. Everyone does. I didn't mean to offend you. Do you think I talk too much about being an atheist?'

'It's not that,' Fisher responded defensively. 'It's just that I'm a friend of Tommie Fox, as you know, and he told me how you wouldn't let him bless your wedding. He was very hurt.'

His look of reproach stung Verity to the quick. She resented being rebuked by someone who had no right to chastise her and felt herself become angry – her normal reaction when corrected.

'I won't try to convert you if you don't try to convert me!' she said with an effort at good humour.

'This is no time for levity, Lady Edward,' he said, ignoring her request to call her by her first name. 'We live in a godless age and we face unimaginable evil. How can we hope to overcome our enemies if we cannot overcome ourselves?'

'You are very severe, Mr Fisher. Did not Christ say forgive your enemies, turn the other cheek?'

'How can you say that to me? Can you really forgive what the Fascists are doing to the Jews in Germany and to the brave Christian priests who protest against an evil regime? Christ is being crucified again even as we speak.'

Verity was ashamed. 'You are right, of course. There can be no forgiveness for that. I have seen enough of it to know its true nature.'

Fisher seemed satisfied. The smile on his thin lips made him suddenly less severe and better-looking. He raised his hat. 'We shall see each other in Sussex, no doubt, but goodbye for now.'

'Good heavens!' Verity exclaimed, perhaps inappropriately, as he disappeared into Broadcasting House. Silently, she added, 'It's a bit much to be dressed down by a bigot and a prig in this temple of free speech. I must ring Tommie and find out what has made him such a Bible basher.' Her experience of Church of England vicars was not great but those she had met tended to be amiable men with liberal views, unwilling or unable to preach hellfire at the non-believer. Paul Fisher made her more certain than ever that she was an atheist.

10

The next few days passed quickly and quietly as time tends to do before any major catastrophe, at least in retrospect. Edward spent a day at the Oval with Tommie Fox watching England draw with the West Indies. A third wicket stand of 264 between Len Hutton and Walter Hammond recalled Hutton's mighty 364 against Australia at the Oval the previous year.

Edward itched to take up a cricket bat again but had to make do with a box of croquet mallets and balls he discovered in what had once been the summerhouse but was now little more than a ruined shed given over to rats and birds. Basil tried to evict the rats but they were too fierce for him so he turned his attention to the birds who protested loudly but otherwise ignored him.

Leonard and Virginia they saw almost every day. Edward grew very much to like Leonard and at his urging made a determined attack on Virginia's *Three Guineas* which puzzled and rather repelled him. Virginia was so complicated and subtle a character that he found it hard to get a grip on her. While he now thought of Leonard as a friend, he still regarded Virginia as something between a seer and La Gioconda – elusive but infinitely fascinating.

Verity was much less struck by Leonard and made no attempt to read Virginia's novels, having convinced herself that she would not understand them. However, she became very fond of her and constantly sought her advice or approbation. It was almost as if she had adopted Virginia as an unpractical but wise older sister – the sister she had never had. Verity accepted her for what she was and her uncomplicated affection seemed to spark something similar in Virginia who, in Verity's company, was cheerful and sometimes merry. She seemed to see in her something of Julian, her beloved nephew. Leonard and Edward would look at each other in delighted surprise when they heard the two women – so different in every way – laughing together.

'When I first knew Virginia, she used to laugh and make jokes but now she laughs so seldom that I treasure each occasion. I owe your wife a lot, Edward.'

'Not as much as I owe her,' Edward responded fervently.

Verity found she was nervous as she pushed through the swing doors of Broadcasting House the following Wednesday. She had stopped before entering to admire the famous window boxes outside the Director General's office on the first floor which, viewed from the street, recalled Sir John Reith's shaggy eyebrows. She might not sympathize with all his views but his creation – the BBC – seemed to her almost perfect.

Frieda met her and took her straight up to the third floor. It was six o'clock and they used the interval until the recording to rehearse some of the questions Verity would be asked. Frieda wanted the conversation to sound spontaneous but found that it helped to prime the pump, as it were. Although Verity was no novice when it came to broadcasting, she had in front of her, as was her practice, a list of the names, dates, facts and figures which could so unaccountably elude her at a crucial moment when she was in full flow.

136

At twenty to seven they went into Studio 3D. Reg Barnes, talking to them from the control room behind a plate-glass window, tested their voice levels and twiddled knobs until he was satisfied with the technical side. The two women sat opposite one another across a table, each with a microphone in front of her. Frieda faced the control room so that she could take instructions from Reg Barnes. Although there was a clock on the wall, he said he would put his hand in the air when they were five minutes from the end and again two minutes before the stop signal. He was a comfortable calm figure and Verity knew she was in good hands. At five to seven she fought down an impulse to run out to the lavatory and the recording began. It was to last forty minutes.

She listened to Frieda's introduction with some astonishment, hardly recognizing herself. Was she really the hard-bitten war correspondent Frieda painted her? There were references to her 'scoop' – her dispatch from Guernica just after its destruction by the Luftwaffe in April 1937 – her deportation from Vienna after the Anschluss and also her recent illness. Verity had not wanted this mentioned but Frieda felt that her recovery from TB might encourage others who had been struck down by the disease to feel that they too could regain their health and return to normal life. Verity had reluctantly agreed but absolutely refused to discuss her marriage so was annoyed when Frieda sneakily mentioned that she was the wife of the celebrated amateur sleuth, Lord Edward Corinth.

After the first questions about how she had become a war correspondent and the problems a woman faced competing with men in a difficult and occasionally dangerous job, she relaxed and rather enjoyed talking about herself. Frieda asked one or two awkward questions about why she had joined and then left the Communist Party but they ended with what was almost a call to arms. She said the Nazis *could* be defeated and that in her experience the worst thing about war was the waiting.

All in all she thought it had gone well. When the red light went off, she got up, stretched and – leaving Frieda to tidy up her papers – went into the control room to see if Barnes was happy with the interview.

He was playing it back on the Marconi-Stille machine. 'Very good! You'll get a lot of sneers from the far right, but take that as a compliment. I think the DG will be pleased.'

Verity listened to the first few minutes of the interview but then begged Barnes to stop the machine. 'I can't bear my voice! I sound quite different in my head. Have I really got that clipped, nasal whine? Please tell me I sound more like Greta Garbo.'

'You mustn't be so hard on yourself. You have a low voice for a woman and that always sounds better on the wireless. Now, where is Frieda? There are a few things I need to say to her about the next interview.'

'Who is that with?'

'E. M. Delafield. She writes in *Time and Tide*.'

'Of course! I love her books, particularly *The Diary of a Provincial Lady*.'

Barnes glanced through the window of the control room into the studio. 'Good heavens! What on earth . . .?'

He got up hurriedly, knocking over a chair. Verity turned round, anxious to discover what had happened, and saw that Frieda appeared to be lying across the table. Her first thought was that she had fainted. The studio was certainly stuffy despite what Frieda had told her about the building's ventilation system.

As she followed Barnes into the studio, a sudden fear gripped her. If Frieda had fainted, she would surely have fallen on the floor and, in any case, she had given no sign of feeling ill. Barnes was already leaning over her as Verity came through the door. She cried out when she saw Frieda's head. She had been hit with something heavy which had caused a terrible wound. Blood was leaking on to the table in an ever-widening pool. There could not be the slightest doubt. Frieda had been murdered.

'Oh my God! Frieda! How can this be possible? I was only out of the room for a minute. Who could have done it? And why?'

Verity found that tears were pouring down her cheeks and she wiped them roughly away. It was the shock of finding someone so alive one moment, dead the next, murdered by some lunatic in the heart of Broadcasting House where, just a short time before, she had felt so safe.

Barnes pointed to a small bust of Sir John Reith covered in blood and worse which had fallen to the floor. There could be no doubt as to what had happened. In the five or six minutes Verity had been in the control room, someone had entered the studio, picked up the nearest heavy object and beaten Frieda to death. It would have been unbelievable had the evidence not been in front of them.

Pulling herself together Verity went to the door and looked into the passage. There was no one and nothing to be seen.

'The killer must still be in the building,' she said. 'Quickly, ring down to security and tell them to stop anyone leaving until the police get here.'

Barnes still appeared dazed by the suddenness with which the horror had come upon them.

'She was so alive . . . I can't believe it . . . for this to happen in the BBC of all places,' he muttered, unconsciously echoing Lady Macbeth. He looked at Verity and seemed to get a grip on himself. 'Yes, the police – I'll telephone the front desk.' Then he added, rather strangely Verity felt, when she thought about it later, 'Well, at least no one can suspect either of us of killing the poor girl.'

'Whoever did this will be covered in blood,' Verity pointed out. 'He must be changing his clothes as we speak or at least cleaning himself up. Where are the nearest washrooms?'

'At the end of the passage but you can't go on your own. If he's killed once, he'll have no hesitation in killing again. Wait while I raise the alarm and then I'll come with you. Oh God, what a mess! I must inform the DG. Murder in Broadcasting House! It's never happened before. Why kill Frieda? What had she ever done to anyone?'

Verity, too, was beginning to recover from the shock. 'We must keep out of here. There may be . . . Look!' She pointed to a bloody footprint. 'Someone needs to be on guard in here.'

Barnes went back to the control room and started telephoning. Putting his hand over the receiver, he said to Verity, 'No one covered in blood has been seen at the front desk. I suppose he must have gone out through the back.'

'Let's go and look at the washrooms. He may be hiding.'

Barnes would much rather have waited for the police but, unable to admit this to Verity, he followed her down the passage. The women's cubicle, containing a basin and a lavatory, was small and rather squalid. It was empty and there was no sign of anyone having used it to wash bloody hands or clothes. Barnes emerged from the men's washroom and shook his head. To his relief, he hadn't had to grapple with a murderer nor had he seen anything to suggest the basin had been used to wash away blood.

He had a sudden thought. 'The murderer . . . he might have gone up the stairs.'

'What stairs?'

'There's a small spiral staircase at the end of the passage that goes to . . .'

'Goes where?'

'To the Silence Room.'

140

Verity remembered Frieda telling her that the Silence Room was where announcements could be made and telephone calls taken without interrupting whatever was going on in the studios.

Grim-faced, her heart racing, she ran down the passage and up the staircase, her leather-soled shoes clattering against the metal. She thrust open the door of the Silence Room not quite knowing what to expect but fearing the worst. She half-suppressed a cry. A heap of bloodstained overalls lay by a chair. Panting, Barnes came up and stood beside her. They both stared open-mouthed at the sinister pile of clothes.

'That knitted thing with eye-holes . . . it's a balaclava, isn't it? He must have put it over his head to disguise himself.' Verity shuddered. It was clear that this was where the murderer had lurked and where he had changed after attacking Frieda. 'If only we had been a bit quicker . . .' she said under her breath.

'We must have only just missed him.' Barnes was sweating from the effort of climbing the stairs and felt rather dizzy. He tried not to show how relieved he was that they had not come face to face with the killer. 'What's that on the floor by the clothes?' he added, bending down to pick up a shiny piece of metal. 'It's a badge, isn't it?'

'Don't touch it,' Verity said urgently. 'We must leave everything exactly as we found it. Quick – let's get back to the studio. We mustn't let anyone in before the police arrive.'

As they reached the studio, they saw two commission-aires running towards them along the passage.

'There's been a terrible accident,' Barnes told them. Verity wondered vaguely why he called it an accident. There was no way of disguising what had happened. For one thing, police would soon be crawling all over the place and, for another, there would be no more broadcasts from the third floor for the foreseeable future. She suddenly

141

felt exhausted and deeply depressed. Why was violent death so often her companion, even here at the BBC, even before war made death a matter of routine? First Byron and now Frieda. Where was Edward? She needed him.

11

'It was terrible. I don't think I've ever been so shocked. I left Frieda as right as rain and five minutes later she was dead – murdered. It was truly horrible. The mess – her blood spattered all over the table we had been sitting at, the floor, even the walls. It was somehow worse, if you can understand me, that it happened at the BBC. I mean, next to being in a church, Broadcasting House is just the most respectable place. To desecrate it . . . as I say, it was horrible.'

'I'm so sorry, V, but at least . . .'

'You're going to say that at least I didn't get *my* head bashed in. Perhaps whoever did it *was* after me. Frieda had her back to the door so she could watch Reg through the control room window. Maybe the killer made a mistake.'

'I don't think so, V. Someone wanted to kill Bryon and his mistress but why Frieda was attacked there, with so many people in the vicinity, I don't know. The murderer risked being caught a hundred times.'

Verity was back at the Old Vicarage and Edward had poured her a strong whisky. She had told Mrs Brendel that she didn't want anything to eat but had been persuaded to drink some broth.

'What was Inspector Lambert like?'

'He was all right. I thought he was stupid at first. He had

a rugby player's frame and a head like a rugby ball with no hair.'

'But he wasn't stupid?'

'No. He asked me some pretty searching questions. I had to tell him about Byron's murder, of course, in case there's a connection. He asked if there might have been anyone in London today who had also been at the fête. I couldn't think of anyone.'

'Well, I can,' Edward said ruefully. 'Leonard and Virginia were in Bloomsbury moving their stuff. You remember them saying they've bought a new house in Mecklenburgh Square?'

'Yes, Virginia seemed to be regretting it.'

'Well, I said I would give them a hand if they needed a car to cart round the small things but they thanked me kindly and refused. They said they had help from a young man who works at the Hogarth Press – you know, their publishing business.'

'No one could possibly believe that Leonard murdered a girl he had never met at Broadcasting House.'

'No, but Mark Redel . . .'

'Was he in London?'

'I gather he was visiting his gallery – the Lefèvre. Apparently, they want to drop him as his last show was rather a failure and he was trying to persuade them not to.'

'Golly, and now I come to think of it, Paul Fisher may have been in Broadcasting House because he said he was taking some of the Daily Services this week.'

'What about Lewis Cathcart, talking of Frieda's lovers?'

'Yes, didn't I tell you? He *was* in Broadcasting House, though, as far as we know, he wasn't in Rodmell when Byron was killed. He came storming into the studio this evening, brushing aside the commissionaire who was trying to keep people out, and was obviously distraught. Reg Barnes told me who he was. There can be no doubt he still loved Frieda. I can see that he might have killed Byron for taking her from him but not Frieda herself.'

'Hm, you can't be sure of that,' Edward said. 'What sort of person was he?'

'Ordinary – mid-forties, I should think – tall, black hair, rather stooping.'

'No, I mean what is he like?'

'How would I know? He was distraught, as I said. You could hardly expect me to chat to him while his former mistress was lying dead on the floor, her brains bashed out by some lunatic.'

Edward saw that Verity was, understandably, still very upset and apologized. 'Who else was in Broadcasting House?'

'I don't know – probably hundreds of people. There were men in suits who arrived even before the police. Who they were, I have no idea – administrators I suppose.'

'One was probably Colonel Rathbone.'

'Who's he?'

'Guy Liddell's man at the BBC.'

'You mean MI5 has someone permanently stationed at the BBC?'

'Yes, Room 305, so I'm told. He vets all appointments, particularly foreigners.'

'But that's disgraceful. The BBC is independent.'

'Grow up, V. The BBC is the most influential broadcasting organization in the world. In wartime, it would be grossly irresponsible for it not to be monitored. What would people say if some spy or traitor was able to use it to aid the enemy? They'd be justifiably furious.'

'But censorship by some colonel no one has heard of . . .'

'You think he should be elected?' Edward asked sarcastically.

Verity looked at him with something like suspicion. She had belonged for many years to a legal organization – the Communist Party of Great Britain – whose every move had been 'monitored' by Special Branch and MI5. It had been a thoroughly unpleasant experience knowing every telephone call was being overheard and every friend watched while this information was being filed in some government department not open to democratic scrutiny or control. Edward had succeeded in convincing her that the security services were doing a necessary job in the circumstances, but to find that another organization, one in which most people had implicit trust, was also being 'monitored' stirred up her suspicion of all government snooping. And she did not like Edward telling her to 'grow up'. There had been an edge of contempt in his voice which she had never heard before.

However, instead of snapping his head off, she said mildly, 'I hope your Colonel isn't responsible for internal security at the BBC. Inspector Lambert was very uncomplimentary about the ease with which people can get in and out of Broadcasting House despite the threat from the IRA. Although the front desk is manned at all times and there are commissionaires on hand, there are at least three other exits at the back and at the side of the building. They are supposed to be locked but . . .'

'An exit can also be an entrance,' Edward commented. 'But fancy the killer using the statuette of Sir John Reith to kill Frieda! If it weren't so awful, it would be funny. I mean, his strict morals . . .'

'I wonder if the killer grabbed hold of the nearest heavy object and killed Frieda or if it was planned?' Verity mused.

'I think it must have been planned. He knew the layout of the studios and had identified the Silence Room as somewhere to change. He brought overalls so he wasn't covered in blood and a balaclava to disguise himself. No, it was planned all right.'

'But how did he know Frieda would be alone in the studio?'

146

'Quite a few people would have known that she was interviewing you in that particular studio. He would just have to wait his moment.'

'True – but to use the statuette . . . If you intended to kill someone, wouldn't you bring a weapon with you?'

'How easy would that have been?'

'You're right. It wouldn't have been very easy, now I come to think about it. They were searching people's bags as I entered Broadcasting House because of the IRA bomb threat. To smuggle in a weapon would be difficult but not impossible, particularly if someone let you in through a side door. If he was already familiar with the studio and had noticed the statuette, he might have decided it was easier to use a weapon already to hand.'

'Would it have been difficult to bring in the clothes he was going to use?'

'No. I asked Reg that and he said a lot of people – announcers for instance – bring in a change of clothes if they are going to be on duty for some time. If the murderer had them on a hanger over his arm, I doubt anyone would have been suspicious.' Verity hesitated and then exclaimed, 'Oh Edward, I'm so sick of people being killed all around us. Do you think we're a sort of ill omen – like the albatross, or do I mean the stormy petrel?'

'I know. You are longing to be away from it all and get on with your job.'

Again, there was an edge to his voice and she was quick to contradict him.

'I'm not looking forward to leaving you, Edward. You know how much I love being here with you although I admit that I do want to get on with the only job I know how to do. Women are going to play a much greater role in this war than the last and, when I see so many girls already in uniform, I confess I feel jealous. I want to do my bit too. You feel the same, I know.'

147

'I'm sorry V, I'm a bit on edge. One just longs for this bloody war to start – if it has to – so we can get on with it, and I admit I'm a bit envious of you. You'll be in the thick of things and I'll be escorting bigwigs to safety or acting as a messenger boy. I don't know . . . Sometimes I feel hopeless and useless.'

He had not told Verity that his first job for the Foreign Office in the event of war would be to escort the Duke of Windsor to safety from his villa in the south of France – he had been sworn to secrecy – but the more he thought about it, the less he liked it. He must obey orders, of course, but it wasn't exactly how he had imagined serving his country. They could surely find him something more demanding to do than playing nursemaid to an overgrown schoolboy.

'Edward, don't!' she said, taking his hand. 'Everyone must be feeling the same sort of anxiety, the same fear of the unknown. We've just got to live from day to day. Let's get back to finding this madman before he kills anyone else. If we can help rid the world of one killer, we'll have achieved something. By the way, Joan Harries seems to be getting on very well,' she continued, changing the subject.

'Yes, I think she's just what we want. Jean and Ada seem to like her and it won't be long now until Mary gets back.'

'We have Paul to thank for that,' Verity said, trying to be 'Christian' about a man she instinctively disliked and distrusted.

'Yes.' Edward shook himself mentally. 'I wish we knew if Inspector Trewen had turned up anything.'

'A bloody axe?'

'Something like that, but I'm sure the murder weapon has long ago been cleaned and possibly disposed of. Byron's killer would be mad to hang on to it.'

'But he is mad, isn't he?'

'Who knows? Leonard says Virginia goes mad sometimes, by which I think he means that she suffers from terrible depressions. She certainly doesn't want to kill anyone.'

'Except, perhaps, herself,' Verity put in. 'I'm sorry, I didn't mean that, but I've seen people feel suicidal with depression. I've got to know Virginia quite well in the last couple of weeks and, though she seems normal enough most of the time, there's a sadness in her eyes which never seems to go away – not even when she's laughing.'

'I know, V. I've noticed it too. I sometimes think we're none of us totally sane. We are about to embark on a war which everyone knows is going to destroy everything we treasure – people, buildings . . . everything. We'll *expect* men to kill then. That can't be sane.'

'It's not madness to fight against evil. Hitler may be mad but he's also evil and, until he's destroyed, we can't hope to lead "normal" lives. Madness may be an explanation of evil but it's not an excuse.'

Edward sighed. 'You're right again. So what do we do? We have very little time and no reason to meddle with the professionals who are investigating these murders.'

'I agree. It's not for us to meddle but we must still keep our eyes and ears open. I feel we owe it to Ada.'

'"My sword glued to my scabbard with wrong'd orphans' tears",' Edward declaimed. He saw Verity's look and apologized. 'I think that, instead of an education, they strung flypapers across my brain and every line of verse I was made to learn at Eton seems to have stuck to them. My tutor used to say that to quote was to continue a conversation from the past in order to give context to the present, but I'm inclined to think I'm just talking to myself.'

'Yes, well, you usually are,' Verity responded unsympathetically. 'By the way, Inspector Lambert wants me to call in at Scotland Yard early next week to go over a few things. I thought of taking Ada and Jean with me to

London. It might do them good to get away from Rodmell and see a bit of life. I could take them to the paper – Jean wants to be a reporter when she's grown up – and perhaps visit the British Museum . . .'

'Good idea! I tell you what, I'll come too. I want to drop in on Ken Hines at the *News Chronicle* and I might see if Cathcart will talk to me. I'll ask Liddell if I can have a word with Colonel Rathbone. By the way, when do we tell Jean and Ada about Frieda?'

'I don't know. I suppose they'll have to be told sooner rather than later – or perhaps they won't. Unless they read something about Frieda and Byron in the press why should they ever know?'

'Do you think it would it upset them very much?'

'You mean finding out that she was their father's mistress or that she was murdered?'

'Both, I suppose.'

'I don't think they ever met her. I got the impression that she didn't want Byron to introduce her to them. She was a good person, even if she was rather promiscuous. She had a kind heart and would have hated to cause them grief. She kept on saying how worried she was about them.'

About eleven the next morning, Edward and Verity strolled round to Mark Redel's cottage. They had an appointment to look at his paintings with a view to buying one or two for the Old Vicarage. He had told them to go straight to his studio and so they walked round the side of the cottage where they met an ashen-faced Adrian Hassel.

'Thank God you've come. Mark's tried to kill himself. Maybe he has, I don't know. I was just going to get help.'

Edward and Verity pushed past him into the studio. Mark was lying on the floor in front of his easel, unconscious but breathing stertorously.

'Adrian, run and get Dr Hind. If he's not there call an ambulance. Redel doesn't have a telephone, does he? He's taken something,' Edward said, picking up an empty bottle with a chemist's label, 'but I'm not certain what it is – sleeping pills, I think. Help me get him sitting up, will you, V? We ought to try and make him sick but I don't like to give him anything to drink in case he chokes.'

As they struggled to get him on his feet, Verity caught a whiff of his breath. 'Ugh! You're sure he's not just drunk? His breath smells of beer.'

'Perhaps, but he's definitely taken pills – luminal, probably,' Edward panted. Redel was a dead weight and difficult to manoeuvre in the cluttered studio. 'The writing on the label is smeared. I'm no expert,' he grunted, 'but I know that a combination of luminal and alcohol leads to coma more quickly than luminal alone. We have to try and get him walking. If he lapses into unconsciousness he may never wake.'

Adrian appeared at the door with Dr Hind. 'I just caught him as he was about to set out on his rounds,' he explained. 'And I've called an ambulance just in case . . .'

Dr Hind said very little other than to ask Edward if he knew what Redel had taken. Edward showed him the pill bottle and mentioned the alcohol on his breath.

'Just what I thought. I gave him those to help him sleep. Now we've got to make him sick it all up.'

He set to work with a professionalism Edward admired. Ten minutes later Dr Hind was sweating profusely but he had succeeded in making Redel vomit up a lot of unpleasant-looking fluid – mostly beer, Edward thought. He was still a bad colour but his breathing improved and it wasn't long before he began to regain consciousness. By the time the ambulance arrived it was clear that he wasn't going to die even though he could barely talk and didn't respond when Verity, mopping his brow with a cold cloth, asked him how he was feeling. She offered to go with him to the hospital but Dr Hind said he would accompany him.

'I want to make sure he's comfortable. There's no need to worry. He's out of danger and should be back home in forty-eight hours. Is there anyone who could look after him? I gather he is separated from his wife.'

'That's so,' Adrian said, 'but I have her address and I'll see if she can be persuaded to come, though I fear she won't. Otherwise, I suppose he'll have to have a nurse. Of course, we'll all be round and about but I expect for a week or so he won't be able to fend for himself.'

'No. Do you have any idea why he might have done this?' Dr Hind inquired. 'I wonder if he knows he could be prosecuted for attempting to do away with himself,' he added with a mirthless laugh.

'You'll have to ask him that,' Edward replied. 'Perhaps it was an accident but, as you know, he had family worries and his last exhibition wasn't a success.'

When the ambulance had gone, its bell ringing as if determined to alert the whole village to what had happened, Edward looked around the studio for a note or anything which might indicate that Redel had taken the luminal with the intention of killing himself. He noticed a leather-bound notebook lying on the table. It was held open by a fountain pen. He picked it up and saw it was a diary or journal. He began to read.

'The greatest crisis of my life? The trouble is my work. What is my value as an artist? What have I in me after all? That is the point. I doubt myself terribly. I have worked so, so hard with my very blood. I have lived and fed upon my work. My work was my faith – my purpose. I am flooded with misery and despair. I feel inferior to all . . .'

Edward turned to look at the powerful self-portrait on the easel, wondering how he could have doubted his talent.

Adrian, who had been reading over his shoulder, answered his unspoken question.

'The gallery had told him they wouldn't represent him any more. And, if that wasn't enough, he told me had written to Marjorie asking her to come home but she had refused. Then there was what he read in the papers about the Jews being persecuted in Germany. He felt he ought somehow to be sharing their misery. I tried to cheer him up and thought I had succeeded. He was excited that you were going to buy some of his paintings but it obviously wasn't enough.'

'And he had received this.' Edward passed him a letter that had been lying beside the diary. It was unsigned and read, 'You dirty Jew. Your pictures are filth and you are filth. You should face it – you are a failure and should die.'

'Good heavens!' Adrian exclaimed. 'Who on earth could have sent him such a beastly thing?'

'The same person who sent us – Verity and me – an anonymous letter in London just a week or so ago,' Edward said sourly. 'You didn't get one, I presume?'

'No, but why would someone do such a horrible thing?'

'It's a question we've been asking a lot recently.'

Edward wished they had come an hour or two earlier to look at Redel's work. Verity's enthusiasm might have carried him over that moment of despair. Perhaps the anonymous letter had been the last straw. Anyway, he would do his best to convince the doctor that Redel had taken an overdose by accident, however unlikely. It would achieve nothing if he were prosecuted for attempted suicide – probably just make him try again.

Charlotte Hassel arrived, having been alerted by the ambulance bell that something was amiss, and Adrian told her how he had found Mark.

'Oh my God!' she exclaimed. 'But he's all right? Thank God you arrived when you did, Adrian.'

Edward said he could do with a drink and suggested that they might walk down to the pub.

'Good idea,' Adrian agreed. 'I certainly need a pint but, hang on, I thought you didn't like pubs?'

'I don't, but this is an emergency.'

When they were seated in the bar parlour, Edward lay back in his chair and closed his eyes. He felt very weary. After a moment or two, Charlotte broke the silence.

'I suppose Mark *did* attempt to kill himself? I mean, he could hardly have taken all that luminal by accident, particularly at this time of day.'

'Might he not have woken very early and, wanting to sleep, taken the pills in a muddled sort of daze?' Adrian ventured.

'We'll have to wait and see what Dr Hind says, but I doubt a man in the state you describe could have downed all those pills without sicking them up,' Edward said, his eyes still closed. 'However, I think it's important we try to persuade Hind not to call it attempted suicide. Redel would not want the police snooping into his private griefs.'

'I'd better go and tell Leonard and Virginia what has happened. Virginia's going to be very upset,' Adrian said. 'No, of course, I forgot, they're in London today. Oh well, bad news can wait, I suppose.'

'Yes, I hate to think how it will affect Virginia,' Edward agreed. 'When you tell her, you must . . . not make light of it, exactly – but not give the impression that Mark was really serious about killing himself. Leonard hinted to me that Virginia has contemplated suicide when one of her depressions overwhelms her and she's very fragile at the moment. This is just the sort of bad news which might tip her over the edge.'

'It's a horrible thing but at least it's not another murder – unless you call that anonymous letter a murder weapon,' Verity said. 'Did you leave it in the studio, Edward?'

'No, I took the precaution of removing it and the diary. I have them here. I may be wrong but somehow I don't think Mark would want the police reading either the letter or the diary. If we want Dr Hind to come to the conclusion that taking the pills was an accident, I thought it wiser to remove any evidence to the contrary. One thing I'm sure of – Inspector Trewen's hobnail boots in his studio won't make Mark feel any better when he returns.'

12

An almost tangible cloud of fear and depression hung over Rodmell. Verity and Edward had an irrational feeling that they were in some way to blame for the violent death and the attempted suicide which had transformed this peaceful English village into a place crawling with policemen and newspaper reporters. Thank goodness, Edward thought, the press had not as yet connected Frieda's murder in London to Byron's decapitation, but it was only a matter of time. Ken Hines had, of course, realized that Frieda and Byron had been killed by the same person but had agreed to hold off publishing the story until the picture was clearer.

'I say, V, did you find anything about the badge – or whatever it was – that Frieda's killer left with the overalls in the Silence Room?' Edward asked as they lay in each other's arms the morning after Mark's attempted suicide, reluctant to rise and face another day of questions without answers.

'Yes, I did. I spoke to Reg Barnes on the telephone and he told me the police had traced it to the Middlesex Hospital. Apparently it was an identifying label. The overalls belonged to a porter at the hospital and had been stolen from his locker three weeks before.'

'I see,' Edward mused. 'So the murderer could either have worked at the hospital or been a patient there?'

'Or visiting a patient.'

'Less likely . . . A visitor wouldn't know his or her way around the place. I assume the locker room is in a part of the hospital that isn't open to visitors?'

'Yes, I asked Reg that and he said it was in the basement. He had overheard Inspector Lambert discussing it with his sergeant. The room was kept locked but, as every porter and quite a few other people had keys, that doesn't mean much. The lockers were also kept locked but this particular one had been left open for some reason.'

'Did you ask if any fingerprints had been found on the statuette?'

Apparently not. The murderer must have been wearing gloves.'

'No surprise there. And no gloves were found in the Silence Room?'

'Not as far as I know but the murderer could have taken them out of the building with him. There was something else I've been meaning to tell you. Reg said that when he played back Frieda's interview with me, he realized the machine had still been running after I left the studio. Right at the end, you can hear Frieda saying something – just a word. He says it sounds like "not he" or possibly "knotty".'

'Knotty?' Edward wrinkled his brow. 'Could she have been saying "not me", I wonder?'

'Did the murderer – if we assume Byron and Frieda were murdered by the same person – write the poison pen letters?'

'Frieda said she didn't think Byron had received one, but perhaps we ought to talk to Jean. She's a sensible girl and might know. I get the feeling that she didn't terribly care for him. Not surprising really except that he obviously liked her rather more than Ada.'

'Yes,' Verity agreed, slipping out of bed and opening the curtains, 'too much, perhaps. Jean is intelligent enough not to want the sort of admiration her stepfather was offering. She might have found it embarrassing – even creepy.'

'True. Look, why don't we tear the girls away from their books and take them for a walk after breakfast? It's a lovely day and they might feel more like talking out in the fresh air. I don't expect Joan will mind.'

'She's a nice girl, isn't she, Edward?'

'Yes. She doesn't ask a lot of questions or talk too much. Just the sort of girl I ought to have married.'

'What would she want with a man almost twice her age?'

'Come back to bed and I'll show you.'

'We mustn't overlook one thing,' Verity said, doing as he asked.

'What's that, Dr Watson?' Edward teased.

'Stop it. You know how I hate it when you call me that,' she protested, punching him. 'We're not detectives and, if we were, I would not be Watson. He was an old fool.'

'No, he wasn't. You're judging him on the basis of Nigel Bruce's ludicrous performance.' They had recently seen the film of *The Hound of the Baskervilles*. 'Would Holmes really have teamed up with such a buffoon? I think not. It would have driven him crazy.'

'That's beside the point. I'm not your stooge or sidekick, so there.' She bit his shoulder.

'You little cat! You know what happens to biters, don't you?'

'And Basil Rathbone is much better looking than you – though I have to say, you do have his nose.'

'Thank you for nothing. Now, stop wriggling and let me have my wicked way with you.'

Afterwards, Verity turned on her back and lit a cigarette.

'No, you don't,' Edward said, taking it out of her mouth and putting it in his. 'You know what the doctor said. Anyway, what was it you were saying we mustn't overlook?'

'Damn you and damn all doctors!' Verity exclaimed but could not be bothered to wrestle the cigarette from him. Instead, she let her mind return to Frieda's murder. She could not admit it, even to Edward, but the way Frieda had died, almost in her presence, and the violence with which she had been struck down had shaken her badly. She was unable to get the image of Frieda's smashed skull out of her mind. 'I was going to say, we mustn't overlook the fact that Mark could have killed Byron and Frieda and then tried to kill himself out of remorse. He had the opportunity. He was in London the day Frieda died and I happen to know that he knew his way round Broadcasting House. He told me he was a chum of Dylan Thomas, the poet, who works at the BBC on and off.'

'Yes, that's a thought. We heard him say how much he disliked Byron and how he had refused to paint Frieda. There must have been some bust-up between them when they were both living in Hampstead. I wonder if it would be worth having a talk with Thomas,' Edward mused.

'On the question of the poison pen letters,' Verity said, as Edward went into the bathroom to shave, 'it's generally agreed that they are normally written by women but Rogers said our letter was delivered to Albany by a man. Though I suppose it could have been a woman dressed as a man.'

'I distrust any rule of thumb about which sex does what. I think the sexes are equal when it comes to nastiness,' Edward shouted from the bathroom.

'Thank you for that unchivalrous thought, but when it comes to murder I can't see a woman having the nerve or the physical strength to tie Byron up and then behead him, can you?'

Edward poked his face, covered in shaving foam, round the door. 'No, I can't. However, if we discover that he

159

did get a letter, then we have to assume that receiving one precedes the recipient's violent death. We – or rather I – had such a letter so I'd better watch out. Mind you, I go armed!' Grinning he waved his razor.

The girls were delighted to leave their school work, and Joan said tactfully that she had some letters to write so would not accompany them on their walk.

Ada seemed to be returning to normal but Edward knew that the kind of shock she had suffered was not easily absorbed and the wound would take many months to heal if, indeed, it ever did. She might suppress her grief but it could have scarred her for life.

Just as they were going out of the front door, a boy in a peaked cap rode up on his bicycle. He had a telegram which he offered not to Edward, though he put out his hand for it, but to Jean. She tore it open and read it excitedly.

'Mother says she's on her way home. Isn't that wonderful?' she told them, waving it in the air. 'The *Aquitania* is due to dock at Southampton next Friday.'

'That's splendid!' Edward said.

Ada tried to look pleased but she was clearly apprehensive. Verity kissed Jean and added, 'I'm so pleased but we'll miss you. I wonder if she'll whisk you both back to America.'

Jean's face fell and Verity wished she had kept her mouth shut.

'Ada, what will you say if Mother wants to take us back to Hollywood with her?'

Ada smiled wanly. 'It'll be all right for you. You're so beautiful. You'll be snapped up by some mogul – isn't that what they're called? – and turned into a film star, but what will I do?'

No one answered. Instead, Verity said, 'Come on! Let's have our walk. It's a glorious day and Basil is mad with

160

excitement at the thought of going on the downs, aren't you, Basil?'

They had no alternative but to tell Jean and Ada about Mark's attempted suicide and, inevitably, it cast more gloom on the girls. They didn't know him well but he had given Jean a sketch he had done of her which she treasured. However, no one could be depressed striding over the downs, a warm wind ruffling their hair and Basil leaping around them like a puppy. Ada was walking with Edward while Verity and Jean followed some way behind discussing what qualifications were needed to be a reporter. Verity admitted she had none at all.

'I hated school, Jean. I was silly, I see that now, but I was bored rigid. It all seemed so irrelevant. I larked about and got myself expelled more than once. My poor father! I wish now I had learnt something. Edward is so well read and remembers what he reads, which is alarming. I think I was lucky to find Lord Weaver. He had faith in me for some reason, or perhaps I amused him. Anyway, he gave me my chance and I took it. When I was telling Mr Churchill about my lack of education, he said, "My education was interrupted only by my schooling," and that's how it was for me. To be a reporter you need luck, enterprise and cheek. If someone says no to you – and, in my experience, they always do – you just take no notice and do it anyway.'

'But you need to be able to write?' Jean suggested.

'You need to be able to write plain English, certainly, but I never learnt how to spell. Fortunately the "sub" – the sub-editor – will correct your mistakes. What else? You need to be alert, thick-skinned – not afraid to be snubbed – and suspicious.'

'Suspicious?' Jean queried.

'You should never believe what you are told. Always check your facts. I remember one old boy I was interviewing telling me all about his childhood and I only discovered by chance that it was all lies. Or rather *he* believed it but it was a fantasy he had concocted without realizing what he was doing. He even told me his mother had died giving birth to him when, in fact, she committed suicide when he was your age . . . Oh, I'm sorry! I hope I didn't upset you. My big mouth!'

'No, after all Byron didn't do that – kill himself, I mean.'

'No, he didn't,' Verity agreed.

'But Mark *did* try to kill himself,' Jean added meditatively. 'I'm glad you were in time to save him. I like him, although he is a bit odd. Sometimes he was really nice to us and let us watch him paint and sometimes he'd shout at us to go away. He was driven – that's what my stepfather said. He said that, if you were a true artist, you cared for nothing but your work. Everything and everyone else – family, friends – could go hang.'

'I don't think that is necessarily true, Jean. Look at Mrs Woolf. She's a true artist, and she and Leonard are very happy together.'

'Yes, but he looks after her, doesn't he? I've watched them together. I think they both agree that her work is the most important thing.'

Verity was impressed by her perceptiveness. 'I'm sure you're right but I believe it proves that an artist or writer doesn't need to be utterly selfish. In my limited experience most marriages – the ones that work – are about mutual support. Artists, strong in one area, can be weak in others and need support but not, if possible, at the expense of the people who love them. I don't know whether I'm making any sense.'

'What about Miss Bron and Miss Fairweather? On the surface, Miss Fairweather is in charge but I sometimes think that actually Miss Bron makes the important decisions, despite giving the impression of being all fluffy and muddled. But you and Edward are equals, aren't you? He respects your work as a journalist.'

'I very much hope so, Jean. I couldn't have married him if he didn't, but it's not always easy. I mean, I may have to leave him for months on some foreign assignment. That won't be pleasant for either of us but particularly for him. I'll be busy doing my job and won't have much time to be lonely. He is going to be working for the Foreign Office but I'm not sure yet how they will use him. Most men expect their wives to be there to minister to them after a hard day's work, which I suppose isn't unreasonable. Edward has had to learn to accept that I'm not like that. I love him very deeply but I can't – and he wouldn't want me to – sacrifice the thing that defines me, my job. That's how it is with Leonard and Virginia. I think that's why we get on so well with them. We're in the same boat, though of course she is a great writer and I'm only a journalist.'

'Do you think that's why Mother was able to leave us with my stepfather while she went off to Hollywood?'

'I don't know, not having met your mother, but don't forget that the money she's earning in Hollywood is a factor. It's easy to pretend money doesn't matter but you can only think that when you have lots of it. They say money can't buy happiness – and I agree with that – but I've seen enough poverty, enough slums, to know that the absence of money can bring misery, and don't let anyone tell you otherwise.'

Jean was quiet for a moment while she absorbed what Verity had said before remarking, 'Thank you for talking to me like an adult and not patronizing me. It's so difficult to get grown-ups to tell you the truth. They always want to protect you and so they tell lies and half-truths which merely confuse.'

They walked on, enjoying the sun and the feeling of being on the top of the world with the larks swooping high above them. They had almost caught up with Edward and Ada but Jean hadn't quite finished her questions.

'And is that what makes you a good detective – being suspicious?' she asked, harking back to what Verity had said about the qualifications needed for being a journalist.

'I suppose so, if I am a detective. I never set out to be one. It was just a series of accidents but then, that's what life is. There's a similarity between the two jobs – both searchers after truth. At least, a good reporter wants to get at the truth.'

'And do you know yet who killed my stepfather?'

Verity was beginning to feel under siege and walked a little faster, wishing she had longer legs. Edward and Ada, chatting away happily, seemed to have forgotten all about them.

'No, I don't know who killed him. That's for the police to find out.'

'Is that why you haven't asked me any questions?'

Verity was taken aback. 'Why? Is there something you know which you should tell the police?'

'It's something Ada knows. She hasn't told me what it is but perhaps she's telling Edward. I do hope so because it's making her very unhappy.'

'I'm not telling that Inspector Trewen anything,' Ada was saying in response to a question of Edward's. 'He's so . . . I don't know how to say it but he treats me like a little girl when I'm almost grown up.' Her voice quavered. 'Anyone could have told him that Colonel Heron didn't do it . . . kill my father. Although he can be bossy sometimes – a bit ex-army – he wouldn't hurt a fly.'

'Is there anything you want to tell me?' Edward asked mildly. 'Anything you don't want to tell the Inspector? If it would help find out who did do it, I think you should.'

'I found a letter on the doormat,' Ada said in such a low voice the wind almost blew it away. 'It hadn't been

164

posted – it had no stamp on it. It was addressed to Dad so I took it to him in his study. He was working so I didn't stay.'

'When was that?'

'The morning of the fête.'

'You didn't see who delivered it, I suppose?'

'No.'

'And you don't know what was in it?'

'Yes, I do. I went back an hour later with a cup of tea.'

'What time was that?'

'About eleven thirty. The letter was lying open on his desk.'

'And you read it?'

'I couldn't help it. It was written in capital letters. It said something like "You are an adulterer and the beast must die." It wasn't signed, which I thought was odd.'

'Did you ask your father about it?'

'I said, "Who sent you that horrible letter?" He told me that it was none of my business. He was quite cross, which was unfair.'

'And did you see it again?'

'No. I think he must have burned it because I saw what must have been the remains in the grate that evening.'

'Do you think he knew who it was from?'

'I'm not sure. I sort of sensed that he did but I might be wrong.'

'And did you understand what the letter meant?'

'Not at first but I looked up "adulterer" in the dictionary. Is that what he was – my father?'

Ada looked up at Edward and he felt his heart go out to this forlorn little girl, alone in the world – probably unloved and desperately unsure of herself.

'Writers and artists have never been good at being faithful and your father was very attractive. He loved women and women loved him.'

'So he was what the letter said he was?'

'I think he was, but even those closest to married people can never know what really happens in a marriage.

Sometimes even the people in the marriage couldn't tell you. You'll learn in time that every marriage is different and we shouldn't judge other people, especially our parents.'

'I don't understand. Do you mean you would forgive Verity if she loved someone else? Oh, am I being rude? Dad always said I was.'

'You need to be a bit careful about what you ask people,' Edward said gently. 'Loving someone is very private and we don't always know why or how we do it. You have to trust people and trust is part of love.'

'Trust them, even if you're suspicious of them?' Ada persisted. Edward looked at her and, seeing that it was a joke, felt a sense of relief. Perhaps she would, after all, survive her father's murder, but was it a good idea for her to go to Hollywood with her glamorous stepmother and desirable half-sister? Oh well, it was nothing to do with him but still . . .

'Have you told anyone else about the letter your father received?'

'Only the vicar. I thought he might be able to explain it to me.'

'And did he?'

'Not like you did. He was embarrassed and said I ought not to have read the letter. Anyway, he said my father shouldn't have done it – commit adultery – and that the Bible says that adultery is breaking one of the ten commandments. He said sinners will be punished. Dad *was* a sinner, I suppose. Do you think he's gone to hell?'

Ada tried to sound unconcerned but Edward could hear the anxiety in her voice and cursed Paul for frightening the girl. Surely *that* was a sin.

'To be honest with you, Ada, I don't believe in hell. Or rather I think bad people create their own hell here on earth.'

'Like Hitler?'

'Like Hitler,' he repeated grimly.

Basil came bounding up, panting after having failed to catch a hare, and they all sat on the grass and admired the view, sharing a bottle of lemonade.

'I wish I had my Brownie,' Verity said suddenly. 'I'd like to have a photograph of us now – this minute.'

'Yes,' Jean agreed, 'when you look at photographs you only want to see people – what they looked like *then*. It's a wonderful view but views are so disappointing in a photograph without the colour and the noise of the birds and the smells . . .'

'I'd like to remember this day when I'm a long way from here,' Verity said dreamily.

13

Given that Edward still maintained that he was not investigating Byron's murder and certainly not Frieda's, he was very busy that Monday in London talking to people and asking questions. At the end of it, he thought he knew who the murderer was but had not a shred of evidence to support his theory.

The train had been late and they didn't get into Victoria until almost eleven thirty. In the end, they had decided not to take Ada and Jean with them as they had so much to do, though Verity was determined to keep her promise to show Jean round the *New Gazette* before her mother returned.

She hurried off to Scotland Yard to see Inspector Lambert while Edward took a cab to Fleet Street. He had arranged to meet Ken Hines at El Vino, a drinking hole familiar to lawyers and journalists and just around the corner from the *News Chronicle* in Bouverie Street. El Vino was dark and rather gloomy. The smell of stale tobacco emanating from ashtrays full of cigarette stubs rather nauseated Edward, but he ordered a pint at the bar and went to sit beside Ken at a table badly stained by many a flagon of thick brown porter.

He had known Ken for some years. He had been a supporter of Verity's – for which Edward was grateful – and had shown her the ropes when she had started out in journalism. In such an all-male world, Verity would have been ignored or elbowed aside without Ken's insistence that she be included in the information-sharing that was *de rigueur* in that unofficial trade union. He was regarded as the doyen of crime reporters and boasted that in a single year he had reported on no fewer than fifty-six murders.

'I'm giving up crime, you know,' he said to Edward as he sat down. 'My bosses have agreed to send me to war. I always envied Verity her experience of covering the Spanish Civil War. I don't want to be left in a backwater when this new war starts. Will a crime, even one as gory as Byron Gates's murder, make the front page when whole armies are fighting? I don't think so.'

'Talking of Byron, Ken, what did you mean when you said on the telephone that Frieda wasn't quite the nice girl we took her to be?'

'Well, I don't like sex gossip but it's well known in certain circles that she didn't only like men.'

'What do you mean?'

'Do I have to spell it out?' He saw from Edward's face that he did. 'All right, she was a lesbian – or rather she liked sex wherever she could get it.'

'Good heavens! I would never have suspected . . .'

'I don't know why you are so surprised. Like most men, you assume lesbians all dress as men and stride about in riding boots like . . .'

'Like?'

'Like Miss Fairweather, of course. Why did you think I was in Sussex? I was fossicking around to find out if the affair was still going on. I was intrigued to discover that Gates and Fairweather both lived in the same village.'

'You're telling me that Frieda and Elsa Fairweather were lovers?' Edward was taken aback. The thought had never crossed his mind that Frieda had known Miss Fairweather. 'But how could they be?' he objected. 'As far as I know, Frieda never came down to Rodmell.'

'I don't think she did. She must have suspected there would be ructions if she showed up there. Even a girl like

169

Frieda wouldn't have wanted her lovers squabbling over her. She worked at the BBC, remember? There are plenty of that kind – male and female – in Broadcasting House but, as long as nothing is done in public to scare the horses, if you understand what I mean . . .'

Edward did. 'I see. And does Miss Fairweather know about Byron and Frieda?'

'I don't know about that. You'll have to ask her yourself. But I do know that she went to London to visit her publisher in Bedford Square on the day Frieda was killed. It's only a ten-minute bus ride from there to Portland Place.'

'And you think . . .'

'I'm not accusing her of anything, but she might have been trying to tempt Frieda back and Frieda might have rejected her advances. It's just a theory.'

'It certainly is. Well, thank you, Ken. I owe you.'

'I know you do,' Ken said with a grin.

Before his meeting with Lewis Cathcart, Edward had taken the precaution of telephoning Reg Barnes to find out more about him. Reg had laughingly described him as a Scot on the make. He had been assistant editor of the *Scottish Bookman* in which he had published some of his own poems and was one of the first to recognize Dylan Thomas's talent. They had met when Thomas came up to Edinburgh and Cathcart had bought a poem off him for the princely sum of two pounds. The two men had taken to each other, perhaps because they were both Celts and felt excluded from London's Grub Street. They shared a liking for pubs, the shabbier the better, and, when Cathcart came to London, they had become drinking partners.

The shoe was now on the other foot and Thomas had found Cathcart freelance work which kept him in funds while he looked for an editorial position with a newspaper or publishing house. Thomas had introduced him

170

to some BBC chums and that was where Barnes had come across him.

'Cathcart wrote quite a good play I used – I think Thomas must have had a hand in it because it had his rather whimsical humour – and he's done several other things for me. Of course, he's not as talented as Thomas. If only Dylan didn't drink so much he'd be one of our leading writers, but perhaps he's one of those unfortunate people who can't write without the drink. He's damned lazy, too. I've got to know him quite well and I like him but I wouldn't trust him an inch. He has charm but he is quite unscrupulous when it comes to money. He'll try and touch you for a pound or two, I guarantee it!'

Barnes had gone on to say that, when Cathcart first arrived in London, he had shared a flat in Hammersmith with another Scottish poet and was soon friends with W.H. Auden, Stephen Spender, Robert Graves and Byron Gates. In fact, it was Barnes who had introduced Frieda to Cathcart and they had quickly become lovers. Frieda liked older men, he explained.

'Frieda thought Cathcart could introduce her to "people that mattered" but it wasn't long before she realized that he wasn't quite the influential poet and editor she believed him to be because of the company he kept. It was inevitable that she turned her attention to Byron. She would have preferred Auden but quickly discovered that he wasn't interested in women.'

'So could the spurned lover have murdered the girl he still loved?' Edward asked.

'I wouldn't have thought so,' Barnes opined. 'Cathcart was jealous all right, and in his cups swore to have his revenge on Byron, but I think it was all talk.'

Lewis Cathcart was not quite what Edward had expected, despite Verity's description of him. He was about forty-five, thin and pasty-faced, with the haggard look of a man who drank too much and could only be bothered to shave every other day. He was sitting at the bar with a cherubic-looking man of about the same age who, Edward guessed, must be Dylan Thomas.

'Lord Edward!' Cathcart said in mock surprise. 'I never thought you'd find this place.'

They had arranged to meet at the Mitre, a rather squalid pub off Fleet Street. The last thing Edward wanted was another drink but he knew he must make an effort to look as though he was at home in pubs and insisted on standing a round. Dylan – which Cathcart pronounced Dullen – looked at him over the foam on his pint with sharp, twinkling eyes and Edward could not help smiling in response. He was like a naughty boy – a plump cherub, Barnes had called him – whom you could not be cross with for long. Cathcart, on the other hand, was surly, his bad temper inadequately disguised behind a thin veil of bonhomie. Here was a man, Edward thought, who could wield a knife if he had to, whatever Reg Barnes might say to the contrary.

'You know,' Thomas said, 'Caitlin – that's my long-suffering wife, Lord Edward – says her mother brought her up to marry a duke. I really must introduce you.'

'I would be a great disappointment,' Edward replied. 'In the first place, the younger son of a duke is worse than useless. His title is empty and, very often, his pockets too. In the second place, I have recently got married.'

Thomas looked at Edward's perfectly cut Savile Row suit and crisp Jermyn Street shirt. 'I hope you aren't really broke because – as I was just saying to Cathcart – I am more than usually hard up and was hoping to persuade you to lend me a fiver.'

The pub was beginning to fill up but they found a small table in a corner where they perched uncomfortably on hard wooden benches. Cathcart must have seen Edward's look of distaste at the table puddled with beer because he made what might have been an apology.

'I can't think why we come to this place, Dylan. It's dirty and uncomfortable and stinks of cigarettes and faeces.'

'That's why we like it. We'd feel out of place somewhere posher. We're not *respectable*, thank God. Tell me, Lord Edward,' there was something mocking in the way Thomas drew out his title that made Edward wince, 'why did you seek us out here in our sordid hideaway? I have heard you are an amateur sleuth. Would I be right in thinking you've come to accuse Cathcart of Frieda's murder? Now, if you were to ask me whether my friend here could have killed Byron Gates, I'd have to say it was more than likely – we've all wanted to kill Byron at one moment or another – but not Frieda. Frieda was a bitch and she treated Lewis like shit but he loved her. He still loves her and he could never have hurt a hair on her head. Isn't that right, my dear?'

It was a mannerism of Thomas's to call his friends 'my dear'. Edward didn't like it and nor did he care for his language. It was both flowery and filthy which was not a combination he found attractive.

'Cathcart, I gather you were there – in Broadcasting House – when Frieda was murdered? My wife said you rushed in when you heard the news,' Edward inquired.

'Yes, I had a meeting with a producer in an office on the third floor. As soon as I heard the sound of pounding feet I sensed something terrible had happened. I rushed out and followed the crowd. I couldn't believe it when I saw Frieda. I loved her – whatever you choose to believe – and to see her lying there with her head smashed in . . . I can't bear to think about it even now.'

'Have you any idea who might have done it?'

'Well, Gates is dead otherwise I might have said him. Frieda could be terribly annoying. They might have had a row but . . .'

'Did she love Byron, do you think?'

'Not really. She was a selfish cow,' Cathcart said bitterly. 'She wanted to "get on". That's why she attached herself to me originally. I fooled myself into thinking she loved me but I soon saw my mistake. She thought – wrongly, as it turned out – that I was a "coming man". I helped her to meet people – people like Byron – and she dumped me when she'd squeezed everything out of me she could. She would have dumped Byron too if she'd met some film producer or the DG or the Prime Minister. I loved the little bitch, as I told you, but I didn't like her.'

Edward was rather shocked at Cathcart's language but tried not to show it. 'So you have no idea who might have killed her?'

'An ex-lover . . . perhaps that lesbian writer – what's her name? Elsa Fairweather. She was pretty cut up when Frieda threw her over. You know about that?'

'I had heard,' Edward admitted guardedly. 'Anyone else?'

'Not that I can think of but . . .'

'You know Mark Redel, I believe? Was he in Broadcasting House at the time of the murder?'

Cathcart looked at his friend. 'I didn't see him. Do you know whether he was, Dylan?'

'Not I, but Mark and she were lovers years ago when we were all young, though he always denied it. She modelled for him and don't painters always sleep with their models?'

'Were you aware that Mark had tried to kill himself?' Edward asked brutally.

'No, I wasn't!' Thomas looked genuinely shocked. 'Lewis, did you know?'

'Not me.' Cathcart seemed uninterested.

'You say he *tried* to kill himself. I take it then that he's all right? He didn't succeed?' Thomas asked, showing what Edward thought was real concern.

'It was a close-run thing. So you don't think he was in Broadcasting House when Frieda was murdered?'

'Not as far as I am aware,' Cathcart answered.

'You see, he was in London visiting his gallery,' Edward explained.

'Was he? I wonder why he didn't let me know?' Thomas murmured. 'We were very close at one time but I'm not very good at keeping up with my friends.' He sighed and once again, Edward thought, donned his armour of quiet amusement and world-weary cynicism.

'Whoever killed Frieda must have known their way round Broadcasting House,' Edward remarked.

'That's true. Dylan, you're quite sure it wasn't you?' Cathcart smiled wryly.

'I really don't think I could do murder,' his friend mused. 'But what about that vicar fellow – the one who was doing the Daily Service the week she was killed?'

'Paul Fisher? Why on earth would he want to kill Frieda?'

'I've no idea but I saw him look at her once in the canteen. It was a combination of lust and loathing.'

'But vicars don't murder people except in books, do they?' Cathcart asked. 'Well, I'm sorry I can't help you, old boy. What with the war coming any day now, I suppose the police have got better things to do than find Frieda's murderer. I notice the investigation hardly makes page six in the *News Chronicle*.'

'That may change,' Edward replied.

'Golly, gosh,' Thomas mocked. 'Is the amateur sleuth going to reveal all and make the police look like fools? I do hope so.'

Edward got up to go. 'No, I'm afraid there's very rarely that sort of denouement in real life – or do I mean real death? In my experience, most murders – other than husbands killing their wives and vice versa – are rather too messy and complicated to be "solved" in that way. But I will find out who killed Frieda – that I promise you.

One last question, Cathcart. Did you receive a poison pen letter? I ask because the murderer appears to send them out before he sets about killing the recipient. Mark Redel received one and it almost killed him.'

Cathcart visibly blanched. 'No, I've not received a poison pen letter. Why should I?'

'I'm glad to hear it,' Edward replied. 'I thought it unlikely but I wanted to be sure.'

'Before you go,' Thomas said in a comical whine, 'you couldn't lend me a fiver, could you? I have to get back to my wife and son in Wales tonight and I seem to be stony-broke.'

Edward took out his wallet and parted with a banknote.

'Why, thank you! You're a gent – but then of course you are. You'll be able to tell your grandchildren that you once gave that great poet Dylan Thomas a sub. Now that's got to be worth something, hasn't it?'

Edward had one final call to make in London. Guy Liddell had grudgingly agreed that he could talk to Colonel Rathbone, MI5's man at the BBC. 'But you won't get anything out of him,' he had added, sounding pleased.

Before mentioning his appointment with Colonel Rathbone, Edward asked the commissionaire at the front desk to put through a call to 'Talks'. When he had spoken to Reg Barnes the day before, he had asked whether he might have five minutes with him while he was at Broadcasting House to clear up a few points he didn't want to discuss on the telephone.

Barnes looked with interest at the tall, distinguished-looking man with a beaked nose and an air of authority as Edward strode into his office. He had met men like him before. They came into the BBC to give talks on the Arab Revolt or the ascent of Everest – army officers or empire-makers for the most part who were more at home in a

Damascus souk or a Kathmandu bazaar than in Portland Place.

'I'm so sorry to bother you, Mr Barnes . . .'

'Call me Reg, please. Everyone does.'

'Thank you. It's very kind of you to see me. I can guess how busy you are, and you were very helpful on the phone. I thought you might like to hear how my meeting with Lewis Cathcart went.'

'What did you make of him?'

'He was just as you described him and, as you prophesied, his friend Thomas "borrowed" a five-pound note off me. But I wonder if I could just ask you a few questions about Frieda's murder which I didn't want to ask on the phone? I'm sure the police have gone through it all with you until you're sick to death of talking about it but you can understand how, with my wife's involvement, I very much want to get to the heart of the matter.'

'To tell you the truth, Lord Edward, I haven't seen much of the police. They don't seem to think I can tell them anything they don't already know.'

'And can you?'

'Well, it was all such a mêlée. I mean, I can't remember who was there and who wasn't. To be honest with you, I was in a blind panic. I couldn't believe that it had happened in my studio. I so admired your wife, Lord Edward. She was as cool as a cucumber. And so brave. She insisted on trying to see if the murderer was still in the building whereas I'd have been happy to leave it to the police. I can see why she is such a good foreign correspondent.'

'I'll tell her you said so. Are you still planning to use the interview? With Frieda dead . . .'

'I think we will – as a tribute, you understand, if your wife has no objection. In fact I was thinking of asking her to say a few words before the interview is broadcast, saying something nice about her. Do you think she would?'

'I'll ask her.'

'Thanks.'

'So did you recognize anyone immediately after Frieda was found dead?'

'We didn't see anyone in the passages or the washrooms.'

'No, I meant when the news got out that something had happened. Was there anyone you didn't expect to see?'

'Not really. I remember Cathcart turning up in the studio almost immediately. And that vicar fellow, Paul Fisher, may have been there as well. In fact, I've been thinking about him. Did your wife tell you that right at the end of the recording one could hear Frieda saying something like knotty?' Edward nodded. 'Well, what if she said, "Not E"?'

'Meaning?'

'Meaning that she assumed whoever had come in had mistaken it for Studio E.'

'And Studio E is . . .?'

'The chapel. It's where Fisher holds the Daily Service which is broadcast to a grateful nation.'

'I see. So you think Paul Fisher might have come into the studio – Frieda turns round to see who it is, starts to tell him he's in the wrong place and then he smashes her skull in with the statuette of Sir John Reith?"

'No, I can see it sounds rather absurd.'

'It is an interesting theory. And you can't recall anyone else? The painter – Mark Redel – do you know him?'

'No, I don't think so but I know his name . . .'

'Well, I've taken up enough of your time, Reg. Here's my card. Could I ask you to telephone me if anything else occurs to you?'

'Of course! Frieda was like a daughter to me, Lord Edward. Whatever I can do to help, you can count on me to do it.'

Colonel Rathbone was almost invisible behind a tall stack of brown files but he would have been easy to miss even if he had not been hiding. He was wearing a brown suit and a brown tie. His obligatory toothbrush moustache was brown and bristly and his toupee – Edward was sure it was a toupee – was also brown. He might have been bald on top but little tufts of brown hair in his ears and on his cheekbones and luxuriant brown eyebrows suggested the monkey, and there was something simian about his eyes which – it must have been Edward's imagination – appeared to be yellow.

There was hardly room in the tiny office for Rathbone to edge round the desk to greet him but he managed it, and Edward tried not to smile as he watched him pull in his stomach to avoid dislodging the mountain of files.

'Let's stroll into Regent's Park,' Rathbone suggested. 'It's a lovely day and it's a sin to be stopped up in here like a fox in his earth.'

Edward looked at the little man sharply. Why that casual reference to the fox? It was true he was more fox than monkey, now Edward came to think about it, but did *he* recognize that?

Apart from a few pleasantries about the weather, little was said until they were ensconced on a bench in Queen Mary's Garden admiring the roses.

'So, what do you want to know and why should I tell you?' Rathbone asked roguishly.

Edward held his temper in check. 'I imagine from what my wife told me that you were in the studio immediately after Frieda Burrowes was murdered?'

'I was in my office and was quickly on the scene when I heard the uproar. I don't know how well you know Broadcasting House but my office is on the same floor as the "Talks" studios.'

'And did you notice anything odd – apart from the fact that a murder had taken place, I mean? Did you see anyone behaving suspiciously?'

'By the time I got to the studio, there was quite a crowd. Two of the commissionaires had arrived and were trying to restore order but they know me, of course, and let me through.'

'What did you see?'

'I saw a young woman lying across the table, her head battered in. The weapon appeared to be a statuette of the BBC's revered but recently evicted chairman, Sir John Reith. It was lying on the floor covered in blood and brains.'

'Do you know if the police found any fingerprints on the statuette? For some reason, they don't seem to want to keep me in touch with developments.'

'No fingerprints. Just blood – Miss Burrowes's and not the murderer's, unfortunately.'

'And who did you see there? I mean, who were you surprised to see?'

'Well, I saw your wife and the producer, Reg Barnes. I saw Lewis Cathcart who I happened to know had been Miss Burrowes's lover until she traded him in for the more influential Byron Gates. A vicar fellow was also there – the one who sometimes does the Daily Service.'

'Paul Fisher.'

'Is that his name? I don't keep track of casual visitors to the BBC. I have enough on my plate dealing with the employees,' Rathbone said a trifle defensively.

'Were there any women there, apart from my wife?'

'No. Wait a moment – I've just remembered that I *did* see a woman, though at first sight I took her for a man. She was dressed like Hamlet – white shirt with black trousers and a black jacket.'

'She was – at least I assume she was – Miss Elsa Fairweather,' Edward told him. 'Did she seem distraught?'

'I'm not sure. No, I think she looked . . . not pleased, exactly but . . . I might be imagining it but I would almost say triumphant.'

'You know Miss Burrowes had a relationship with Miss Fairweather?'

'It's on her file,' Rathbone admitted.

'Anything else you can tell me? In those files of yours – is there anything to suggest who might have murdered the girl?'

Edward spoke lightly but Rathbone took his question seriously.

'No, I'm afraid not. I'm only interested in criminals where there is a political connection. That man Cathcart, for instance – he consorts with some rather odd characters.'

'You mean like Dylan Thomas? I met him with Cathcart at lunchtime.'

'In the pub, I imagine. He's more or less an alcoholic so I don't take him very seriously, but he's a troublemaker. He's not employed by the BBC but he often gives talks and reads his poems – the most awful stuff. I've always had a distaste for the Welsh – they're all goats. Look at that man Lloyd George, a dishonest goat if ever there was one.'

Ignoring the slur on the Welsh nation in general, Edward asked why he particularly disliked Dylan Thomas.

'He's open to blackmail, though I doubt whether anyone would bother to blackmail him when they could buy him for a few bob. He's married but he goes after every girl he sees. And he's a coward.'

'A coward?'

'I intercepted a letter of his . . .' Edward was shocked but said nothing. 'He was writing to one of his literary friends. I remember his words exactly. "What are you doing for your country? I'm letting mine rot." He's registered as a conscientious objector but he's admitted to friends that he's just an escapist. One of the people who drinks with him told me he brags that he can't "do Brooke in a trench".'

'Rupert Brooke?' Edward said. 'I suppose he means he can't be a "patriotic poet" – I don't blame him for that. I think we are a bit too cynical to take that sort of verse in this war. Anyway, that's by the by. He may be rather "artistic" for my taste but it doesn't make him a murderer.'

'No, but Cathcart would do well to choose his drinking companions more carefully.'

'Is there anything on Reg Barnes?'

'The producer?' Rathbone sounded surprised. 'No, though he does give a voice to some undesirable characters on the left – that odious man Guy Baron for one. But Reg is all right – even given me a tip or two. Why, do you think he had a relationship with Miss Burrowes which went wrong?'

'He claims it was a father/daughter thing but he might not have liked seeing his little girl play around with people like Byron Gates and Lewis Cathcart, let alone Elsa Fairweather.'

'Yes, but Barnes was the wrong side of the glass when the murder happened and your wife was with him.'

Edward sighed. 'I know. I was simply trying not to rule anything – or anyone – out. But you're right, Barnes isn't a murderer. Well, thank you, Colonel, you've been most helpful,' Edward said, suddenly tiring of the man and getting up from the bench.

'Do you have your suspicions as to who killed the girl?' Rathbone asked.

'I have, but no evidence as yet. I need to think it through.'

'Mike Heron – I knew him in the war. I'm glad you were able to get him off the hook. I read all about it in the papers.'

'You know Colonel Heron?'

'Don't sound so surprised. We were both Indian Army. He's a good fellow and a brave man. I kept my head below the parapet but he led from the front. A man of honour.' Rathbone barked out a laugh.

'And do you still see him?'

'Mike? He's been up to see me a few times. Had a few pints – showed him around Broadcasting House.'

'Did you see him the day Miss Burrowes was murdered?'

Rathbone wrinkled his brow. 'Nope. As I said, we don't meet very often. Dash it all, you surely don't suspect Mike, do you? I thought you had proved he was innocent. I tell you, he's a good man. Wish there were more like him. I can't stick these artistic types and the politicians are even worse. The truth is, there aren't many kindred spirits at the BBC. I'll be quite glad to be shot of it.'

'You're leaving?'

'Yes, I've got a posting in Hong Kong. Rather more my cup of tea. Even the war has a silver lining, what? Well, good luck then, Corinth.' They shook hands. 'Or should I say "Good hunting". I don't suppose we'll see each other again.'

As Edward watched him stroll off between the banks of roses, he wondered if the England they were going to have to fight for was really the free, democratic country of his imagination. There was something second-rate about Rathbone which made Edward feel dirty. He considered going to the Turkish bath in Jermyn Street but, looking at his watch, realized he would miss his train. It would be good to be back in the fresh country air, he thought.

Verity had caught an earlier train home. Lambert had, she told Edward, grilled her for almost an hour but in the end had seemed satisfied with her account of Frieda's killing.

'He even said I was a good witness,' she ended.

'Did he discuss Byron's death with you?'

'He made me go over it all again. I get the impression he doesn't think much of Inspector Trewen but he gave very little away. I came out feeling as though I had been wrung out like a wet rag.'

'The sign of a good interrogator,' Edward remarked. 'I must say, I'm pretty exhausted too. It's been a long day. What say you to an early night?'

183

'Good idea. By the way, you haven't forgotten that Tommie's coming tomorrow?'

'No. I'm looking forward to it. I've hated him being angry with us.'

'With me,' Verity corrected him.

As they got ready for bed, Edward asked, 'What was it you said that made Tommie "forgive and forget"? I thought he'd never come round.'

'I didn't tell you but I telephoned him after I met Paul Fisher at Broadcasting House. I said we needed him to give us his blessing before the war fractured our lives and sent us spinning off who knows where, like a croquet ball.'

'That was good of you, V. "So shines a good deed in a naughty world." We'll sleep well tonight, I think.'

14

'It's lovely to have you here.' Verity nudged her ball through a hoop and croqueted his.

'You are one of my oldest friends and you are married to an even older friend. I just couldn't let it go on any longer. I say, isn't that cheating?'

Tommie Fox watched her apply a sharp tap to her ball which shot his off into the flower bed.

'It was making Edward unhappy. He didn't say anything but I know it was.'

'What's he been up to down here? I'm probably wrong but somehow I don't see him as a countryman. Does he garden?'

'No, he doesn't garden but he loves walking on the downs with Basil and the girls. They'll be back soon. In fact, he ought to be back by now but he loses all sense of time when he's roaming.'

'Is he sleuthing? He told me about the murders.'

'Of course he's sleuthing. I encourage it. It gives him something to think about while we wait for this war to start.'

'I thought he wasn't going to do any more of that?'

'He tried not to get involved but what could he do? One murder right on our doorstep and then Frieda Burrowes a few minutes after she'd been interviewing me. It's personal, you might say.'

Verity let Tommie croquet her and then, trying to sound neutral, said, 'Edward wants to ask you about Paul Fisher.'

'Yes, I know. He's an odd fish, that's for sure, but I don't see him as a murderer.'

'Because his collar buttons at the back?'

'No, because he's a true Christian and Christians don't go about murdering people.' Verity bit back a remark about the Crusades. 'I telephoned and told him I was coming to Rodmell,' Tommie went on. 'He didn't seem particularly interested. Anyway, I thought I would go and see him tomorrow.'

'He probably didn't like it that you were staying with us. I asked him to supper but he wouldn't come. He shares your view on unbelievers. He thinks I'm the devil and, worse still, that I have tempted Edward from the path of righteousness.'

'Oh no! Surely not . . .' Tommie protested. 'I tell you what, I think he's ill. I happened to meet a friend of his and she said he had cancer. But he's the most reserved of men and would never admit it. He couldn't bear to be pitied.'

'I know the feeling.' Verity remembered how, when she had TB, she had hated anyone feeling sorry for her. 'If he is ill, it would certainly help explain his behaviour. When you see him tomorrow, try and persuade him to come to supper. I've invited Virginia and Leonard. I know he respects Leonard.'

'I'll do what I can, Verity, but I can't force him. I remember him as very intense, very sincere, and it's not an easy time to be a priest and have to explain why God allows so much evil in the world.'

'Without wishing to be flippant, Tommie, when war comes the churches will be full. At least, that's what happened in 1914.'

'True, and in this case we can be sure that we are fighting for a just cause. In 1914, many of us had doubts and

186

hated seeing the Church of England become patriotic to the point of jingoism. We asked ourselves why God should be on our side and not the German. No doubt Germany prayed for victory as hard as we did. This time there can be no doubt that we are fighting against a great evil. The church in Germany has, for the most part, spoken against Nazism and suffered for it.'

'I know,' Verity said, resting a hand on his arm in sympathy.

'You're hoping to be sent abroad for the *New Gazette* before war breaks out?' Tommie asked, although he knew the answer.

'I am. According to Mr Churchill, instead of being pinned down in trenches, the new army will have to move fast. He believes the German tanks will race across Europe, but who knows? The only thing I *do* know is that I have to be in position before everything goes up in smoke. I can't afford to be stuck in England. It's all very frustrating. I had expected to get my marching orders a week or more ago. Oh well, I must be patient – though it's not something I have ever been good at. Anyway, what about you? Tell me, how are you getting on in Kentish Town? It's a poor area, isn't it? You must have your work cut out?'

Tommie talked eagerly about the challenges he faced and about the plans which had been made and rehearsed for evacuating the children in the event of London being bombed.

'We can take some evacuees here,' Verity offered. 'As you know, we have Ada and Jean here now but their mother is back later this week and she'll want to take charge of them, I am sure. I may not be here much but Mrs Brendel, who you met, is all ready to do her bit. As a refugee herself, she feels it's her special duty.'

'I'll have a chat with her, if I may,' Tommie said, expertly knocking his ball through a hoop but, so Verity informed him, in the wrong direction.

'And you must speak to Leonard – he's very involved with placing refugees and preparing for evacuees.'

Edward was delighted to see his old friend when he finally returned, apologizing for not keeping track of the time and being there to greet him. He introduced Tommie to Ada and Jean, whose pink cheeks and happy smiles suggested that they were recovering from the shock of Byron's death. Jean was excited that her mother would soon be home and even Ada seemed to be looking forward to seeing her stepmother again.

At dinner, and afterwards over brandy and cigars, Edward told Tommie everything he had found out in London. It was useful, he decided, to lay out all the facts so they could be examined by someone impartial and uninvolved. It helped to order his thoughts.

'It's not conclusive but . . .'

'Don't jump to conclusions,' Tommie warned him. 'You thought on other occasions that you had it all worked out only to find that you were wide of the mark.'

'Very true, Tommie. I promise not to rush to judgement. It is so good to have you here. How long can you stay?'

'Just two nights, then I'm going to stay with a Cambridge friend, Noel Symington. Do you remember him, Edward?'

'Of course! He sent me his book, *The Night Climbers of Cambridge*. He used to make me curl up with fright. Do you remember when he scaled King's College Chapel? I think it was one of the finest, or stupidest, things I have ever seen. He had no equipment, no rope, but he made it. He slipped once, I recall, and knocked away half a gargoyle.' He mused. 'I expect in this war his sort of courage and foolhardiness will make him an ideal soldier if they know how to use him.'

'Yes, but he was never very good at obeying orders, I seem to remember – a bit like Verity – and I gather discipline's a sine qua non in the army. I thought I might try to persuade Paul to come with me to Cambridge. He was a great friend of Symington's and a climber himself. Do you remember, Edward, how his gyp had to get him off the roof of Trinity when he got stuck one night? From what you say, he needs a break but I expect he'll refuse.'

They sat in the garden until it was almost midnight and the ashtrays were overflowing but even then it was not completely dark. Edward and Tommie tossed away their cigars and gradually their conversation gave way to the silence of contemplation and tranquillity. They let the garden scents calm them – the almost overpowering sweetness of jasmine and, beneath and above it, the delicate scent of roses.

'I shall always remember this evening,' Verity said as they rose from their deckchairs and made their way back into the house.

'It's the sort of night which must have reminded Old Adam of what his and Eve's foolishness had deprived him,' Tommie agreed.

Edward, predictably, quoted his beloved Shakespeare. '"In such a night Troilus me thinks mounted the Trojan walls, and sighed his soul toward the Grecian tents where Cressid lay that night." '

'Only tonight you are fortunate in having your Cressid with you,' Verity pointed out, down to earth as usual.

'I do, and I thank God for it,' Edward replied, taking her hand.

The following morning, Verity left Tommie with Edward and went up to London with Ada and Jean on their long-promised visit to the *New Gazette*. They were to have lunch at the Lyons Corner House on the Strand and then, if there was time, go to *Jamaica Inn*, Jean's choice. There was a Spanish film – *Barrios Bajos* directed by a friend of hers,

Pedro Puche – at the Academy Cinema in Oxford Street, which Verity very much wanted to see but she could not disappoint the girls. It would be a long day but they were looking forward to being in London again.

Verity's heart always beat faster when she entered the *New Gazette*. The energy that flowed through her when the great doors swung open gave her hope and purpose. Jean seemed to feel it too and looked about her awestruck. The building was mostly glass and flaunted its modernity. In the magnificent foyer, they could sense rather than hear the rumble of the mighty printing presses below them like the engines of an ocean liner.

Verity had telephoned Miss Landon, Lord Weaver's secretary, who had arranged a tour of the building for the girls while Verity had an interview with the great man. However, just before she went up to his suite of offices on the fifth floor, she paid a visit to the *New Gazette*'s archive. She wanted to ask Tom Balcombe, the librarian, if he could find any mention of Colonel Heron's war service. Balcombe seemed doubtful but said he would look through the index and leave a message for her at the reception desk if he found anything.

'It's a good index,' he explained, 'but it certainly doesn't list every war hero – how could it? – unless it was a story which was reported at some length.'

Joe Weaver was in a sombre mood. 'War will be declared within two weeks,' he told Verity.

Hitler had made it clear that he would annex the Baltic port of Danzig, Poland's access to the sea. In the House of Commons, the Prime Minister, Mr Chamberlain, had promised to support the Poles if they had to resort to force to keep Danzig a Free City under the League of Nations mandate.

'And I have just heard that Stalin has signed a Non-Aggression Pact with Hitler. When two devils make peace with one another, then it's time to worry,' Weaver declared with a flourish. He was well aware that, as a former Communist, Verity would be horrified at this betrayal.

'I can't believe that!' she exclaimed. 'Are you absolutely sure it's not just a propaganda lie by the Nazis? I have known for some time that the Communist Party will do anything, however cynical, if it thinks it is in its interests, but to sign a pact with the devil . . . surely not.'

'I'm afraid it's a fact, Verity, and one that makes a European war inevitable. If Poland is attacked, we will go to her aid and so will the French.'

'And if that's not enough,' she lamented, 'the IRA are still killing people in English cities. I see in the paper that five people have been killed and fifty wounded in a bomb attack in Coventry. It's too horrible. Just when we're facing a fight to the death with Nazi Germany the Irish decide to kick us in the teeth.'

'Indeed. Bus conductors won't let you take a suitcase with you when you board a bus in case it contains a bomb,' Weaver said, waving his cigar in the air for emphasis. Verity wondered when was the last time her boss had been on a bus. 'How we could have got to this pass, I really don't know,' he added, shaking his head.

They looked at one another blankly. War had been expected for two years but now it was on the point of being declared. It was hard to believe.

'The Prime Minister is heartbroken,' Weaver continued. 'Between ourselves, Chamberlain's not cut out to lead this country in war. It's only a matter of time before Lord Halifax or Winston takes over. Neville's too closely associated with the policy of appeasing Hitler. He'll not be forgiven for its failure.'

'Lord Halifax! You must be joking.' Verity found it impossible to accept that a member of the House of Lords could lead the country through the perils it faced.

'I know what you are thinking. I doubt the Foreign Secretary could take over given that he's just as much associated with appeasement as the Prime Minister.'

Verity thought wryly that, despite Weaver's friendship with Mr Churchill, appeasing Hitler had been the policy the *New Gazette* had espoused and promoted for the last three years. Apparently that was now to be forgotten.

'And me?' she asked timidly.

'You are to leave for Paris the week after next. Depending on what happens, you'll stay there to help Curtis or go on to Madrid.' Curtis was the *New Gazette*'s chief correspondent in Paris. 'Miss Landon has your tickets. What can I say but good luck? You're on your own. I can't give you any instructions. You must just be where it's happening, that's all.'

'I won't let you down, Joe,' Verity said earnestly.

'I know you won't, and try not to get yourself killed. Edward would never forgive me – nor would I forgive myself,' he added gruffly.

'I'll probably be safer than you will be here. The bombing . . .'

'Yes, they will bomb London. We have to accept that many historic buildings like St Paul's,' Weaver turned to look out at the dome of London's greatest church, 'will be destroyed and goodness knows how many civilians will lose their lives. It was bad enough in the last war with the Zeppelins but this will be on a very different scale. If the Germans unleash total war, they will regret it in the long run. If they bomb London, we can bomb Berlin. We have the wherewithal . . .'

They talked about the international situation for another ten minutes until Miss Landon arrived with Ada and Jean who had finished their tour of the building. Verity introduced them to Weaver and she could see that he was taken with Jean. She was on the cusp of womanhood and Verity wondered which lucky man would drown in her green eyes. According to Byron, she had inherited her mother's creamy skin and auburn hair. It was a stunning combination and Verity was momentarily jealous. But then she remembered what a bore it was fending off men who only had one thing in mind.

She hurried to make a fuss of Ada. The poor child seemed subdued in the shadow of her glamorous step-sister but, when Weaver asked her what she thought of the newspaper, her eyes lit up and she spoke with a fervour and eloquence that surprised them all.

As they were leaving the building, Verity was handed a note from the archivist, Balcombe. He had, after all, been able to find a reference to a Captain Mike Heron who, in 1916, had apparently led an attack on a machine-gun nest which was holding up the British advance in his sector. The attack had been successful but Heron had been wounded and as many as thirty of his Indian troops had been killed. Just as they were celebrating victory, they had seen a noxious cloud of yellow gas coming in their direction. Although they had time to put on their gas masks, several of Heron's men had breathed in enough gas to leave them gasping. He had personally carried one of his badly wounded men back to the dressing station under fire from the enemy.

He had been recommended for a VC but, in the end, had been awarded the DSO. Mike Heron was no fraud, as Verity had suspected, but a genuine hero.

Although she was longing to get home and begin preparing for her assignment, she knew she could not do the girls out of their treat. At Lyons Corner House, Verity could only manage coffee and a bun but she watched with pleasure as, to the amusement of the 'nippy' who served them, the girls ate themselves silly for 2/9d. She half-listened to their chatter as she went over in her mind the implications of what Weaver had told her. She was excited but also apprehensive. She lusted after a cigarette to calm her nerves but managed to restrain herself from buying a packet from the display case by the till. This was what she had longed for – a foreign posting – but would she be up to it physically and mentally? In Spain, she had witnessed the devastation caused by bombing from the air and Weaver's words about what might happen to London frightened her. She had to suppress an image of the restaurant in which they were eating being flattened by a bomb and all the innocent men, women and children sitting around her being killed.

She turned once more to the tempting rows of cigarettes piled up beneath a poster advertising Player's Navy Cut. It featured a pensive-looking sailor staring out to sea and she immediately thought of Frank, Edward's nephew, aboard HMS *Kelly*. She shivered and lowered her eyes. Her gaze was arrested by the sight of a familiar face – or rather two familiar faces. At a small table in the corner of the restaurant, Lewis Cathcart was deep in conversation with Colonel Heron. She was about to get up and go over to them when she had second thoughts. What did these two have to talk about so earnestly? She thought back to the moments after Frieda's murder. Cathcart had been genuinely distraught – or at least she had thought his anguish was genuine – but what if it had all been an act?

She didn't fully understand how Cathcart and Heron had got to know each other. According to Heron, they had met by chance in a pub near Broadcasting House. It seemed unlikely but Verity knew only too well that real-life coincidences could be even stranger. Had Heron told Edward about Cathcart's relationship with Frieda to give him a motive for killing her in revenge for being thrown over for Byron Gates? It was all a bit too obvious, she decided. If he really believed Cathcart had murdered Frieda, what was he doing cosying up to him?

By the time the girls had finished their lunch, Cathcart and Heron had disappeared. Verity didn't know if

194

they had seen her. She thought they probably had but, if so, why didn't they come over to say hello? It was a puzzle that occupied her all through *Jamaica Inn* – viewed through a haze of cigarette smoke – and on the train back to Lewes.

While Tommie went off to see Paul Fisher, Edward – rather reluctantly – walked round to see Miss Fairweather. He wasn't looking forward to the interview but it had to be faced. To his relief he found that she was in London.

'She's there a lot at the moment,' Miss Bron explained, 'but do come in and have some tea. The kettle's on.'

'Are you sure I'm not disturbing you?'

'No, of course not. In fact, you are a welcome distraction. Not a lot happens in Rodmell – well, I mean not usually.'

He was shown into a little parlour decorated with rather severe paintings by Gwen John, the sister of Augustus. When Edward went over to examine them, Miss Bron said, 'Gwen is a friend of ours. Elsa prefers her paintings to her brother's though not many people agree.'

'I'm afraid I never knew he had a sister but I think they are very good indeed. To be honest, I'm not much good with modern art but these I do like. This painting of a woman in black is very powerful and that one of the girl with the cat on her lap . . .'

'That's a portrait of another friend of ours who died young, so we treasure it.'

'Why is Miss Fairweather in London so much?' Edward asked innocently when they had sat down.

'Her publishers are being very difficult. They want her to cut some things from the novel she has just finished which they consider will – what's the phrase? – "offend public taste". Ridiculous, really. Radclyffe Hall published *The Well of Loneliness* ten years ago and Elsa's book is quite inoffensive in comparison.'

Miss Bron pursed her lips in the bitter-sweet smile the French call a *douce-amère*.

'May I ask what it's about?'

'I shouldn't really tell you because Elsa likes her novels to break on the unsuspecting world with a bang, but I'm sure you won't run to a newspaper and cause a scandal, Lord Edward.'

'I give you my word.'

'It's about two women teachers who live quite innocently together but are accused of vicious behaviour by a parent of one of their pupils. It's very strong and will, I think, make a good play or film if . . .'

'If people don't find it too shocking?'

'Precisely.'

Miss Bron was noticeably less mouse-like in the absence of her friend. Her hands did not quiver and her voice was firm. She fixed Edward with intelligent eyes and waited for him to speak.

'I did enjoy the pageant, Miss Bron. You read Miss Fairweather's words beautifully.'

'I'm glad you liked it but one must hope that nothing I said influenced the murderer of Mr Gates. There are so many executions in English history, I'm afraid.' She shuddered. 'I really don't see how we can ever have a pageant again.'

'I'm sorry to have to say that I believe we will be at war next summer so there probably won't be a fête or a pageant.'

Miss Bron paled and Edward wished he had kept his mouth shut.

'You know,' she said fearfully, 'in Germany they have been sending homosexual men to their terrible concentration camps – I think that's what they are called. We have many friends in Berlin. We used to go to Germany a lot in the old days. We have had some pathetic letters asking for help in getting to England. I show them to Mr Woolf. He has performed miracles spiriting people out of Germany but it's becoming more and more difficult. Fortunately, the regime is very corrupt and one can sometimes buy people's freedom. We heard only the other day that two of our friends – actors, not political in any way – were arrested by the Gestapo three weeks ago and no one has heard anything from them since.'

She looked so stricken that Edward thought she might burst into tears but she managed to control herself. 'There are evil men ruling Germany now,' she said fiercely. 'We must fight them but – you'll think I'm being melodramatic – Elsa and I do have poison which we intend to take if the Germans invade. We won't wait to be sent to a camp. We'd rather die by our own hands.'

Edward looked grave. He would have liked to reassure her but he could not in all conscience bring himself to do so.

They were silent for a minute as they considered the state of the world. 'But, Lord Edward, what is it you wished to say to Elsa? Perhaps I can help, or is it very private?'

Edward shifted uneasily in his chair. 'May I speak to you in absolute confidence, Miss Bron? Please don't hesitate to stop me if you think I am being impertinent, but I was hoping to ask Miss Fairweather if she knew about . . .'

'About what, Lord Edward?' Miss Bron looked aloof and almost frightening.

'About Frieda Burrowes's murder – and particularly where she was that day. You read about the murder in the papers, no doubt, but perhaps you weren't aware that she was Mr Gates's . . . his girlfriend. That was kept out of the press.'

'His girlfriend! But he was married, wasn't he?'

Edward detected a tremor in her voice. It made him sure that she was lying if she intended him to believe she knew nothing about Byron's womanizing. He decided, however, to play along and see where the conversation led.

'Apparently, he and his wife had some sort of arrangement. She is sometimes away in Hollywood for months at a time and . . . well, they had an understanding.'

'I see.' Miss Bron looked severe and then suddenly started to giggle. 'Don't they call it "dcol – doesn't count on location" in the film world? I'm sorry, I shouldn't laugh at such a horrible thing. That poor girl . . .'

'Did you know Frieda, Miss Bron?'

'Know her? Why on earth should we have known her?'

Again, Edward was certain from the tremor in her voice that she *had* known Frieda. He decided not to beat about the bush.

'I heard that Frieda might have been a friend – a lover – of Miss Fairweather's and that she might have resented her relationship with Mr Gates.'

There was a stunned silence while Miss Bron considered what she had just heard. Edward was quite unable to forecast her reaction. Would she order him out of the house, break down in tears or faint? He waited to see with interest and, when she finally spoke in quite a normal voice, he was almost disappointed.

'Lord Edward, correct me if I am wrong but are you accusing Elsa of killing Frieda Burrowes? You are suggesting that she was a jealous lover taking revenge for a betrayal?'

Although this was precisely what he was accusing Miss Fairweather of, he said, 'No, certainly not, but I wanted to be sure that she had an alibi for the time Frieda was murdered. It would ease my mind to know that she . . .'

'What time was the girl murdered?' Miss Bron asked coolly.

'It was quite early in the evening just after she had finished an interview with my wife.'

'Well, I accompanied Elsa to London and, at the time you mention, we were having an early supper before catching the train back to Lewes. And, before you ask, there would have been dozens of witnesses but none we could call on to support my – our – story. Before that, we were in Bloomsbury with Elsa's publishers. Will that do?' Her voice was icy.

'The strange thing is that I have talked to someone who said they saw Miss Fairweather in Broadcasting House immediately after Frieda was murdered. They said she seemed . . .' Colonel Rathbone had described it as 'triumphant' but Edward decided to use another word. 'They said she seemed distraught.'

Miss Bron was silent for a full minute while she debated with herself whether or not to deny that her friend had been at the BBC. She came to a decision at last.

'Lord Edward, I do not suspect your motives in asking me these questions though I would have thought that this investigation was a matter for the police. In fact, I rather admire you for having the nerve to ask them. I feel, therefore, that I should be frank with you. I would ask that this should be the last time we discuss Elsa's and my private life. You are right. Elsa was for a short time in love with Frieda Burrowes but I can assure you that there was never anything . . . there was no physical side to the relationship. I admit I was . . .' She hesitated. 'I was unhappy when Elsa became infatuated with her. The irony was that I introduced them. I did a little acting in the past and one of the last plays I appeared in was a production of Chekhov's *Three Sisters*. I was cast – you might say "typecast" – as Olga, the schoolteacher who never loves and is never properly loved. Frieda was playing Irena and she was absolutely enchanting. She wasn't a great actress – far from it – but she had the naivety, the freshness, to play to perfection a young girl full of life and hope.

'I admit to being a little in love with her myself but Elsa was completely bowled over by her when I introduced them at the first-night party. I suddenly found myself forgotten, disregarded, cast out by the woman I loved. I don't know whether you can understand this, Lord Edward, but to find oneself lonely while living with the person one loves is to plumb the full depths of desolation. That was my condition. I felt sorry for Elsa because I knew that Frieda wasn't serious and would eventually betray her. And she did. In the end, as you can imagine, she had enough of being pursued by a woman who no doubt seemed to her old, ugly and ludicrous.'

'So what did you do?'

'All I could do was wait. Elsa was convinced that Frieda would come back to her. For a time she still accepted presents from Elsa – sometimes quite expensive ones. Once, on Frieda's birthday, we took her to Paris. After dinner at the Ritz, we went on a tour of the clubs – you know the ones I mean? – the Monte Cristo, the Melody, Le Monocle, and drank brandy cocktails until five in the morning. A few weeks later Frieda said she never wanted to see Elsa again. There was the most almighty row but that was the end of it. Elsa never saw her again – at least not until the day she was murdered. Frieda had at least two male lovers, Lewis Cathcart and Byron Gates, at the same time as she was teasing Elsa. Inevitably, in the end, she decided to devote all her time to them. These were men who could do things for her career, you understand. And she was afraid of scandal. It would do her prospects no good if word got out that she had "tendencies", as she put it to me once.'

'Did Byron Gates know that Frieda and Miss Fairweather had been . . .?'

'No, I don't think so. At least, he never said anything to suggest that he knew. I was afraid he might bring her down to Rodmell but, thank God, he never did. When we heard that he had been murdered after the fête, we were shocked, of course, but not too disturbed. I don't think either of us actually said, "He deserved to die," but I don't disguise from you that we thought it.'

'But you are now saying that Elsa did see Frieda the day she died?'

'I'm afraid she did. I shouldn't have lied to you. It was stupid but I wanted to protect her. She discovered that Frieda was interviewing your wife and said she wanted to call in to say goodbye. I couldn't stop her even though I told her she was just punishing herself and she would be made to look a fool. She managed to persuade a commissionaire at Broadcasting House to let her through. They knew her as she did occasional work for the BBC – writing scripts or advising producers on how to improve other people's scripts. I waited down in the foyer, fearing the worst.

'A few minutes later, she came rushing down to tell me that Frieda had been murdered. I didn't know what to do to calm her. In the end, we went to a pub and I made her have a double brandy. When she had pulled herself together, we went to Victoria and caught a train home. I told her we must never tell a soul that we had been to Broadcasting House and she agreed, but here am I telling you everything.' Miss Bron shrugged as though accepting defeat.

'Did she kill Frieda?'

'No, Lord Edward, she assured me she hadn't. I believed her then and I believe her now.'

Edward sat with bowed head considering what Miss Bron had told him. Both women had a motive for killing Frieda and Byron and had the opportunity to carry out the murders, but Edward was inclined to think that neither of them had in fact done so. On the other hand, one of them might have sent the poison pen letters. How painful it must have been for Miss Fairweather to learn that Byron

201

Gates was parading around London with the girl she had loved.

Having gone so far, he thought he might as well ask the question. He knew that Miss Bron would never voluntarily talk about these matters again.

'As you have been kind enough to speak so frankly about things – painful and private things – which, as you pointed out, are not strictly my business, may I ask one last question and then I shall leave you in peace?'

'If you think you must.'

'You may have heard that someone has been sending rather unpleasant anonymous letters. I believe that person lives in Rodmell. I received one, as did Byron Gates and Mark Redel. I believe the letter Mark received upset him so badly that it tipped him over the edge and he decided to kill himself.'

Miss Bron got up and went over to a desk. She opened a drawer and pulled out a sheet of paper.

'You mean a letter like this, Lord Edward?'

He scanned the sheet. The anonymous author accused Miss Bron and Miss Fairweather of disgusting practices and of being perverts who deserved to die.

'Yes, like this one. May I ask when you received it?'

'The day after Frieda was murdered. Do you think our lives are in danger, Lord Edward? Ought we to tell the police?'

'I think you should,' he said reluctantly, 'but I can understand how unpleasant that will be for you both.'

'I suppose you thought, as most people would, that as rather ridiculous women – lesbians, let's call a spade a spade . . . *we* might be authors of this filth. You thought two embittered, perverted spinsters were the most likely people to have written poison pen letters. But in this instance you were wrong, Lord Edward.'

There was a nobility in the way Miss Bron held herself that made Edward admire her strength of character. 'As it happens,' he said, 'I thought you were much more likely to have been a recipient of one of these letters than to have written them yourselves but I decided it was better to ask you face to face. I apologize for upsetting you. My only wish is to discover the truth before anyone else gets hurt. I am pretty sure that whoever wrote these letters considers himself, or herself, to be a moralist and feels bound to admonish anyone he or she believes is leading an immoral life. I'm not a psychologist but my reading of Freud leads me to think that people who write letters like these hate themselves most of all.'

'As well they might,' Miss Bron retorted.

'Byron Gates, Verity and myself, Mark and now you ... I can only say that I regard it as an honour to be one of such a group. I believe I know who is spreading this poison and I shall now do my best to put an end to it. There is enough unhappiness in the world already without some madman adding to it.'

'Lord Edward,' Miss Bron said as she showed him out, 'I am not going to tell Elsa about ... about our conversation. I think it would be for the best. I take it that you do not believe either of us killed Frieda or Mr Gates?'

'I'm not quite sure why but, yes, I do not believe either of you to be a murderer. And I agree that it would be quite unnecessary to distress your friend any further. You have answered all my questions frankly so let's leave it at that, shall we?'

Edward raised his hat and breathed a sigh of relief. He very much hoped he was not deceived.

15

Dinner that night was strained even though it was warm enough to eat out on the terrace, which should have soothed the most untranquil breast. Added to which, Mrs Brendel had surpassed herself with roast pork followed by her special jam pancakes which Edward blamed for the few pounds he had added to his rangy frame in the short time she had been cooking for them.

Virginia, he was pleased to note, seemed less worried about the possibility that her world might soon be destroyed by German bombs and Leonard, too, was almost relaxed though he constantly watched his wife out of the corner of his eye, like a bird guarding its nest. Edward thought this vigilance might actually unsettle her. Of course, it was understandable that, in her fragile mental state, Leonard should be always looking for signs of nervous collapse but at least tonight Virginia seemed at peace.

Edward thought how beautiful she was. Not pretty – her face was equine and her skin sallow – but there was a languor in the way she moved which was sensuous in the extreme and her eyes, when she shot a glance across the table, were brilliant. It was as though the power of her intellect was such that it had to be shaded but, when unveiled, shed a cool, clear beam – like that of a light-house – over what she observed. It could be disconcert-ing and Edward noticed that even Verity occasionally checked herself in mid-sentence, feeling that what she was saying was not as clever or profound as she had thought.

Tommie Fox and Paul Fisher were almost silent, hardly listening to the conversation, and Edward wondered whether there had been some sort of row when Tommie had gone over to the vicarage that morning. What argument had he used to try and get Paul to overcome his dislike of Verity and his disapproval of her way of life? Whatever it was, it had been enough to get his friend to the dinner table even if he would not join in the conversation. He had shaken Verity's hand when he arrived but had not looked her in the eye and Edward felt that he ought not to have come if he were going to be so boorish. He could see that Verity was hurt and Tommie's stumbling attempts to cover his friend's silence only made things worse.

It was not until they got on to the subject of women's education that Paul spoke. Virginia had been complaining that, although there were now women's colleges at Cambridge, women were not awarded degrees or regarded as full members of the university.

'Dorothy Garrod, Pernel's predecessor as Principal of Newnham,' she said, referring to Pernel Strachey, one of Lytton Strachey's sisters, 'was elected Disney Professor of Archaeology last year. She is the first woman to hold a Professorial Chair but, can you believe, she's not permitted to speak or vote on the affairs of her own department let alone the university as a whole! Quite absurd but there you are – at least at Cambridge – it's still a man's world.'

Paul grunted that, in his view, educating women to university standard was even more absurd and hardly prepared them for a life looking after their husbands and children. 'I have a niece at Newnham – Catherine, my sister's child,' he said. 'I have often argued with her but she's a strong-minded girl and was adamant that she should take the place offered her despite my saying that she was wasting her time. I only permitted it because my sister lives in Cambridge and can keep an eye on her.'

There was a hint of pride in his voice, perhaps at the idea that she had proved to be as intransigent as her uncle. Verity and Virginia exchanged glances but managed to restrain themselves. Leonard and Edward were less inhibited by good manners and did not hesitate to tell Paul that he was behind the times. When Tommie made it clear that he, too, approved of women having an equal opportunity to benefit from a university education, his friend retreated into a sulk.

Later, over the pancakes, the conversation turned to the new divorce laws. Predictably, Paul disagreed with the general view that easier divorce was in general a 'good thing'. He declared that adultery was unforgivable and particularly to be condemned in a woman.

'What father,' he asked rhetorically, 'would regard fornication with the same horror if his son was the sinner as he would if his daughter had besmirched herself?'

When Edward declared it was iniquitous that divorce did not necessarily ruin a man's reputation but meant that a woman could never regain her position in society, Paul interjected, 'That's exactly as it should be.'

'So you don't agree that divorce should be granted on the grounds of desertion, cruelty or drunkenness?' Leonard put in.

'I do not,' Paul replied emphatically. 'There is no divorce in the eyes of God.'

'Well,' Tommie said bravely, 'I can't agree. Marriages do break down and staying together unhappily is not what the God I believe in would want. And, more often than not, the children suffer when their parents are unhappy.'

'Certainly, anything is better than the absurd charade couples have to go through at the moment if they want to divorce,' Leonard continued. 'To prove adultery to the satisfaction of the divorce court, a husband has to spend an uncomfortable night with a prostitute in Brighton. He also has the indignity of having to pay a private detective to witness the "adultery" so he can protect the reputation of a completely different woman. In my view, the hypocrisy is worse than the sin which gave rise to it. I suppose, Paul, that means you don't agree with birth control either?'

'I certainly do not. Sex within marriage is for procreation and there's an end of it.' For a moment, Edward was sure Paul would throw down his napkin and storm out of this godless household but for some reason he remained seated, looking thunderous.

Edward was quite certain some personal tragedy under-pinned Paul's views on sex and marriage but could not begin to guess what it might be. Paul had never been married, according to Tommie, but maybe the sister he had mentioned had been betrayed in some way.

Talk of Cambridge led Virginia to mention that she had accepted an invitation to lecture at Newnham later that week.

'I have lectured there before but this is rather differ-ent. Pernel's a very old friend and during the long vac-ation she has been given permission to experiment with adult education for women who did not go to university but now want to educate themselves. As you probably know, Morley College does the same sort of thing. I have given the scheme my whole-hearted support. It's much better than leaving the college buildings empty during the summer vacation. I'm not a good lecturer but Pernel says it is important that they are given by . . . well, by people who have something worth saying. The students must not be fobbed off with something inferior. Better not to offer the courses at all than make do with second-rate lectures by second-rate lecturers, as I'm sure you would agree.'

'But are they just for women?' Verity asked.

'At this stage, it's thought better not to be too ambitious and invite men. Perhaps some of the men's colleges will eventually offer similar courses to those who have missed out on a university education. I like to do what I can because I know how difficult it is being an outsider in a world where, despite the efforts of Mrs Pankhurst, the male of the species is king.' She glanced at Paul but he would not meet her eye. 'I want to tell them that they must never let themselves be bullied by men into thinking that they are freaks or failures and that women deserve to be educated to the same standard as men. Any sensible man,' she looked at Edward, 'finds a woman with a brain much more interesting than one content to be a mere appendage.'

Edward nodded his head in agreement. 'As you can see, it's not Verity's looks which attracted me to her.'

Verity laughed. 'I don't think all women should go to university. I've never felt the absence of a university education myself.'

'Your spelling might be better if you had been to university,' Edward joked.

'Who cares about spelling?' Virginia rebuked him. 'My spelling's atrocious, isn't it, Leonard?'

'Creative, certainly. Look, I have had an idea – why don't you two come with us to Cambridge? You could show Verity your old haunts, Edward, and dine with us and Pernel after the lecture.'

'Do you really mean it?' Edward asked. 'To tell you the truth, I had thought about doing just that while there's still time. What about it, V?'

'Why not? I'd enjoy seeing the place which stamped itself so indelibly on you. As far as I can see, if you haven't been to Eton or Winchester, Oxford or Cambridge you are not permitted to rule this country.'

'And don't forget, you have to be male,' Virginia added.

'Well, that's excellent.' Leonard sounded genuinely pleased. 'Virginia and I will go separately because you'll want to get to Cambridge earlier than us, but we could meet at Newnham at five fifteen. Virginia's lecture is to begin at five thirty. After it's over, we repair to the Common Room for drinks and then dinner. Of course, it won't be grand but the food will be eatable even if the wine isn't up to much and it's a very worthy cause. Then you can either drive home or . . .'

'We could stay with an old friend of mine. He's the don who put me on the right track when I very nearly got derailed,' Edward said.

'That's fixed then. I shall warn Pernel that we'll be two extra for dinner. Paul, would you or Mr Fox . . .?'

'As it happens, I will be in Cambridge on Friday,' Tommie said. 'I was telling Edward yesterday that I am spending a few nights there with a friend.'

'Then you'll come?'

'Thank you, Mr Woolf, I'd be delighted to attend the lecture but I won't come to the dinner if you don't think it rude.'

'What about you, Paul?' Leonard asked.

'No, thank you,' Paul replied gruffly. 'I must stay here and tend my flock.'

Edward wasn't sure if he was being ironic because Paul's 'flock' could very well manage without its shepherd for a night. However, he was relieved that Paul would not be there, glowering at any mention of women's rights, so he didn't press him to change his mind and nor did Leonard.

'Will you, Edward and Tommie be the only men in the audience?' Verity asked Leonard.

'No, this particular lecture is not part of a course and is open to everyone. Given Virginia's reputation, I can guarantee it will be well attended by men and women alike.'

'Now you are making me nervous, Leonard. I hardly know why I agreed to speak. Pernel can be very persuasive . . .'

It was another in a sequence of beautiful nights and they lingered on the terrace chatting, their guests reluctant to go home. Edward lit a cigar and Verity took a puff. When she had stopped coughing she said, 'I shall never forget this night – all these nights.' She stretched luxuriously, stifling a yawn. 'When I was a Communist, I think this was the vision I had of utopia – intelligent conversation among equals under the stars.'

'That's it exactly,' Virginia agreed. 'A society of friends. I think friendship is the epitome of what it means to be civilized. Any man or woman can love but friendship is half an art and wholly a pleasure. Isn't that something we can agree on, Paul?'

'I have no need of friends, Virginia. I have God and He is my world.'

'But surely Christ's apostles were a group of friends?' Edward saw Paul wince as if he considered this blasphemy. 'I do not believe in God,' Virginia continued, 'but, if I did, I would find Him in my friends. Before the war, as I expect you know, there was a group of friends, including friends of mine such as Lytton Strachey and Morgan Forster, who called themselves The Apostles.'

'Were women allowed to join the group?' Verity inquired.

'They were not,' Virginia replied with a smile, 'but then, any institution can be reformed and improved.'

Paul rose slowly from his chair. 'I cannot stay in this house a moment longer. To call your godless friends The Apostles is a calculated profanity and an insult to all good people. I was persuaded to come tonight so I could be made to understand that you were not the loose-living, anti-Christian so-called "free thinkers" I believed you to be. I know now that I should not have allowed myself to be persuaded. I shake the dust of this place off my shoes, grateful to be gone. And you,' he said, pointing an accusing finger at Tommie, 'ought to come with me.'

Leaving the company shocked and silenced, he stumbled off into the night.

16

Edward always felt his heart beat faster when he came back to Cambridge. As Verity had often remarked, he was what Eton and Cambridge had made him. Eton had given him security – the 'family life' of which he had been deprived at home. At Mersham, the attention had been focused on his eldest brother Frank who was killed in the first months of the war. After this tragedy, Gerald became heir to the dukedom. Edward, as the youngest of the three brothers, was ignored.

He was packed off to school where he thrived. He worked hard and entered sixth form as someone to be reckoned with – the equal of the scholarship boys, or 'tugs' as they were called at Eton. In sport his straight eye and natural athleticism had been recognized with a bouquet of coloured caps and ties. He had been elected to Pop – the group of senior boys who effectively ran the school – and had left Eton in a cloud of privilege and popularity.

Cambridge had been altogether more difficult. He could see in retrospect that he had done well at Eton in order to prove to his father that he was as worthy of attention as his elder brothers – particularly Frank, who had made the ultimate sacrifice. He had failed to make his point. His father had taken his success for granted. So, when he went up to the university he was, defiantly, intent on failing. He was bored by the work and hardly troubled to prove himself on the river or the cricket field. He was moody and made no real friends, content to lounge around with a few Etonians who had come up with him. In short, there was a very real possibility that he might 'go to the bad', get 'sent down', achieve nothing.

Fortunately, one of the dons, George Greyshott, a medieval historian of some note, had taken him by the scruff of his neck and made him 'buck up'. He had got the boy interested in his namesake, King Edward I – nicknamed 'Longshanks' and the Hammer of the Scots.

Greyshott, or GG as he was known to the undergraduates, was now retired but, whenever Edward was in Cambridge, he went to see him in his cottage on the outskirts of the town. He had a spare room and Edward had used it once or twice when attending a dinner and was in no fit state to drive back to town. Like many dons, GG wasn't a ladies' man and Edward was a bit nervous about introducing him to Verity but thought there was a chance that these two rather awkward, sharp-edged people might get on.

When Edward had telephoned to say he was going to be in Cambridge, he explained that, now he was married, he would quite understand if GG would find it more convenient if he and Verity put up at an hotel. To his delight, Greyshott had insisted that they stay with him. Apparently, he was an admirer of Verity's journalism and wanted to hear her views on the Spanish Civil War and the current European crisis.

The hall at Newnham was packed to the rafters but Edward and Verity had seats reserved for them in the front row. Just as the lecture was about to begin, Tommie rushed in, looking rather flurried, and sat down beside them.

'It's Paul,' he hissed in Edward's ear. 'He's in Cambridge and in a bad way. I'm very much afraid that he might do something stupid. He says he's going to tell his niece that she must leave Newnham.'

'Is there anything I can do?' Edward hissed back.

'No, nothing, thanks. I'll go and keep an eye on him after the lecture.'

Edward tried to concentrate as Pernel Stachey – pleasant-voiced, earnest but not without humour – opened the proceedings. She spent a good five minutes talking about her friend Morgan Forster's newly formed National Council for Civil Liberties before introducing Virginia in glowing terms.

Verity looked about her with interest. It was the first time she had been in a Cambridge college and it reminded her of being back at school. The smell of unwashed girls was noticeable if not overpowering. The college bathrooms and lavatories were totally inadequate although the previous Principal had been heard to remark that she couldn't see what the fuss was about as the summer term only lasted eight weeks.

Perhaps predictably, Virginia had called her talk 'A Room of One's Own'. Ten years earlier, she had given a series of lectures at Newnham and Girton examining whether women were capable of producing work of the quality of William Shakespeare's and suggesting that – until they had space and time for anything other than domestic work, and that usually meant a measure of financial independence – it was almost impossible for them to be writers and artists.

This time she spoke about what had been done in the last decade to improve the lot of women, particularly those who wanted to participate in worlds which, until recently, were reserved solely for men. To Verity's pleasure and embarrassment, she mentioned her by name and her work as a reporter of world events. Without having to turn his head, Edward could feel the audience craning to get a glimpse of her and felt proud.

214

When the lecture was over, Virginia answered questions and was amused rather than offended when two questions were directed at Verity.

'You must invite Verity to come and lecture,' Virginia whispered to Pernel. 'I think you would find that they would flock to hear her.'

Pernel brusquely informed the questioners that they could talk to Verity later, insisting that, as a guest, she could not be expected to take questions from the platform and was certainly not *obliged* to answer any questions.

When Virginia left the platform, she was immediately surrounded by a group of students – mostly women in their twenties or thirties but some older – who were eager to ask her about her work. She was even asked to sign copies of her books. Pernel frowned at this and would have stepped in to prevent it had not Virginia indicated that she did not mind.

To Edward's amusement, Verity was surrounded by a rather larger group of admirers. He was delighted to see his wife lionized by intelligent young people and tried to make himself invisible. She deserved to be fêted and he knew it would do much for her fragile self-confidence. He retreated to a corner to talk to Tommie but he made his excuses and went off in search of Paul Fisher.

Much to his surprise, one girl – rather younger than most of the women – came up to Edward and introduced herself.

'I believe you know my uncle. He said you were coming to Newnham for the lecture.'

'Your uncle?'

'Paul Fisher.'

'Of course! You must be Catherine?'

'Yes, Catherine Fisher . . . or rather, Catherine Gates.'

'Catherine Gates? I don't understand.'

'I call myself Catherine Fisher but actually Byron Gates was my father.'

215

Edward was nonplussed. 'How could he have been your father?'

'I can't tell you now, there's no time. You're about to be called in to dinner. I say, I don't want to be a bore but I wondered if we could meet later? It's important. I need to talk to you about my uncle.'

'About Paul? Of course we can meet. When and where do you suggest? If there's anything I can do . . . though I'm afraid he doesn't have a lot of time for me. By the way, my friend Tommie Fox – he's also a friend of your uncle's – has gone to look for him. I don't know if you met Tommie? He came to the lecture but slipped out afterwards. I know he was worried about Paul.'

'Yes, I do know him and I'm very grateful but, Lord Edward, my uncle needs *your* help. He seems to be in trouble. He won't tell me exactly what but I think it's to do with a murder in his parish. He said you would know. I think he may have wanted me to talk to you though he wouldn't admit it. The truth is I'm afraid of what he might do.'

'I see. Well, I hope he can be persuaded to talk to me but I wouldn't count on it. As I say, he doesn't approve of me. Look, shall I cut this dinner and come with you?' Edward offered, sensing the girl's distress. 'I'm sure the Principal would understand.'

'Thank you but no. You must stay for the dinner. I'm probably getting het up about nothing.'

Pernel was beckoning the guests to follow her. 'Where's Paul staying?' Edward asked hurriedly.

'With Aunt Gladys and me.'

'Give me your address.'

'No, we can't meet there. I don't want my aunt to know that I've talked to you. She wouldn't understand. I'll meet you on the Backs, behind King's College Chapel – say about eleven?'

'Are you allowed out so late?'

216

Catherine looked at him pityingly. 'I am grown up, you know.' Then she added conspiratorially, 'I can get out of my bedroom window without my aunt knowing – a convenient drainpipe.' The tension left her face for a moment and she looked younger and prettier.

'Who was that you were talking to?' Verity asked as he caught up with her.

'Paul Fisher's niece, Catherine. Do you remember him mentioning he had a niece at Newnham? She lives with her aunt in Cambridge. I'm not sure where exactly – she wouldn't give me the address. She's worried about Paul. Apparently he's in rather a state. I haven't had a chance to tell you but Tommie says he's in Cambridge and he's gone to see if he can do anything to help. Catherine says she needs to talk to me so I've agreed to meet her on the Backs about eleven.' Verity looked puzzled so Edward had to explain. 'That's by the river. Come on, Pernel is looking cross with us for lagging behind.'

On any other occasion, Edward would have enjoyed the evening. The dinner was good and the dons friendly. There were several from other colleges most of whom seemed to be spending the long vacation in Cambridge researching or writing books – as well as some favoured students, all women. If this was the kind of female who wanted to fill in the gaps in her education, Edward decided that he was all in favour of it. But try as he would to be interested in the burning issues of the day, he could only join in half-heartedly. Would Newnham be closed down in the event of war? When would women be awarded degrees? What did he think of women in the House of Commons? Had he met Nancy Astor or Ellen Wilkinson ? Although he found himself stimulated and entertained, his thoughts constantly strayed to his meeting on the banks of the Cam and the girl who might hold the key to the identity of the Rodmell murderer.

Several hours later, he escorted Verity through narrow arches, down little-used passages and across damp grass towards the river, their way lit only by the occasional lamp and an almost full moon. Verity was reminded of Venice, which she had only seen in pictures but imagined having this same air of floating through time, above and beyond reality. The spires gleamed ghostly pale in the silvery light and, clinging tightly to Edward's arm, she felt very much a stranger.

Cambridge was not her natural habitat – she was not an academic and found it difficult to understand the intellectual urge that made women shut themselves away to study as though they were nuns. True, their host, Pernel Strachey, was active in what Verity thought of as the real world and fought doughtily for women's rights, but she was an exception.

As they passed beneath the shadow of King's College Chapel, a vague feeling of foreboding made her shiver. Suddenly, the bells of Cambridge began to chime eleven. Verity had never liked the sound of church bells, perhaps because they challenged her lack of faith or reminded her how short life could be, but these chimes were different. Yes, they seemed to say, we are living on the edge of a precipice and these are almost certainly the last days of peace, but England will survive as it has survived so many trials in its long history. Her anxiety was replaced by an equally irrational optimism. Surely the Luftwaffe could never triumph over so much beauty and wisdom? She was being sentimental, she knew, but there it was – she was calmed and reassured.

They had no difficulty in seeing Catherine, a single white figure on Clare Bridge, gazing up at King's College Chapel as though expecting to see something or someone appear among its elegant spires and turrets. To Verity, the Chapel seemed too large for its surroundings, as though the medieval Christians who had built it had committed an error of taste, but Edward seemed entranced.

His mood changed as soon as Catherine ran towards them, waving and pointing.

'Lord Edward, thank God you're here.'

'Why? What's the matter?'

'It's my uncle. He's . . . I think he's gone mad. We were walking up from the river . . . he wanted to talk to me in private. He told me he had decided that Cambridge was a godless place and he wanted me to leave . . . He wouldn't listen to anything I said. Then we saw the Chapel and I asked him how Cambridge could be godless with a church as beautiful as that.

'He went all silent and began to breathe in a strange snorting sort of way. I thought he might be having a heart attack but suddenly he started running towards the Chapel. I caught up with him when he stopped for breath. I tried to put my arms round him but he shook me off. He said . . .' Catherine was crying now and her voice was hoarse. 'He said God had commanded him to come to Him. He started to run round the Chapel as though he was looking for something. I tried to stop him but he's surprisingly strong. Then he seemed to find what he was looking for. It's in a corner over there . . . a sort of ladder. He started climbing up it. I tried to drag him down but I couldn't. Look . . . there!'

Edward looked up at the Chapel and groaned. He knew that without ropes it was almost impossible to climb the forbidding turrets that sprang from the roof, delicate as crystallized sugar, but it was just possible to climb on to the roof itself. Several undergraduates had managed it in his time but it was dangerous. If you fell halfway up, you could break a limb or worse.

They ran towards the corner of the Chapel where Catherine had seen her uncle start to climb and stared up into the darkness. A black shape like a monstrous spider seemed stuck to the wall about fifteen feet above them.

219

'You see, Verity, this corner of the Chapel forms a sort of chimney. I remember trying to climb it once. I'd had too much to drink and nearly killed myself.'

'Shout to him to come down,' Verity said. 'Tell him you want to talk.'

'I'm afraid of distracting him. If I made him look down or lose his footing he could easily fall and break his neck. Oh God, I think he's stuck. No, he's moving again.'

The first part of the climb was made easy by bands of stone that acted like a ladder. After that, Paul had taken a grip of the lightning conductor – little more than a copper wire attached to the wall by clamps. He had managed to loosen one of them, get his fingers around the wire, and was now pulling himself up, using the conductor as a rope. It was a painful and exhausting business. The width of the 'chimney' down which the wire ran was scarcely more than that of a man's thigh. As they watched, Paul levered himself up on to a broad sloping ledge and stopped to draw breath.

Edward sighed with relief, judging that it was now safe to urge him to come down. Just as he was about to do so, Paul began to climb again, his feet pressed against a stone flange about four inches wide, his back taut against the side wall at right angles to the main wall of the Chapel. Edward saw that he had taken off his shoes so he could grip with his bare feet. He climbed rapidly and was soon eighty feet above them. Then he was on the roof and Edward breathed a second, more profound sigh of relief. Provided Paul did not attempt one of the Chapel's four turrets, he was safe. He knew he needed to keep Paul talking until the authorities could be summoned and the Chapel opened. There was, he remembered, a stone staircase inside which led on to the roof.

'Catherine, call to him and ask if he's all right,' Edward said, as calmly as he could.

'Please, Uncle, come down! You are frightening us,' she cried, cupping her hands to her mouth to make her voice carry. If Paul heard, he gave no sign of it.

They watched in amazement as he began to take off his clothes. He was soon naked and they could hear that he was singing. He spread his arms wide, either in imitation of Christ on the Cross or perhaps to show himself to his God without a fig leaf behind which to hide himself. It was a ludicrous sight, almost funny if it had not been tragic. Paul – so tightly wound up – had finally snapped like an over-stretched rubber band.

'The Nunc Dimittis,' Edward muttered. 'Now let us depart in peace . . .' Was he now preparing to depart from the world he despised?

'Paul, it's me, Edward . . .' he called, cupping his hands to make a trumpet. 'You wanted to talk to me, remember?'

He shouted so loudly that he was sure Paul had heard him. He looked down and almost fell. He righted himself but Edward had no idea if he knew who was calling to him. In his madness he might think it was God or, more likely, the devil.

He made a decision. 'Paul, wait!' he shouted. 'I'm coming up. You said you wanted to tell me something.'

Paul seemed to recognize him for the first time and beckoned with his finger as though tempting him to join him on the roof.

'No!' Verity said. 'I won't let you, Edward. It's too dangerous. It's not worth the risk. They'll come and rescue him.'

'It's not dangerous – not that first bit. I want to talk to him face to face. Catherine, you run and get help – call the Proctors – while I keep him occupied. Take this, will you?'

He took off his jacket and gave it to Verity to hold. She bit her lip, knowing that once Edward had made up his mind there was no point in trying to get him to change it. Quickly, he pulled off his shoes and socks and swung

221

himself up the first few feet. He then began to climb, using the slender wire as a rope. It was harder than he had thought and he found it difficult to get a grip. Being much taller than Paul, he was unable to use his feet against the stone wall where the chimney was narrowed. He had to drag himself up using just his arms and, though he was strong, he was not as fit as he had once been. He wondered how long his muscles would do his bidding before they weakened or cramp set in.

The stone was soft and, as he fought to gain a foothold, a sizeable piece came away, narrowly missing Verity. The sweat poured off him and, when a cloud briefly obscured the moon, he missed his footing and was a second away from falling. He struggled on, feeling his strength ebbing, but at last he reached the low stone balustrade which encircled the roof and scrambled over it. He lay on the lead platform panting, unable to move. He was as exhausted as he had ever been climbing in the Drakensberg as a young man. His legs and arms trembled uncontrollably but he had made it. A sense of triumph turned him light-headed. He was not too old yet, he thought grimly.

He had met the physical challenge but now a new, psychological, challenge faced him. He had to prevent this crazed man from killing himself. Paul stood, stark naked, on the very edge of the roof swaying backwards and forwards as he communed with his God.

'Paul!' he called urgently when his chest had finally stopped heaving and his heart racing. It was more of a grunt than a voice he recognized and Paul ignored it. Edward struggled to his feet and called again. 'Paul! Tell me what has made you do this.'

It sounded feeble but how to ask a man on the point of jumping from the roof of King's College Chapel whether he was a murderer? 'Paul, is it because of Byron Gates . . .? Is it because of Catherine . . .?'

As he had hoped, the directness of his questions caught Paul's attention.

'There's an axe in the belfry covered in blood,' he almost chanted.

'And did you put it there, Paul?'

'I don't think so.' He sounded uncertain but then he added in a stronger voice, 'Guilty as charged.'

Edward felt nauseous. 'Why did you do it?'

Paul wiped a hand over his eyes as though he was puzzling something out. He swayed and Edward put out a hand to steady him, but Paul pushed him away.

'God told me to . . . to write and warn people . . .'

'So you wrote those letters to Byron, to Miss Bron and Miss Fairweather, and to me . . .?'

'I had to . . . immoral lives . . .' Paul was mumbling now. Then he said quite firmly in a normal voice, 'But I didn't kill . . . I'm sure I did not kill. Christ forbade vengeance.'

'Then you aren't a murderer!' Edward felt relief overcome his weariness.

'I did kill . . . I wrote a letter to Mark Redel and he killed himself.'

'He *tried* to kill himself but he survived. He will soon be out of hospital.'

'He's alive?' Paul sounded disbelieving.

'You've forgotten. You've been ill. Yes, Mark survived. You haven't killed anybody.'

'I've been ill . . .?' Paul repeated doubtfully.

'Yes, you've been ill but now you will get better,' Edward said with gentle urgency. 'Please understand, you are not a murderer.'

'No, I remember now. He confessed to me kneeling at the altar so I could not tell anyone. The burden was intolerable.'

'Who confessed? Mark? Did Mark confess? You can tell me now and lay down your burden.'

'"Seeing we are compassed about with so great a cloud

223

of witnesses, let us lay aside every weight, and the sin which doth so easily beset us . . . Almighty God who desireth not the death of a sinner, but rather that he may turn from his wickedness and live . . ." I told him . . . I told the Colonel . . .'

Paul was looking inwards and in another moment might have collapsed on to the roof. But that was not to be. There was a sudden noise far below them. A police car's strident bell broke the silence . . . a blue light flashed.

Paul turned his head and took a step back. Puzzled by the lights and the noise, he seemed overcome with giddiness. Turning to Edward, he stretched out a hand, whether in appeal or apology Edward would never know, and toppled back over the parapet, thudding against the stone as he fell.

Edward rubbed his forehead as he always did under stress and then knelt, his head pressed against the cold stone, but in that holy place no prayer came to solace him. Rather a few words of Horace, *'Premet nox alta'*, 'Deep night will cover it.' Paul Fisher was dead. Edward had failed.

17

Edward drove Verity back to Rodmell in the Lagonda on the Monday. Tommie had returned to London by train the night before. He had been waiting anxiously for Paul and Catherine on the Friday evening at her aunt's house and had been horrified when he heard what had happened. He blamed himself for not having been able to help his friend but Edward told him that Paul's brainstorm had been so sudden that it could not have been foreseen.

Privately, Tommie believed that Paul might have benefited from psychoanalysis but this was probably wishful thinking. He would never have let his deeply held faith be explained away. He believed he knew what God was asking him to do and, surely could never have been persuaded that this was a delusion. He had confessed to Edward, on the roof of King's College Chapel, that he had sent poison pen letters to people of whose morals he disapproved and that he was tormented by the notion that Mark Redel might have tried to kill himself after receiving one, but that was all. He could admit to no other sin. He was doing God's work and that was all there was to say about it.

Tommie tortured himself with the thought that persuading his friend to come to dinner with Edward, Verity and the Woolves had tipped him over the edge but, as Edward said, had it not been that it would have been something else. In his view, if there was anyone to blame for Paul's descent into the hell of madness, it was the murderer who had confessed to him at the altar and left a bloodied axe in the church. This man had murdered Paul just as surely as he had murdered Byron Gates and Frieda Burrowes.

Greyshott had been shocked when Edward returned with Verity in a police car at three o'clock in the morning, utterly exhausted, his clothes torn to shreds. He had sat in his pyjamas, his head in his hands, as they told him what had happened. Afterwards, GG had looked at Edward as though he was responsible for the tragedy and Verity had had to work hard to persuade him otherwise.

After a few hours tossing and turning in GG's rather uncomfortable guest bedroom, Edward had bathed, eaten a hurried breakfast and driven round to the police station. He had a lot of explaining to do but was finally able to convince the Cambridge police that Paul's fall from the roof of the Chapel was an accident, not suicide, and that he had done everything he could to prevent it. Paul's broken body was to be returned to Rodmell for burial as soon as the police had completed their inquiries.

There would, of course, have to be an inquest but, with the police offering no evidence to the contrary, the verdict would be accidental death. No one wished to muddy the waters and encourage the press to speculate on how a respected Church of England vicar came to die in so dramatic a manner. Edward had hinted to Ken Hines that Paul had drunk rather too much and then tried to emulate a youthful exploit which had gone tragically wrong. Ken had his own suspicions – the connection with Rodmell was too much of a coincidence – but, at Edward's urging, he kept them to himself. None of the papers, to Edward's relief, mentioned that he had been present when the accident occurred.

On the Saturday morning, while Edward was being interviewed by the police, Pernel Strachey had gone to see

226

Catherine. Verity had telephoned Newnham first thing that morning to let her know what had happened. She had grasped immediately how important it was that Catherine should be comforted and supported and had offered to go round straight away.

She found Verity and Catherine going over the events of the previous night, trying to decide if there was anything more they could have done to save Paul. Catherine's aunt, a cold woman who seemed unmoved by her brother's death and her niece's distress, had made it more than obvious that the invasion, however kindly meant, was unwelcome. She pursed her lips and informed Verity and Pernel that she had known for some time that her brother was mentally ill but had not been able to make him see a doctor. It was clear she thought her niece was making a fuss about not very much.

'I can't think why she is taking on so. She hardly knew Paul and he had done all he could to stop her going to Cambridge, so why should she mourn him?'

She had no patience with sentiment, she told them, and repeated that her niece ought to pull herself together and get on with her life. To their relief, she disappeared into the kitchen, without even offering them a cup of tea. Disgusted, Pernel and Verity decided to ignore her and concentrate on giving Catherine the support she so desperately needed and would not get from her aunt.

They set out to convince her that she could not have prevented Paul's death. She had gone to Edward for help as soon as she understood that his mind was disturbed. There was nothing else she could have done. Pernel, who often had to deal with undergraduates suffering breakdowns of one kind or another – usually the result of pressure from their families to achieve more than was possible academically – knew only too well the damage that could be done to a young mind if that guilt was not expunged, and she encouraged her to tell them everything.

227

'When Uncle Paul arrived here without any warning, I thought he had come to tell me that I must leave Newnham – which he did. However, there was something much more important he wanted to tell me – who my father was. He said he was a man called Byron Gates. I knew the name because I'm keen on poetry and had read in a newspaper that he had been murdered in a rather macabre way, but you can imagine how amazed I was to be told that this man was my father.

'According to my uncle, he had been teaching at a preparatory school where my mother was the under-matron. She was seventeen and very pretty and Byron – I can't seem to think of him as Mr Gates – was unable to keep his eyes off her. When she eventually had to confess everything to my uncle, she told him that she had resisted him at first but Byron could be very charming, very persuasive. He was much older than her and a published poet. She fancied herself in love with him and it was inevitable that she would let him seduce her – at least, I think so. My uncle was much more severe in his judgement.

'Anyway, as I understand it, all might have been well except that my mother became pregnant with me. When she told Byron, he said it was nothing to do with him but offered her fifty pounds to have the baby aborted. My mother was horrified and saw for the first time the true nature of the man whom she thought she loved and who, she had believed, loved her.' Catherine sighed. 'I'm afraid my father – I must call him that and not evade the issue – was that all too common figure, a practised seducer, selfish, cold and without any compassion. Nothing bored him more than a needy woman, I am sure. I think I have enough of him in me to understand how he thought.'

She spoke with dry eyes but her voice was hoarse with suppressed emotion. Verity nodded her head but did not interrupt. She wanted Catherine to tell the whole story, as she had heard it from Paul, convinced that it would ease her heart to repeat it to a comparative stranger. It was as though, as she spoke, she was testing the validity of the story. Was it convincing or was it a fabrication of her uncle's?

'When my mother's pregnancy became so advanced that it was visible,' she continued, 'she was interviewed by the headmaster. He called her a silly trollop but was relieved she hadn't become pregnant by one of the boys – something which had, apparently, happened some years earlier. When she mentioned Byron, the headmaster refused to accept that he was to blame. I expect having Byron on the staff attracted parents to send their boys to the school and, if his name was tarnished, so would the school's be. The headmaster's one concern was that Byron should not be caught up in a scandal which might result in boys being withdrawn from the school. He told her to leave, refused her a reference and threatened her with legal action if she spread any rumours that a member of staff was responsible for her condition.

'My mother did not dare go to her parents, who were set in their ways and deeply religious. They would not have been sympathetic, she knew, and would probably have made her have an abortion. For some reason, she was determined to have me even though she knew that she would become a social outcast. She went instead to her brother, my uncle Paul, who was five years older than her. He had been brought up, my aunt says, to regard the sins of the flesh with the same horror as my grandparents and, furthermore, he was about to take holy orders.

'Nevertheless, he did what he could. He persuaded his elder sister, my Aunt Gladys,' she nodded towards the kitchen, 'to take me in. My aunt is not religious. I've never asked her but I have always felt that, as soon as she was able to, she rejected the family's stern Calvinist views. I know she left home when she was only twenty-one and became a teacher here in Cambridge. She's retired now but I love her and owe her everything.

'According to my aunt, my mother died giving birth to me, although now, when I think about what Uncle Paul told me, I can't help wondering whether it could have been a sort of suicide. Why would she want to live with so much shame heaped on her?'

'She would have wanted to live for you,' Verity told her gently. 'You mustn't believe that your mother rejected you. If she had wanted to do that, she would not have had you. She resisted what sounds like considerable pressure to have an abortion. What does your aunt think?'

'You've met her.' Catherine shrugged her shoulders. 'You can see she's not one to speculate about someone's state of mind. She's pretty tight-lipped and she has told me a very little.'

'Did you grow up thinking your aunt was your mother?'

'No, she explained to me when I first asked – I must have been about eight – why I did not have a mother or father that my mother had died having me.'

'Did she say anything about your father?'

'She said she didn't know who my father was. I accepted that, as a child does. It came as a shock when my uncle told me the truth.'

'I'm sure it did!' Verity said with feeling. She thought how difficult it must have been for the child to come to terms with being so alone in the world. Catherine had said she loved her aunt but, from what Verity had seen of her, she was inclined to doubt it was possible. Gladys Fisher seemed to be as unlovable as her brother.

'Did Paul tell you that you had a half-sister?' she asked Catherine as gently as she could.

'No! Have I? I never thought of that, though of course my father must have had other children.'

'He had a child by his first wife who died of cancer a few years ago. Her name's Ada and she's twelve. His second wife has a fifteen-year-old daughter – Jean – by her first husband.'

'Jean and Ada!' Catherine exclaimed. 'Well, I suppose I had better get used to the idea. It's rather exciting actually. I never liked being on my own. I always wanted to be part of a big family and now I am.'

'Jean's mother is the actress, Mary Brand. Have you heard of her? She's appeared in some Hollywood films.'

'No, but then we don't go to the cinema much – my aunt and I.'

'She's very pretty, like you.'

Catherine looked startled. 'Do you think I'm pretty?'

'I do, and clever as well. Not very fair.'

'You're teasing me!'

'I'm not. I suppose what I mean is that you have a lot going for you. You mustn't let this terrible tragedy spoil Cambridge for you. You must do well, get a good job and marry Prince Charming.'

'Now you *are* teasing me.'

'A little, perhaps. Anyway, you and your aunt must stay with Edward and me when you come to Rodmell for Paul's funeral. You'll meet Ada and Jean then. By the way,' Verity added, 'how did your aunt explain you to the neighbours? They must have thought it strange when she suddenly acquired a baby – do you know?'

'I think she always gave people the impression that I was some sort of orphaned cousin or grandchild – my origins left to be guessed at.' Catherine managed a smile. 'As I said, she's always been tight-lipped and certainly isn't someone who gossips with the neighbours.'

'But she's been good to you?'

'She took me in and loved me in her fashion. Otherwise I might have ended up in orphanage. She can be stern but she's been a true mother to me. It was a bit of a surprise to her when it turned out that I was clever – or at least clever enough to get a scholarship to Newnham. As you know,

231

my uncle doesn't – I mean, didn't – approve of girls being educated, but my aunt insisted I should have my chance.' Catherine shrugged. 'So here I am. By the way, I am right, aren't I? You don't really think that Uncle Paul murdered anyone, do you?'

'I don't,' Verity said firmly.

Leonard and Virginia had returned to Rodmell on the Saturday when it became clear that there was nothing they could do to help but, before leaving, they visited Catherine and her aunt to offer their condolences.

Despite her other responsibilities, Pernel told Verity that she would see Catherine on a daily basis and Verity left feeling confident that Catherine was in good hands.

Edward had telephoned Inspector Trewen and informed him that Paul Fisher, his chief suspect, was dead. Trewen, rather reluctantly, confirmed that, after an anonymous tip-off, the axe used to decapitate Byron had been recovered from St Peter's Church the previous week. Byron was blood group AB and the blood on the axe belonged to this fairly rare group. Trewen volunteered the information that, although the only fingerprints on the shaft were Paul's, he had not arrested him. There had been something about the way Paul looked at the axe when it was shown to him and his admission that he might indeed have killed Byron Gates that made even Trewen, whom Edward did not credit with much imagination, feel that a guilty man would not behave in this way. The Inspector had recognized that Paul was confused and disturbed and he had asked Dr Hind to examine him, but Paul had refused to see him.

'You don't believe Paul was the murderer, do you, Edward?' Verity asked, as the Lagonda sped away from Cambridge. 'I told Catherine we didn't.'

'I don't, but we know he wrote those poison pen letters. He had convinced himself that it was his duty to reprimand those of his parishioners he believed to be leading an immoral life.'

'And that included us?'

'It did, V. He even followed us to London. He must have overheard me say something to Leonard about having a last night on the town.'

'It must have been a terrible shock to Paul when the axe was found in his church,' Verity mused.

'Yes,' Edward agreed. 'He must have known the police would assume that he had killed Byron. Unbalanced by the strain he was under, he convinced himself – temporarily at least – that he might indeed have used the axe. As a man who put such a high value on morality, he might well have been unable to cope.'

'But before he fell from the roof, he told you that Colonel Heron had confessed to the murders?'

'He said "Colonel" not "Colonel Heron" but I think we can assume that was whom he meant.'

'And you think Heron is the murderer?'

'I'm afraid I do. There's no evidence, of course – just the word of a man suffering a nervous breakdown, but still . . .'

'So he wasn't the innocent man we thought him?'

'In my defence,' Edward said, 'I merely pointed out that the only evidence against Heron was the bloody sword and it obviously wasn't the murder weapon. It was possible, I thought, that he might have been framed by the real murderer – but it was just possible it was all an act. At the time, I doubted whether Heron was capable of acting the innocent so convincingly, but I was mistaken. I believe now that Heron *wanted* to be suspected. He wanted his motive to be *too* obvious. He had made no secret of hating Byron, knowing full well that there would be others – like Paul – with equal reasons for wanting to – how did he put it? – "mete out justice".

'Heron also knew that it would quickly become obvious that Byron had not been executed with his sword. I should have been suspicious that he made so much of the sword and how it had been in his family for generations. Anyway, had I not pointed out that Byron was killed by a sharp-edged instrument like an axe, the doctor doing the post-mortem would have spotted it. I have to confess, it does rather hurt my pride to think how easily Heron fooled me. He played me like a salmon, knowing my vanity would make me want to score over Inspector Trewen.'

'When you spoke to the Inspector on the telephone, did you tell him what Paul said about Heron just before he fell?'

'No, I didn't. It was hearsay and nothing more. Before I tell Trewen anything, I need to have some hard evidence.'

'Ah, so you are investigating Byron's murder after all,' Verity could not help teasing. 'Heron certainly had the measure of you.'

'I think I must finish the job,' Edward said calmly, refusing to rise. 'There are the three innocent girls – Ada, Jean and Catherine – who deserve to know the truth, and I don't anticipate Inspector Trewen finding that out very soon.'

'I must say, I find it difficult to feel sympathy for Byron. The man was a monster.'

'Maybe, although he would be hurt and puzzled to hear you say that. He would have said he had a healthy sexual appetite and, as a poet and a liberal, he could not pay too much attention to middle-class morality.'

'I don't have much time for middle-class morality myself, particularly if it drives people mad – as it seems to have done to Paul,' Verity said defiantly. 'What I do object to is Byron's selfish, callous betrayal of one woman after another.'

'I agree with you, V, but he still didn't deserve to have his head cut off.'

'Not his head . . .' Verity agreed.

18

The first thing they noticed when they entered the house was that Basil was unwell. Instead of the enthusiastic rough and tumble that normally greeted them – Basil sometimes almost knocking Verity over – he lay in his basket hardly able to wag his tail. He was panting hard as though he had just chased a couple of hares over the downs. Verity threw down the bags she was carrying and rushed over to kneel beside him.

'What's the matter with Basil, Mrs Brendel?' Verity asked as the housekeeper appeared from the kitchen. 'Has he been like this long?'

'Good heavens, no! He was all right a moment ago when Colonel Heron dropped in the gas masks.' She indicated a pile of respirators near the front door. 'He wants us all to try them on for size. Basil was jumping up and down with excitement and the Colonel remarked on how well he was looking.'

'I think we should take him to the vet immediately,' Edward said. 'It looks to me as though he's been poisoned. You see his tongue is an odd colour and his breathing is affected.'

'Poisoned?' Verity exclaimed. 'But how?'

'No time to discuss that now,' Edward said grimly, glancing at the gas masks. 'I'll get him into the car. You telephone the vet and make sure he's there.'

Mrs Brendel and Edward had quite a struggle getting Basil into the Lagonda. He seemed to weigh a ton and was incapable of standing upright, let alone leaping on to the seat as he normally did.

Edward drove the Lagonda dangerously fast into Lewes. The vet took one look at the dog and confirmed his suspicion.

'Is there anything you can do?' Verity was close to tears.

'How long do you think he's had the poison in him?' the vet asked.

'Only a few minutes. Thank God we came back when we did.'

'I'll have to rinse out his stomach and his mouth. I don't know what he could have swallowed but it's obviously pretty unusual – not something he could have picked up naturally.'

'Look, V, you stay with Basil,' Edward said. 'I'm going back to the house to see if I can find out how this happened.'

'No, I'll come with you. I'm not good in hospitals – not even animal hospitals – and I'll go mad waiting to hear if he's going to be all right.'

When they got back to the house Edward stood in the hall sniffing, his long, beaky nose twitching. There *was* something in the air – something poisonous. He had no difficulty in locating the source of the smell – it was the pile of respirators stacked next to the elephant's foot which held his walking sticks and umbrellas. He leant over and then backed away quickly.

'Go outside, will you, V. I don't know what there is here but it's deadly and could be infectious.'

'But I . . .' she began to protest.

'Outside! I mean it, V'

There was something in his voice that made Verity obey without further objection.

Edward had a moment of fear that Heron might have used anthrax or some other deadly bacteria on the gas

236

masks, but he had never heard that anthrax smelled like this. Could one of them have been contaminated by something left in it from the war? No! He remembered reading that all the gas masks which were being distributed had been manufactured recently. It was one of the few preventative measures the government had taken in 1937.

One thing he did know was that, having only just recovered from TB, Verity must be prevented at all costs from breathing in noxious fumes. He put on gardening gloves and gingerly picked up one respirator, then the next . . . They looked so sinister with their tiny Perspex windows, long black snouts and rubber tubing. Ugh! He inadvertently breathed in before pressing his handkerchief over his mouth and nose. The last gas mask in the pile was the one which was stinking. He took it out into the garden, holding it as far away from his face as possible, and dropped it on the lawn.

'Get away from it – it's poisoned!' he shouted as Verity, ever inquisitive, came over to look at it. The gas mask lay there, black and sinister on the innocent green grass, like some not quite dead, deformed animal. Edward suddenly felt a pain in his lungs and throat. He hurried back to the house. His eyes were streaming and his throat was burning by the time he reached the bathroom. He splashed cold water over his face time after time and when the basin was full, he plunged his head in and held his breath for a full minute.

'Are you all right, sir?' Mrs Brendel inquired, handing him a towel. She had followed him upstairs, alarmed by his coughing and the sight of the tears streaming down his cheeks.

'I am all right now, Mrs Brendel, thank you. I have found the source of the poison – it's one of the gas masks Colonel Heron delivered. I've taken it out into the garden. I'll call the police.'

'Sir, you aren't well,' she said as he began coughing again. 'Shall I call the doctor?'

'No, I'm all right, I promise you, but it must be pretty powerful stuff. I only got a whiff of it and it's made me weep worse than peeling onions.'

He tried to make light of it, not wishing to alarm her unduly.

'But how could this have happened?' she wailed. 'How could one of the masks be poisoned?' She shuddered. 'I never liked the look of the things. Now I swear I'll never put one on.'

'You didn't put one on, did you, when the Colonel was here?'

'No, he wanted me to try one on for size but I said that, if it was all right with him, I would prefer to wait until you came home. I hope I did right, sir?'

'You certainly did, Mrs Brendel. You wouldn't be standing here now if you'd tried on the one I've just taken outside. Now, I must find a flowerpot or something to put over it. No one must go anywhere near it.'

He went down to the hall to telephone the police but, as he lifted the receiver and was about to dial the operator, a thought occurred to him. 'I say, Mrs Brendel, do you know whether the Colonel had other gas masks to deliver?'

'Yes, sir. He said he had some he was going to drop in at Monk's House.'

'Here,' he said, thrusting the receiver at her, 'you call the police and explain what has happened. Tell them there is a poisoned, possibly infectious, gas mask on the lawn which must only be touched by someone who knows what they are doing – someone wearing protective clothing. Tell them I have gone to Monk's House. I must warn Mr and Mrs Woolf not to touch the gas masks.'

A terrible fear gripped him. If he and Verity had been there when Heron delivered the gas masks, they might very well have tried them on for size. In their absence, Heron had had to leave them in a heap by the front door. Basil had clearly been rifling through the pile, perhaps curious about the smell, and disturbed the poisoned mask. He had inhaled some of the gas but, in doing so, had alerted them to the danger. Basil, Edward thought grimly, had almost certainly saved their lives.

He stumbled into the garden to find Verity approaching the poisoned respirator, drawn to it as though by some evil attraction.

'I told you to stay away,' he said, more roughly than he had intended but his lungs and throat still hurt. 'Sorry, V, but this thing is designed to kill. Pass me that flowerpot, will you. I want to cover it.'

Without a word, she passed him the pot he had indicated. As he dropped it over the mask, he looked at it again with disgust and anger. He saw it was a small size – obviously too small for him and probably for Mrs Brendel too. It was the one Verity would have selected to try on.

He now knew for certain that Heron was a killer. He must be quite mad or completely reckless and have abandoned any idea of escaping detection. Perhaps he had guessed that Paul Fisher had 'spilt the beans'. If Edward knew that Paul wasn't Byron's killer, then he would also know that the murderer had to be Heron. He must have decided he had nothing to lose and that before he was arrested he would take his revenge on us, but why the Woolves? Edward could understand why Heron might want to hurt him through Verity. It was he who was Heron's nemesis, but Leonard and Virginia had befriended him for no other reason than their kindness to a man adrift and alone in the world.

'Verity, I want you to go round to Monk's House as quickly as you can and stop Leonard and Virginia putting on any of the masks Heron may have left with them.

239

Explain about the poison and say we have called the police.'

'But what are you going to do, Edward?' Her eyes were wide with anxiety.

'I want to pay Colonel Heron a visit. I won't be long but I've got a score to settle with that man.'

'Why not wait for the police?'

'Please, V, you must go now! We'd never forgive ourselves if we were too late and Virginia . . . hurt herself. You know how she dreads gas attacks so she might decide to try them on.'

'All right, I'll go but, Edward, please be careful.'

Five minutes later, Edward was beating on the locked door of Seringapatam. He banged the knocker again and again, angry and frustrated. He stood back and tried to see if there was anyone watching from a window. The house had never seemed so gloomy and forbidding. He ran round the back of the house and found an open window. After a moment's hesitation, he swung his leg over the sill. He found himself in the dining-room. The Munnings seemed to glare at him but he ignored it. He sniffed the air. Yes, there was a smell of gas and it seemed to be coming from somewhere beneath him.

He went out into the passage and into the kitchen. There was a dirty plate, a meat pie and a half-empty glass of whisky on the table. Heron had either been interrupted in his meal or suddenly decided that there was something he had to do without further delay. In the corner of the kitchen, partly hidden by a wooden bench, Edward found some stairs leading down to a cellar. After a few steps, his way was blocked by a heavy oak door. He shook the handle but it was locked and there was no sign of the key. He put his shoulder to the door but it would not budge. Returning to the kitchen, he picked up a heavy chair he had noticed. He swung it against the lock like a mallet and, after half a dozen blows, felt the lock begin to give. Sweating hard, he picked up his battering ram again. At the fifth blow, the lock broke and the door opened with a crash.

The smell of gas was now so strong that he had to take out his handkerchief and hold it over his nose and mouth. There was no doubt about it – he had found Heron's secret laboratory, but the place was in disarray. There was broken glass all over the floor, the remains of several bell jars. Rubber tubes and metal pipes lay everywhere like the tangled and twisted entrails of a dead monster. This was not the debris from some accident or explosion, as Edward had first thought. Heron had made an attempt to destroy his laboratory but had given up before completing the job. Worst of all, the pathetic corpses of rabbits and rats lay in a pile in a corner – the victims, no doubt, of his experiments.

Edward was finding it hard to breathe and realized he must get out before he was overcome by the fumes. As he turned to leave, he saw Velvet, the Colonel's retriever, lying dead under a workbench. Edward knew that, if there was one living thing Heron loved, it was his dog so he guessed Velvet had not died a painful death like the rabbits and rats. Gingerly, he turned the corpse over and saw that she had been shot in the head.

It could only mean that Heron had decided it was all over. Having shot Velvet, he would surely now shoot himself but what if, before he did so, he claimed one more death? Edward ran up the stairs two at a time and gratefully reached the fresh air. Doubling up, he vomited the poison he had ingested. His head dizzy and his eyes streaming, he went back to the lane. Monk's House . . . Verity was in danger. He must get to Monk's House before it was too late.

Verity, meanwhile, had knocked on the door of Monk's House and been told by Louie that Mr and Mrs Woolf were

241

in the garden. Filled with trepidation, she ran round the house to the writing-room at the end of the garden. The doors were open and Colonel Heron was standing just outside offering Virginia a gas mask to try on.

'No!' Verity screamed, as she saw her raise the gas mask to her face. Virginia stopped in surprise and then saw who it was.

'Verity! What's the matter?'

'The gas mask – it may be poisoned,' she gasped. 'Throw it on the ground . . . please!'

The mask dropped from Virginia's fingers and lay like a huge spider on the grass. She went very pale and seemed about to faint as Leonard went to support her.

Verity turned to Heron, furiously angry. 'Is this the way you return all the kindness they showed you? You kill Byron . . . well, I can sort of understand that. You held him responsible for his first wife's death . . .'

'For my *sisters*' deaths,' Heron corrected her. 'Both my sisters.' He seemed quite calm, almost resigned, and made no attempt to deny the accusations Verity was making.

'What do you mean – your *sisters*' deaths? I don't understand. Didn't you tell my husband that you and Marion had been engaged?'

'That was a lie. You see, I had to keep it secret that she was my sister otherwise the police would have known I killed Gates. Marion died of cancer knowing that Gates was sleeping with her own sister – Beatrice. She was the youngest and a silly girl but we both loved her. She killed herself out of despair and guilt when, immediately after Marion's death, he abandoned her and married the actress.'

Heron's voice was hoarse and there was look of such utter despair in his eyes that, just for a second, Verity pitied him.

'So Marion was your sister! I understand now why you hated Byron so much.' Then, remembering that he had

242

been within a whisper of killing Edward and might well have killed her beloved Basil, her heart hardened.

'If what you say is true – and you are such a liar I can't be sure – but, if it is true that Byron was responsible for the death of both your sisters, I can see you had a reason to hate him, but why kill Frieda? What had she ever done to hurt you?'

'It was Frieda who had taken him – worthless as he was – from Beatrice. It was she who made Beatrice commit suicide.'

'But you said yourself that he left your sister to marry Mary Brand. He didn't start an affair with Frieda until after he had remarried.'

Heron shook his head like a bull bewildered by his tormentor in the ring. He seemed to make an effort to try and explain himself.

'Well, his new wife was often away in America and I couldn't reach her. Frieda was a tart and, anyway, Cathcart wanted her dead. He said she betrayed him – that Gates had taken her from him. She deserved to die. We agreed she deserved to die . . .' He shook his head again like a confused animal. 'I could not allow Gates to betray his second wife with her as he had betrayed Marion.'

'But how did you know your way round Broadcasting House?'

'It wasn't difficult. An army friend of mine had an office at the BBC. He showed me round once when we met in London for a drink.'

'And why try to kill us and . . . Mrs Woolf? Did you intend her to be your next victim?'

'Your precious husband had everything I didn't have – a job, a place in society, someone to love . . .'

'And you also knew that, in the end, we would hunt you down?'

'I knew that silly, half-mad vicar of ours would blab and

blab until even you and your husband – always so patronizing to those less well-off than himself – would work out
who the murderer was. I had hoped to convince Fisher that
he had committed the murders in his madness . . .'

'But it was you – in *your* madness – who killed and
killed again.'

'And you, Mrs Woolf . . .' Heron turned to Virginia,
whose eyes were wide with disbelief. 'You and your
friends with your claptrap pacifism . . . It was people like
you who betrayed the generation who died in the war.
I could not bear the thought that comrades of mine had
given their lives so that stupid so-called "intellectuals"
could spout pacifist poison. Unlike Gates and all you other
"intellectuals", I'm not one for poetry – most of it strikes
me as being pretty silly – but one poet I do like is Julian
Grenfell. Do you remember this? "And he is dead who will
not fight, and who dies fighting has increase."' Heron's
eyes blazed and Verity's anger turned to fear. This was a
man gripped by an obsession.

'I expect you despise men like Grenfell, Mrs Woolf,
who fell in battle so you could live your comfortable lives
undisturbed by the real world. You can write your boring,
empty books – I tried one and had to chuck it in the river
before I had read fifty pages – because soldiers like us had
suffered and died. And then, instead of standing up to
Hitler, you and your like gave him what he wanted and
brought this new war down on us. So I thought – how best
to punish you for your pusillanimity? Of course! I recalled
the dread we felt in the trenches when we heard the gas-
gong and the anger when I saw my men gasping for breath
in a cloud of poison gas, tearing at their eyes, ripping
their flesh to try and scrape the poison off them . . . That, I
decided, was how people like you should die. That's how I
am dying.'

Verity thought Virginia was going to collapse. She
was as pale as the moon, now visible in the sky above

them, and seemed almost as serene. Leonard had put his arm round her but she did not seem to notice. This was the evil she had long dreaded and now she was face to face with her nightmares. Without a word of protest or complaint, Leonard led Virginia away. She had suffered a severe spiritual wound but at least she had not been poisoned.

Verity watched them walk away and then turned back to Heron. 'What do you mean? How are you dying?'

'I was diagnosed with cancer of the throat a month ago. They gave me just three months to live so I knew I had to hurry if I was to take my revenge before I became too weak.' He coughed – a rasping, cruel explosion of breath. 'I told Gates at the fête that I had something important to tell him and – rather reluctantly, I must say – he agreed to meet me on the green after it was over.'

'Did he know who you were?'

'He knew who I was all right. He knew I was Marion's brother. We had never met before he moved to Rodmell but he knew she had a brother in India and that she and I had the same surname.'

And you threatened him in the pub . . .?'

'I warned him that I would exact vengeance for what he had done.'

'Why didn't he go to the police or leave Rodmell?'

'I didn't want that. I wanted him to stay until I was ready, so I went and saw him the next day and apologized. We agreed to keep the whole thing a secret. He didn't want me telling everyone that he had seduced his sister-in-law as his wife lay dying. He didn't want Ada to know.'

'Oh my God – Ada is your *niece*. How could you have done what you did to her?' Verity was appalled. 'Is that what your sister would have wanted? You are a monster.'

'I . . . I'm sorry,' Heron mumbled. 'I did not mean to hurt Ada . . . I did not think . . . but I *had* to do it, don't you see? I had to . . .'

'So you lured Byron to the green after the fête?'

'Yes, he came. He did not dare not to. He needed to know what I was planning to do but he never guessed I was going to kill him – not until I told him. He blustered and then blubbed – it was disgusting. He pleaded with me and I enjoyed that most of all. I made him kneel and then I bound his hands. When he understood what I was going to do to him, he wet his pants. I told him it was only justice and I didn't know why he was making such a fuss. I dragged him over to the block I had erected. I felt that I was his executioner and that this was Tower Green. He was a traitor and deserved to die. He had betrayed two women who were very dear to me and no doubt many more I did not know. I can die happy now. I have done what I set out to do.'

'And you will hang for it,' Verity said grimly.

'The hangman will never loop the rope round *my* neck.' A throaty chuckle turned into a cough that shook his whole body. 'Another of his kind is squeezing the life out of me.' He coughed again and almost fell.

'The police will be here shortly, Colonel Heron,' Verity said, 'and it's no good appealing to our sympathy. You have caused terrible suffering to Ada. Byron may not have been the best of men,' she continued remorselessly, 'but he did not deserve to die – certainly not in the way you made him die. You drove Paul Fisher mad and yet you both had something in common, had you but known it. He, too, had a sister who suffered and died because of Byron Gates. And now you are trying to kill someone who has only done you kindness. You deserve to be hanged and if the cancer kills you first, I hope it will be a painful death.'

He lunged at her and she stepped back. 'I'm not afraid of you, Colonel Heron.'

At that moment, Edward stumbled into the garden. He looked like death and Verity started to go over to him but he raised his hand to stop her. His expression was adamantine.

'I have been in your infernal laboratory, Heron . . .'

'He was trying to poison Virginia with that . . .' Verity pointed to the gas mask lying at their feet. Edward bent over and picked it up.

'He was, was he?' he snarled. 'Well then, I think it is his turn now. Try this on, Heron, why don't you?' He spoke with the gentle insistence of a knife at the throat. 'I think it's your size.'

Heron looked at him and smiled calmly. 'You know, Corinth, it was Gates who gave me the idea – that ridiculous detective story of his in which a worthless creature has his head cut off. I don't remember what he called it but at the beginning he quoted a line or two from Shelley – his detective was named Shelley, if you remember – "I met Murder on the way – he had a mask like Castlereagh – very smooth he looked, yet grim; seven bloodhounds followed him . . ."'

He took the gas mask from Edward and pressed it to his face, not bothering with the straps. Then he pulled a little catch and a horrible smell made them all step back a pace. Heron started to choke and, as he did so, he stumbled and fell to the ground still holding the mask to his face.

Edward and Verity stared down at him and watched him die.

At last, when he was quite dead, Edward took Verity's hand and said, 'You are safe – that is all that matters.'

As he spoke, they heard the bell of a police car. Inspector Trewen came round the house at a brisk trot but stopped when he saw Heron's body.

'I'm afraid you are too late, Inspector,' Edward said coolly. 'Your murderer has just taken his own life. Before he died, he quoted the poet Shelley and so shall I. "Last came Anarchy: he rode on a white horse, splashed with

247

blood; he was pale even to the lips, like Death in the Apocalypse." I don't know about you, Inspector, but I have always preferred Shakespeare to either Byron or Shelley.'

19

Tommie came down from London to take Paul's funeral. The whole village turned out and there were several reporters standing at the back making notes. Paul had not been a popular vicar – he was too austere for that – but he had been respected, and his death had been so unexpected and dramatic there was a fascination about it which Edward considered morbid if understandable.

The night before the funeral, Edward and Verity had invited Jean and Ada to the Old Vicarage to meet their new sister. They had decided that Ada should never know that her father's murderer was her uncle. It was too much for anyone to have to deal with. Heron was dead and it could be assumed that Inspector Trewen would not waste time looking for stronger motives for his hatred of Byron than the reason he had provided at the time of his arrest. If Trewen ever did find out that Byron's first wife had been Heron's sister, Ada would be thousands miles away.

Mary Brand had explained that she was planning to take Jean and Ada back to America.

'I have a five-year contract with a new film company called Mayflower Pictures. I wasn't looking forward to having to tell Byron that I was moving to Hollywood with or without him. Now I don't have to.'

Edward and Verity had explained to both girls that Catherine was Paul Fisher's niece and Byron's unacknowledged daughter. It had been touching to see the three of them get to know one another.

'Perhaps, Catherine, when you have finished with Cambridge, you might like to come and visit us?' Mary suggested.

'Yes, please do,' the girls echoed her. 'We could be a proper family at last.'

'I'd like that very much,' Catherine said, 'but, of course, it all depends on the war.'

There had been one difficult moment when Ada had attempted to defend her father but Catherine had begged her to say nothing more.

'Let's leave the past to bury the past,' she implored her. 'Our father was not a good man – it would be stupid to pretend that he was – but, like it or not, he *was* our father. It's up to us now to make the best of our lives. We can't alter the past but we can make something worthwhile of our future. I am very happy to know that I have sisters like you and I hope we can be friends. I've always wanted a family and now I have one. It makes me very happy.'

What with the visit to Cambridge and Heron's death, Edward had not had time to get to know Mary Brand but, sitting next to her at dinner, he discovered that she was an intelligent and imaginative woman, surprisingly unshocked to find another of her late husband's progeny suddenly thrust upon her. She was very different from the silly, selfish actress he had expected. He had vaguely imagined she would be a brassy, red-haired, green-eyed Irish temptress like Maureen O'Hara, the star of *Jamaica Inn*, and was at first rather disappointed to find her 'ordinary'. Though her hair was auburn and her eyes green, she turned out to be a demure, soberly dressed woman who would hardly turn heads in the streets. Verity suggested later, when they were discussing her, that she must have one of those faces which the camera loved and a personality which came alive on the screen.

By the end of the evening, Edward had got to like her and was relieved to find that he had no misgivings about leaving Ada in her care. He saw the girl frequently look towards her stepmother for approval and reassurance and sensed that, with Byron gone, the three might develop a new relationship uncomplicated by his need always to take centre stage and play off one of his women against the other.

When the party broke up, Verity kissed Jean and Ada and said how much she hoped they would keep in touch.

'If you don't become an actress, Jean, I think you could make a very good journalist. And, Ada, promise not to undervalue yourself. Remember, I had no qualifications and was only half as clever as you but I never let it stand in my way. Most people will take you at your own estimation so make sure it's always that much higher than, in your heart of hearts, you think it should be. Then, one day, you'll wake up and find you are the person you'd like to be. Oh dear, am I making sense?'

Ada kissed her and said, 'You have been so kind to us. May we write to you? It would be so thrilling to hear about your adventures.'

'Yes, please!' Jean added. 'I'm not sure we could have survived without you and Edward.'

'We've loved getting to know you both, and we'll certainly keep in touch with Catherine. I'd like to get to know Cambridge properly and Edward always enjoys going back to old haunts, don't you, Edward?'

Edward agreed and asked Catherine if she would treat him like an honorary godfather and come and stay at the Old Vicarage from time to time.

'I may be lonely,' he joked, 'with Verity careering about the world getting into all sorts of scrapes.'

Hugging Catherine, Verity riposted, 'Sorry to disappoint you but I'm not going to take unnecessary risks. I've decided to play safe. I just want to enjoy a ripe old age without feeling I have let myself down.'

'I don't believe that!' Catherine exclaimed. 'You promise you won't forget me, will you?'

'Of course not! We'll often see you and, as Edward says, you must come and stay at the Old Vicarage. It will stop him getting middle-aged and pompous.'

Even Catherine's Aunt Gladys melted to the extent of thanking Edward and Verity for trying to help her brother.

'He meant to be a good man,' she said defensively, 'but the world was too wicked for him.'

Unexpectedly, Mary Brand leant forward and kissed Edward on the cheek before she left and, for a moment, Verity was jealous.

'When are you going back to Hollywood?' she inquired, innocently.

'Next week, I'm afraid, on the *Queen Mary*. I can't be away from Hollywood too long. One is so quickly forgotten.'

Before going up to bed, Edward and Verity let Basil out in the garden and made a fuss of him as he settled back in his basket. He had still not entirely recovered from the poisoned gas and Edward doubted whether he ever would. He seemed to find it hard to get his breath, particularly on one of his favourite walks on the downs. He would start chasing a rabbit but then give it up and pretend he couldn't be bothered, coughing almost like a human. It was stupid, Verity knew, possibly even wicked and she would not confess it even to Edward, but she minded much more that Heron had hurt Basil than that he had killed Byron and Frieda.

As they were getting ready for bed, she said, 'So Trewen was right after all when he arrested Heron at the scene of the crime. Perhaps, by interfering, we merely obstructed the course of justice?'

'I don't accept that. It's a very serious matter, charging someone with murder. They deserve to be properly defended and condemned only when the case against them is proved beyond all reasonable doubt.'

'But Frieda might still be alive if the police hadn't released Heron after you told them the sword couldn't have been the murder weapon.'

'They would have had to release him anyway because the case against him was so thin. I don't believe I was wrong to raise the point with Trewen.'

Verity sensed that Edward was on the defensive and changed the subject. 'I'm still puzzled by what Heron and Lewis Cathcart were doing that day I saw them together at Lyons Corner House.'

'You think Cathcart was in on the plot to murder Frieda?'

'I don't really care, but one thing is certain – by telling Heron about Byron's affair with Frieda, he gave him the motive to kill her. I hope I never see Cathcart again.'

'But it seems to have been Colonel Rathbone who showed Heron around Broadcasting House so he knew where the studios were. I wonder whether it was pure chance that he decided to kill Frieda on the evening she had arranged to interview you?'

'So he would have seen the statuette in the studio?'

'Yes, he probably picked it up and noted how heavy it was.'

'But how could he possibly have known that Frieda would be sitting with her back to the door?'

'I don't think he did. He saw you leave the studio and go into the control room – perhaps he was watching from the Silence Room or lurking in the passage – and then rushed in and killed her. It made it easier that she had her back to him but, even if she hadn't, it wouldn't have stopped him. He was a strong man and Frieda would have been taken completely by surprise.'

'But if we had seen him from the control room I would have recognized him and at least been able to try and stop him.'

'It was a risk, but don't forget that he was wearing a balaclava.'

'And what was it Frieda said just before she died which was captured on the recording – "knotty"?'

'I think she may have cried, "Not me!" but we'll never know for sure.'

'I can't forgive him for that,' Verity said. 'Frieda may have been manipulative and sexually unprincipled but she did not deserve to die.'

'No one deserves to be beaten or gassed to death,' Edward said grimly. 'It's why we cannot ever do a deal with the Nazis. It's inhuman – the sort of treatment they mete out to their prisoners. It is pure evil and nothing can excuse it.'

Verity nodded her agreement.

'Do you remember when we first went to Heron's house, we thought it smelt stale and unpleasant?' Edward continued, putting on his pyjamas. 'That must have been because he was brewing his poison gas in the cellar.'

Verity shuddered. 'And the hospital boiler suit we found in the Silence Room . . . He was being treated for cancer so he would have had no difficulty stealing it.'

'And, as churchwarden, he'd have a key to the church so he would have no trouble hiding the bloodied axe in the belfry. You know, V, he had me fooled at the beginning. I really thought he had been framed.'

'And that was exactly what he wanted you to think. I hate the man and I'm glad he's dead. I never want to think about him again. I still can't believe that he could cause such grief to his own niece – a girl he should have loved and protected . . . He was wicked.'

'Well, come to bed, my darling, and I'll try to distract you from brooding about all that beastliness.'

There were now only a very few days before Verity was due to leave for France. She tried to put behind her the violent deaths of Byron Gates and Frieda Burrowes. There would be more deaths and worse deaths to come, she knew. She had more important things to worry about.

She spent two days in London at the *New Gazette* conferring with the editor and trying to get a firm grip on the quickly moving international crisis. Edward found himself alone with Mrs Brendel and Basil for company. He tried to make the best of it but missed Verity even before she had left for Paris. At Leonard's insistence, he had replaced Heron as ARP representative for the area, which at least kept him occupied, and he embarked on Trollope's 'Palliser' novels which, he hoped, would last him out the war. Adrian and Charlotte Hassel saw him most days, and Leonard and Virginia almost as frequently, so, as he often told himself, he had nothing to complain about.

Mark Redel was back home painting, seemingly none the worse for his attempted suicide – indeed, he was rather more cheerful than before. Edward bought the self-portrait and also two of his small landscapes. Better still for his self-esteem, Mark had been approached by another Bond Street gallery interested in representing him. He and Edward forged an unlikely but genuine friendship despite having very little in common. Edward overcame his distaste for pubs and he and Mark met most days for lunch at the Abergavenny Arms where they ate bread and cheese washed down with a pint or two of the local brew.

Edward desperately wanted to contact the Foreign Office to find out when he was to join HMS *Kelly* to fetch home the Duke of Windsor but restrained himself. He knew that men of his age were pulling every string they could think of to find a job, in or out of uniform, and making a thorough nuisance of themselves. He also knew that the war would not be a short one – no one thought it would be over by Christmas as they had in 1914. There would be plenty of time to find his place in the great effort that the country would be called upon to make if it was to defeat Nazi Germany.

At last, the time came for Verity to leave. She had declined a farewell party, thinking it inappropriate, but Leonard and Virginia insisted on hosting a dinner in her honour and to wish her luck. Virginia was still not herself. The murders, Heron's attempt on her life and the coming war had all combined to make her more than usually nervous and depressed. However, the evening was a success, though Verity was hardly able to eat. Whenever she was excited or nervous, her stomach closed up and she lost her appetite. She longed to smoke but, remembering that the doctors had made it clear that cigarettes would be the worst thing for her health, she had promised Edward she would not.

Whenever Edward looked at Basil, he silently blessed him for nosing out the horror which Heron had prepared for her, even though it had cost him his own health. With her weak lungs, Verity might easily have succumbed to just a breath or two of poison gas.

The gas Heron had cooked up in his makeshift laboratory had been identified as a chlorine-based chemical. It was the type which he had seen used to such devastating effect when he had served at the front. The stinking yellow smoke had killed and maimed so many in the trenches. Heavier than air, it lay low over the battlefield of Ypres in 1915, a miasma of death. That Heron had tried to use it on innocent civilians seemed to Edward evidence of the derangement that war always brings in its wake.

The night before Verity left, they made long lingering love and, satisfied, fell into a deep sleep in each other's arms. Verity was woken about four by the sound of creaking floorboards. She disentangled herself from Edward who was snoring gently, and immediately thought of the ghost which Leonard had told them haunted the Old Vicarage. She remembered with relief that it was a friendly ghost. She lay rigid as she heard a scratching on the bedroom door and then the creak as it was pushed open. She listened to the pad, pad of footsteps across the wooden floor and jumped as she felt a damp nose on her hand. It was Basil, of course. It seemed he could not sleep and had come to his mistress for comfort.

'You know you are not allowed upstairs, Basil,' she whispered, trying to sound cross. He coughed and immediately she felt conscience-stricken. Basil had saved her life and shortened his own in the process. How dare she be cross with him? She sat up and stroked him – he was so big she could fondle him without moving and waking Edward. 'Lie down and try to sleep,' she instructed him. 'I love you.'

Basil appeared to understand for he collapsed on the rug with a sigh and almost immediately began to snore. Verity lay awake for a few minutes, soothed by a gentle susurration of snores from man and dog. She was lying between the two living things she loved most in the world and the sound of their breathing comforted her. At last she, too, slept but her dreams were all of missing trains and losing luggage and people. She was up at six to shower and sort through her things for the hundredth time.

Basil had gone downstairs ahead of her and they breakfasted together, enjoying being alone and having the chance to say goodbye to one another. It was nine before Edward padded into the kitchen, yawning, to make himself a cup of coffee. Seeing Verity and Basil both looking distraught, he quickly came over to hug them.

'It'll be all right,' he said meaninglessly. But how could anyone know it would be 'all right', he wondered? 'It'll be all right,' he repeated, hoping that somehow his empty words would comfort her.

Verity had forbidden Edward to drive her to Croydon where she was to catch her flight to Paris. She told him she loved him too much to bear it.

'Best to say our goodbyes here,' she said, stroking his face. 'What was that poem you read me yesterday which made me cry? "Since there's no help, come let us kiss and part." I'll get the train and it'll save a long, painful farewell which will do neither of us any good. I want, as I board that plane, to imagine you with Basil on the downs – the peace, the fresh air and the sound of the wind in the trees. I shall know you will be thinking of me and it will give me the strength to go forward. We have had some happy times together, haven't we?'

'And will again,' Edward said fervently.

'If I believed in God, I would thank Him for it but, since I don't, I must thank you, my dear,' she said, kissing him.

At eleven Edward, with a heavy heart but trying to look and sound cheerful, prepared to drive her to the station. Her luggage – and in the end there wasn't much of it – was loaded into the Lagonda. Charlotte and Adrian had come to see her off but had tactfully left Edward and Verity together in the house to say their final goodbyes in private. They stood in the hall and looked at each other, suddenly at a loss for words. When would they meet again? was the unspoken question. Verity wiped away a tear. Edward held open his arms and she came to him as bravely as she could.

'*Nunc dimittis*', he said in her ear, and his voice betrayed him.

She put a finger to his lips. 'If you dare say anything about parting being such sweet sorrow, I promise you I will dissolve into a puddle on the floor. We have said everything and not even your beloved Shakespeare can say it better.'

Edward managed a smile and let her go. 'I shall say not another word, I promise you,' he managed.

'Then come, husband,' she said, smiling up at him, and together they walked out into the sunlit garden.

Note

Virginia Woolf drowned herself in the River Ouse on 28 March 1941.

For those interested in the dangerous sport of night climbing, *The Night Climbers of Cambridge* by 'Whipplesnaith', first published in 1937 and republished in 2007 by Oleander Press, is essential reading. It recounts the courageous – or foolhardy – nocturnal exploits of a group of students who climbed King's College Chapel among many other university and city buildings and whose exploits prefigure the modern urban sport of 'Free Running'.

I am most grateful to Richard Reynolds at Heffers for bringing the book to my attention and reading my 'Cambridge' chapters.